"Are you enjoying y

asked her.

"Very much so." She smiled up at him and then felt her stomach lurch as she saw that his eyes were on her lips and he was moving his head closer to hers, as he had before they'd gone to see the Cascade.

And then, all of a sudden, their mouths met and his lips felt warm and—just—glorious against hers.

After a few moments, he parted her lips with his tongue and somehow she felt sensation through her entire body. He pulled her in tightly against him with the arm that had been around her shoulders and pushed his hand into her hair. His other arm reached around her waist so that his hand was against her back.

As their kiss deepened, in a way that Eloise had never before experienced, she found herself reaching her arms around his neck and pulling his head against hers.

When, sometime later, Marcus shifted position a little and raised his head and smiled at her, Eloise was simultaneously disappointed right to her very core and hugely grateful that she'd experienced such a kiss, at least once in her life.

Author Note

As with my debut Regency romance, *How the Duke Met His Match*, I wanted in this story to celebrate one of the Regency-era women who, despite having very few rights or career options, did their best to gain independence for themselves and their daughters. These women's lives were made even more complicated by the fact that they had to ensure that their reputations were spotless. A man might have as many extramarital affairs as he liked, while a woman of course had to be (or appear to be) above any moral reproach.

Eloise, my heroine in *The Secret She Kept from the Earl*, has a huge secret. Its discovery would ruin not only her reputation, but, more importantly, that of her entirely innocent daughter. She has also, after a lifetime of unhappy subservience to her family and then her elderly husband, become a wealthy, widowed duchess, a woman of huge independence.

I also wanted to touch on the difficulties soldiers faced in returning from war in an era when mental trauma was not widely understood. Marcus has left the army to take up his earldom and is struggling a little to come to terms with what he witnessed on the battlefield.

The last thing either of them wants is to fall in love, and yet they do. I loved exploring how each completed the other, and how they gradually came to realize that they were better off together than alone.

I also enjoyed the opportunity to write about both London Society and a country house party set in the beautiful southern England county of Sussex, and to delve into the world of Regency masquerades...

Thank you so much for reading!

SOPHIA WILLIAMS

—

The Secret She Kept from the Earl

HARLEQUIN®
HISTORICAL™

Recycling programs
for this product may
not exist in your area.

ISBN-13: 978-1-335-59603-1

The Secret She Kept from the Earl

Copyright © 2024 by Jo Lovett-Turner

Harlequin Enterprises ULC
22 Adelaide St. West, 41st Floor
Toronto, Ontario M5H 4E3, Canada
www.Harlequin.com

Printed in U.S.A.

Sophia Williams lives in London with her family. She has loved reading Regency romances for as long as she can remember and is delighted now to be writing them for Harlequin. When she isn't chasing her children around or writing (or pretending to write but actually googling for hero inspiration and pictures of gorgeous Regency dresses), she enjoys reading, tennis and wine.

Books by Sophia Williams

Harlequin Historical

How the Duke Met His Match
The Secret She Kept from the Earl

Look out for more books from Sophia Williams coming soon.

Visit the Author Profile page
at Harlequin.com.

To Edward

Chapter One

Eloise

July 1808

As the coach she was travelling in joined the queue to enter Vauxhall Pleasure Gardens, Lady Eloise Grantham adjusted her mask and pulled her domino more tightly around herself with a little wriggle of pleasure. She was delighted with her clothing choice.

Before she and her grandmother had left her grandmother's mansion in Berkeley Square, her looking glass had told her that the mask made her quite unrecognisable, and that knowledge was giving her the most delicious feeling of freedom. If no one was going to recognise her, then she might do anything she liked on this one last night before she had to leave London to prepare for her marriage next month to the elderly Duke of Rothshire.

And the domino was ideal for entirely covering the very risqué shepherdess gown that she was wearing, which she was sure would assist her greatly—once she took off the domino—in achieving her aim of doing whatever she liked this evening. When her friend Lady Anne Crane, from whom she had borrowed the gown, had seen her in it she had screamed with laughter at the way in which Eloise almost spilled out of it.

'On me, that was just quite risqué; on you it's *indecent*,' she had told Eloise. 'You look *ravishing*. You will certainly have no shortage of partners at the masquerade.' Which was exactly what Eloise wanted, because if she was about to be bound in marriage to a not-very-nice seventy-two-year-old man, she wanted just a little bit of diversion first, so that she had some good memories to sustain her through the years ahead.

It seemed that they had arrived at exactly the same time as many hundreds of other persons attending the same masquerade. The cacophony from all the people and horses was immense, the profusion of lamps around the entrance stunning. Eloise *loved* it.

'Come back from the window.' Her grandmother tugged Eloise's elbow as she peered out at the hordes. 'Try to remember that you are a lady.'

'Mmm, sorry.' Eloise didn't move. She didn't care if people saw her, and she wanted to drink in as much of this experience as she could.

As she gazed at the scene before her, one of a group of unmasked young bucks walking towards the carriage caught her eye. He stood a little taller than the others, his shoulders were a little broader, his smile was charming, and there was just something about the way he carried himself.

As they passed the carriage, he glanced into the window, and then took a second look, his smile widening and his eyes dancing.

Eloise smiled back at him and then, secure in the anonymity of her mask, pouted at him. He laughed and gave her a little salute, before wandering away with his friends.

Well. She hadn't ever pouted saucily at a man before, and she clearly wasn't going to have much occasion to pout in that way once she became the Duchess of Rothshire, but for this one evening, sauciness might suit her very well.

She smiled and pouted at another two young gentlemen as they passed the carriage, and both times the pout had an excellent effect, although neither of the gentlemen took her fancy in the way that the first man had.

And then their chaise juddered forward with the rest of the queue of carriages, and her grandmother instructed her in such forbidding tones to move away from the window and draw the curtain that she decided it would be wise to comply.

When they alit a few minutes later from the chaise and began the walk towards the box her grandmother had taken for the evening, Eloise saw that the pleasure gardens were everything she'd hoped for. They were faced as they entered by a quite superb orchestra and a large pavilion. Everywhere, there were coloured lights and chattering groups of people dressed in a range of stunning costumes. The whole effect was one of excess and intoxicating gaiety.

'Is this not delightful, my dear?' her grandmother asked her perhaps half an hour later, as they supped on muslin-thin ham and assorted tarts with their friends.

'I am particularly taken with the paintings here. One could look at them for hours.'

'Certainly,' Eloise murmured. The wall behind them was hung with paintings by both William Hogarth and Francis Hayman. Eloise did enjoy visits (short ones) to art galleries, but she had had higher hopes of this evening than art appreciation.

'Perhaps we might take the young ladies to dance?' one of the men in their group suggested.

Eloise almost had to bite her lip to prevent herself from cheering.

'Yes, my dear, you may go.' Her grandmother smiled at her and then narrowed her eyes. 'Is your gown under that domino quite proper? You are not in fancy dress?'

'My domino is fancy dress in itself.' Eloise didn't like lying to anyone, especially her adored grandmother, but a small untruth at this moment couldn't possibly hurt anyone. She pulled the domino tightly around herself once again. She would leave it somewhere once she was out of sight of their box. There could be no benefit to anyone in her grandmother seeing the full glory of her shepherdess costume before Eloise had had the chance to reap the benefits of wearing it. It was fortunate that her grandmother was a habitually late person and had appeared below stairs some time after they were due to leave the house, so there had been no time for her to inspect Eloise too closely.

Her grandmother leaned closer to her. 'You know that I cannot condone your marriage.'

Eloise nodded. Her grandmother had engaged in a particularly vicious epistolary argument with Eloise's father on the subject of marriage between a nineteen-year-old young lady and a very elderly man, which had culminated in her travelling to their home in Kent and demanding that, if her father persisted in his self-ish plan to sell Eloise to 'that lecherous old dog'—her grandmother's exact words—he should at the very least allow her to spend this one week with her in London before the wedding.

'It would, however, be disastrous for you if the duke were to jilt you now.' Her grandmother's face scrunched a little in the way it did whenever she men-tioned the duke. 'And, therefore, it is my duty to remind you that you should of course act with decorum at all times. No word of gossip or scandal concerning you must reach his ears.' She leaned even closer and kissed Eloise's cheek. 'Enjoy yourself but be sensible. I see a little twinkle in your eye that reminds me of myself at your age. And therefore I do not entirely trust you.'

'I will be sensible.' It wasn't entirely a lie; it couldn't really be at all risky to amuse oneself a little indeco-rously when disguised in a shepherdess costume and mask, because no one would ever recognise her. Elo-ise kissed her grandmother and stood up. 'Thank you. I love you.'

She and her grandmother had been sharing that emotion with each other a lot this week. Eloise had never really experienced love from anyone else, and it was wonderful. She didn't want to think about the reason that her grandmother was being so open about her affection for her; it seemed as though it might be related to how horrified she was about Eloise's impend-ing marriage, and that wasn't something upon which it would be good to dwell now.

As she descended the steps from their box, her friend Lady Anne whispered into her ear, 'Let us slip away from our escorts at the earliest opportunity and *enjoy* ourselves.'

Eloise nodded and then pasted an innocent smile onto her lips as one of their escorts, a very proper young man, a Mr Dryburgh, who apparently eschewed all form of costume, said, 'Perhaps you would care to take a turn about the gardens, Lady Eloise?'

'Certainly. First, though, I must just...' she looked around vaguely '...go over there.' She pointed into the distance and grabbed Lady Anne's hand and pulled her into the midst of the crowd of people on whose edge they had been, so that they were very soon swallowed up.

Once fully surrounded by the crowd, Eloise found herself gasping a little, her eyes on stalks.

A lifetime with her aristocratic, albeit severely impoverished parents, followed by a veritable whirlwind of social activity in the past week, from breakfasts to soirées to ridottos to balls, accompanied by a lot of hissed instructions from her grandmother, had given her a strong impression of Society's rules.

It appeared that those rules were being very much bent here. It was unusual to find earls with an income of ten thousand pounds a year, with whom Eloise had been conversing only the evening before in the extremely strait-laced and much more boring surroundings of Almack's, dancing publicly with a person whom her grandmother would term a demi-rep, or— goodness—to see that earl now equally publicly doing *more* than just dancing with her.

The earl wasn't the only one. They were surrounded by people—*bodies*—dancing, *pulsing* together, people screaming with indecorous laughter, people dressed extremely indecently or just outrageously, many sorts of people, almost as though the highest in Society were dancing with their own servants and tradespeople.

'This is wonderful,' Eloise breathed into Lady Anne's ear, smiling at a very jolly-looking Julius Caesar, who was accompanied by a similarly jovial-looking devil and a purple-robed man wielding a bishop's mitre.

'Domino off.' Lady Anne twitched at Eloise's cloak from behind and Eloise nodded and pulled at the ribbons at her neck to untie it.

Lady Anne whisked the domino away and Julius Caesar's eyes widened, and he stepped forward and said, 'Would you care to dance?'

Eloise would indeed.

'I'd be...' she began. And then she stopped short, because just over Julius Caesar's shoulder she could see the man whom she'd seen walking past when they were queuing in the chaise. He was equally striking at closer quarters, and he was smiling at her too. And if she'd be pleased to dance with Julius Caesar, she'd be ecstatic to dance with this man.

She aimed another pout at him—the one she'd done in the carriage had definitely been a success—and saw him laugh, which made her laugh too.

And then he moved round Julius Caesar, held his hand out to her, and said, 'Dance?'

'No, no.' Julius Caesar wasn't looking so jolly now. 'The young lady had just agreed to dance with me.'

'I'm so sorry.' Eloise turned her masked face slightly in his direction. 'I am going to dance with this man.' The *power* of anonymity: you could behave as badly as you liked—withdrawing acceptance of an invitation to dance would be quite unacceptable in any *ton-*

nish ballroom—and no one would know it was you. Especially when, in addition to your mask, you were wearing a gown quite unlike any you had ever worn before, or indeed would ever wear again. Eloise pushed that sad thought from her mind and beamed at her new dance partner, as he led her away from Julius Caesar and right into the throng.

'I'm Marcus,' he told her, taking her in a *very* close waltz hold, which made her squeak a little.

'I'm El…la.' It seemed prudent not to tell him her actual name. From the way he spoke, the way he was dressed and his demeanour, she was sure that he was a gentleman, and her grandmother's words had reminded her that her future self, the Duchess of Rothshire, probably wouldn't *really* want anyone to know that she'd worn quite such a daring shepherdess costume and danced the night away in a quite abandoned manner with a succession of dashing young men, as she was determined to do. It would be best to ensure that she was completely unrecognisable.

'Well, good evening, Ella.' Marcus smiled at her as he tipped her back in a way that made her breathless and particularly aware of how very low-cut and slightly too small for her the bodice of her gown was.

'Good evening, Marcus.'

'Do you come to the pleasure gardens regularly?'

'No.' She very much liked the way his hand was nestled into the small of her back as they danced. 'This is my first time. And also my first time at a masquerade.' There could be no harm in admitting that. 'Do you come here often?' There could also be no harm in leading the conversation a little herself, in a way that her mother had always said would be most off-putting to gentlemen seeking to court her. 'You don't enjoy wearing a mask?'

Marcus laughed and nodded. 'Yes, I do come here quite often. And I don't mind wearing a mask but I have just had all my affairs packed up, including my domino and mask, and did not have time to procure new ones.'

'You're leaving London?'

'Yes. I leave tomorrow for the Peninsula, to fight.' His smile tightened for a moment, before he said, 'And you? Why is this your first time here? Are you usually too busy with your sheep to attend?'

'That's right.' Eloise smiled at him. 'I am a most devoted shepherdess.'

'And where do you normally tend to your sheep?' He wiggled his eyebrows a little as he spoke.

Eloise laughed. No one ever spoke to Lord Grantham's daughter or the Duke of Rothshire's fiancée in such a way.

'Wherever my fancy takes me,' she told him. And then she smiled saucily and said, 'Do you own sheep? Maybe I will choose to tend to them at some point.'

Marcus pulled her hard against him and she gasped again—he was making her gasp a lot, which was definitely something she'd been hoping for this evening—and bent so that his mouth was close to her ear, his breath whispering across her skin. 'You would be welcome to tend to my sheep—or to me—whenever you choose.'

Eloise gasped yet again and shivered quite deliciously from his proximity. 'Sir!'

Marcus laughed, and danced her in several quick steps into a slightly larger space. He opened his mouth to say something further but was prevented from speaking by their being jostled by a couple tussling.

Marcus let go of Eloise and stepped towards the couple just as the woman—a Cleopatra, with a huge wig and a bejewelled mask—dealt the man—a monk—a resounding slap, and picked up her skirts and walked fast away from him.

'My goodness.' Eloise knew that she was round mouthed. 'I believe that that was the Countess of Strathclyde.'

'You know her?' Marcus was frowning.

'I've seen her.' Maybe Eloise should disguise her voice a little, perhaps speak with the accent of the villagers near her home in Kent, so that Marcus wouldn't think she could possibly be a friend or acquaintance of the countess's. 'In the distance.' Yes, that was a good accent.

Marcus stopped frowning and smiled again. 'While tending to your sheep?'

'Exactly.'

As they continued to dance, buffeted by other couples and making light conversation of the type Eloise was used to making at more decorous social events, Marcus pulled her closer and closer, which was, frankly, quite exhilarating.

After some time—Eloise could not have told how long; she was enjoying herself far too much to count minutes—Marcus said, 'If this is your first time at the gardens, perhaps I should show you around.'

'I should like that very much.' Eloise beamed at him.

With his broad shoulders and superior height, he had no trouble in forging a path through the many dancers until they reached the edge of the crowd and he drew her towards a path lined with trees and lanterns.

'My goodness.' Eloise was impressed by the space

around her and by how beautiful the walk was. 'I hadn't expected to see something like this in London.'

'So you don't usually live in London?'

'No. Well, sometimes.' She really did not wish to give him any details about herself.

'Ella, you are a woman of mystery.'

She nodded. 'Yes, I am indeed very mysterious.'

'I think I'd like to solve some of those mysteries.' He reached for her hand and took it in his and pulled her gently towards a side path. Ella *loved* the feel of her hand in his large—perfectly warm but not too hot—one. It was shocking to think that this was the first time she'd ever held the hand of a man like this, and that the next time would probably be on her wedding day, with the elderly duke.

She clenched her free hand for a moment to try to dispel any thought of the duke and said, 'Maybe you will,' as mysteriously as she could, and then giggled.

'Are you here with a large party this evening?' Marcus asked as they continued to walk down the path, passing two couples doing things together that caused Eloise to blink.

'My grandmother and some friends.'

'Your *grandmother*?'

Oh, dear. 'She's a very…mysterious grandmother,' Eloise offered in her best Kent accent. It was quite possible that Marcus knew her grandmother.

Marcus laughed. 'You're funny.' He pointed to a little bench in a nook in the hedge. 'Shall we sit down?'

'Certainly.' Eloise was sure that sitting with a man in such a secluded place was even more improper than dancing with him and walking with him as she had been. And that was the beauty of a masquerade: she was very much enjoying herself and no one would ever know it was her.

She was even more sure of the impropriety of her behaviour when Marcus sat very close to her and placed an arm around her shoulders. As he hugged her against his side, she leaned right into him, because his hard body felt deliciously comfortable against hers and also because he was warm, and the evening air was turning very cold.

'You're shivering.' Marcus ran his hand down her arm, which caused Eloise to shiver even more, but not with cold. 'Take my jacket.' Before she had a chance to consider whether or not she should agree to his suggestion, he was in his shirt sleeves and wrapping the jacket around her shoulders.

It was warm from his body and, as she breathed in, she caught what must be his scent, something indescribable but extremely alluring. Maybe it was woody. The jacket was huge on her and warming her up very well and, now that she was no longer freezing cold, she couldn't imagine a more enjoyable way to spend an evening than sitting here with Marcus.

'My grandmother told me that there would be fireworks later,' she said.

'Your mysterious grandmother is correct, I believe.' He smiled down at her and she felt her breath catch in her throat. His eyes—which she was sure had been a quite regular green when she'd seen them in bright lamp light—now looked like deep pools in the shadows. He had quite perfect cheekbones and a delightfully strong jaw; really he was the personification of a hero in one of Fanny Burney's novels.

He moved his head a little closer to hers, looking into her eyes the entire time.

Eloise couldn't have removed her gaze from his for all the pin money in the world. She swallowed as he moved even closer, and then his lips were almost on hers, their breath mingling in the cold air.

And then a loud bell began to ring and Eloise jumped so much that she nearly banged her head against Marcus's.

'What *is* that?' she asked.

'It's for the Cascade. Come.' Marcus took her hand and pulled her to her feet and begin to hurry her along several paths until they arrived at an area of woodland to see a bridge, a watermill and a waterfall, accompanied by the noise of roaring water, all of which effect, Marcus explained, was mechanical.

'That was marvellous. Quite the best spectacle I have ever seen.' Eloise opened her mouth to say that it was much better than the play she had been to a few days ago at the Theatre Royal but then stopped herself short, unsure whether the non-aristocratic woman she was trying to impersonate would have been to the theatre that week.

'Let me show you some of the other attractions of the gardens.' Marcus put his arm around her shoulders in a most improper way and guided her through the milling crowd to a wide walk, and then down a deserted side path.

There was much to look at—pillars, statues, wonderful coloured lights—and much to enjoy—Marcus's proximity and quite audacious conversation—as they walked.

Eloise was not at all upset, though, when Marcus

suggested they sit down again, on a bench quite hidden from view.

'Are you enjoying your evening?' he asked her.

'Very much so.' She smiled up at him and then felt her stomach lurch as she saw that his eyes were on her lips and he was moving his head closer to hers, as he had before they went to see the Cascade.

And then, all of a sudden, their mouths met and his lips felt warm and, just...*glorious* against hers.

After a few moments, he parted her lips with his tongue and somehow she felt sensation through her entire body. He pulled her in tightly against him with the arm that had been round her shoulders and pushed his hand into her hair. His other arm reached around her waist so that his hand was against her back.

As their kiss deepened, in a way that Eloise had never before experienced, she found herself reaching her arms round his neck and pulling his head against hers.

When, some time later, Marcus shifted position a little and raised his head and smiled at her, Eloise was simultaneously disappointed right to her very core and hugely grateful that she'd experienced such a kiss, at least once in her life.

She'd kissed precisely two men before: a very decorous and brief pressing of lips with the squire's very shy son at a dance in their village in Kent, and an unpleasant fumble with a much less shy young baronet on a terrace outside another dance, which had ended in her boxing his ears and running inside. She hadn't imagined before that a kiss could be quite so...*wonderful*.

She smiled at Marcus and he reached further into her hair and said, 'Your mask,' his voice much hoarser than it had been earlier, which made her want to laugh but also to kiss him again. She needed to be careful, though.

'No.' She pulled back so that he couldn't reach to untie her mask strings. 'My mask stays on.'

'Indeed? Genuinely a woman of mystery.' Marcus was laughing now.

'Yes.' She nodded and pouted again.

Marcus immediately leaned forward and kissed her again. The power of the pout!

Aware now of how good his lips felt against hers, Eloise sank straight back into the kiss, sighing out loud with pleasure.

Marcus reached inside the jacket that he'd earlier wrapped around her, to pull her against him again, and then… And then she found herself pulling at his shirt and he looked at her and raised an eyebrow and she nodded, quite sure that whatever he might like to do now she would be *very* happy to experience. And then she felt his hand move up to her shoulder, and caress it, and then he did something clever with his fingers because she felt the straps of her dress move, and then he slid his fingers inside the bodice and weighted her breast in his hand, before pinching a little and caressing with his fingers and *oh*. He shifted his hand further, to take the heaviness of her breast fully in his palm, and then took his lips away from hers, to kiss down her chest ever closer to her breast until he took it in his mouth, nipping with his teeth, licking, and, *oh*, the sensation.

As he leaned her back and pulled her dress down and took her other breast in his other hand, stroking and playing, Eloise was dimly aware that this was certainly the kind of thing that would quite ruin her if anyone saw. But no one could see and she was masked, and now called *Ella*, and perhaps she should ask him to stop and take her back—which she was sure he would, because he seemed very kind—but she didn't *want* him to stop.

Indeed, she was quite desperate for him to continue.

She ran her own hands over his very solid chest and then he suddenly lifted her so that she was on his lap, facing him, straddling his legs. And under her, she could feel…hardness, pressing against her.

Continuing to kiss her breasts, Marcus ran his hand up under her skirts until he was touching the inside of her legs.

Eloise could hardly breathe. She had never really known before what exactly men and women did together, although she did know that it was deeply, deeply improper for a man to be touching her like this, but she was certain—*certain*—that she didn't want this experience to end yet. Her whole being was flooded with pleasurable sensation and *want*, and just for this one evening, masked, as Ella, before she became a duchess with a much older and very unpleasant husband, she was going to take that pleasure.

Marcus was moving his fingers closer and closer to the area between her legs and suddenly he touched her there and she almost screamed.

'You're so wet,' he gasped, beginning to grind his body against hers.

'Mmhmm.' Ella had no words. She reached down to his hardness—he didn't know her so why should she be shy?—and pulled at his breeches.

And then he pushed a finger inside her in a way that she'd never even imagined could happen and it was as though her very own fireworks display was igniting.

And then Marcus drew back a little and looked at her.

'May I?' he asked.

'Yes. Please.' Ella could barely speak.

'Are you sure?'

'Very sure.' If anyone knew about this she was already ruined and now she just wanted as much pleasure as she could get out of this night, and, oh, *oh*, he was moving his fingers more, and biting her gently again as she finally managed to open his breeches.

'Please,' she instructed him, and then he shifted her again so that she was next to his nakedness.

Chapter Two

Marcus

'Are you sure?' Marcus asked Ella one more time as he held her above him. There was something about her… Was this, could it possibly be her first time? If so, surely they shouldn't…

She wriggled against him and said, 'Yes,' before reaching down to take him in her hand. That felt… wonderful. *God.*

He kissed her again and then adjusted her on his lap so that he could enter her.

He should check with her one last time. 'Are you certain that you want to do this?'

'Very certain.'

He moved, and Ella gasped and then sighed and then said, *'Yes,'* as he began to move inside her.

And, God, he was sure it *was* her first time. And damn, that was good. She was moist, and tight, and pliant, and *God.* And then he stopped thinking.

'Ella,' he grunted as he climaxed, holding her tightly to him on his lap.

'Marcus,' she panted in response.

He pulled back a little from her before easing himself out of her and then adjusting her in his lap again. He'd been with a number of women in the past few years—what twenty-four-year-old man of his acquaintance had not had a number of sexual experiences—but this evening had been something different, quite exquisite.

He reached to tip her chin up and kiss her on the lips one more time and… Her mask had come off at some point and she was *beautiful*. At this moment she *looked* as though she'd just made—quite abandoned—love, her eyelids heavy and her eyes glazed. Beneath her quantities of now extremely dishevelled red-blond hair, she had a small, very pretty face, with the naughtiest of smiles. And yet…now that he could see all of her face, the smile looked a lot more innocent. Yes, naughty, but not in an experienced way.

And he was certain that that had been her first time.

'Are you…all right?' he asked.

'Yes, thank you.' She smiled at him. 'Quite all right.'

'Was that your…?' Considering what they'd just done and some of the more risqué comments he'd made in her ear in the past hour, and how she'd giggled at those comments, it was surprising that he was finding it now so difficult to frame his question.

'Yes, it was, and thank you.' She smiled again, and then did her adorable pouting thing again, which made him laugh, but also made him *think*.

She had been completely innocent beforehand, it seemed. And the country accent that she'd been using before had completely gone and her tones were now those of a lady. And she just, there was just, she just… God. She really did just somehow have the *bearing*

of a lady. She was pulling her—quite ridiculous—
shepherdess dress up over herself, to cover her—quite
magnificent—bosoms, and the way she was straightening her shoulders, the way she was moving…it reminded him quite forcibly of the way every young lady
of quality moved at Almack's, after their years of de-
portment lessons.

Was she…? Good God, had he…? Had he just made
love to a virgin young lady of quality?

'Ella, where did you get that costume?'

'From my wardrobe.' She twinkled at him.

Marcus did not entirely feel like twinkling back
at her.

He shook his head. 'Ella, I…'

She reached up and kissed him on the cheek.

'Marcus, I've had a truly lovely time with you, and
I needed to have a good time this evening. So, thank
you. Truly. Thank you.'

Marcus had needed to have a good time too. He
was more than ready to go and fight on the Continent
for what was right, and he was excited to go, and he
needed a purpose in life beyond inane London Society, but this evening he'd suddenly realised that tonight
could be the end of his life as he'd always known it,
and he'd wanted to enjoy himself.

'I've had a wonderful time too.' He took Ella's hand
in his and kissed it. 'May I know your full name?'

'No.' She twinkled at him again and he had to laugh.

'May I at least escort you home tonight?'

'No.' And there was the twinkle again.

'Could we…?' Could they what? Now that he suspected that he'd just made love to a young lady of quality, he was a lot more confused than he had been half

an hour ago about what he'd like to do for the rest of the evening.

'Could we perhaps walk a little together? If you'd like to?' Her smile was less confident now. 'And could you perhaps refasten my mask for me so that it's quite secure?'

'Of course.' Marcus almost leapt off the bench in his eagerness to do her bidding.

His fingers seemed to be all thumbs and he kept getting the ribbons caught up in her hair, so it took him a long time to fasten the mask, but eventually he had it done. Ella turned round to thank him, and yes, she did look very different—much less innocent, and slightly older—with the mask on.

As they walked, they talked about the most inconsequential matters, almost as though their lovemaking earlier had never happened, other than that Ella was wearing his jacket and they were walking arm in arm and he felt his entire body respond to her whenever her wonderful softness brushed against him.

'Oh, look.' Ella stopped in her tracks as they saw light from the first fireworks, followed very shortly afterwards by cracks of sound.

Marcus had always enjoyed fireworks, but they were even better when viewed with someone as excitedly impressed as Ella.

'They were wonderful,' she breathed when eventually the display was finished. 'A fitting end to the most perfect evening.'

'I'd like to see you again.' Even as he said it, Marcus knew that his words were ridiculous. He was leaving in only a few hours' time and, even if he'd been stay-

ing, Ella had made it quite clear that she didn't wish
to share even her surname with him.

'In another life, perhaps.' Ella wasn't smiling now.
'But this is my life, and your life. It's been one evening
and I've had the most wonderful time with you. Thank
you again and I think I should like to find my friend
now. And my domino.'

They barely spoke as they walked back towards the
crowds, as though their moment together was already
over.

They moved together amongst the crowds for several minutes, until Ella saw her friend and tugged on
Marcus's sleeve and pointed. He made to walk towards
the friend, but Ella tugged his sleeve again.

'I will bid you farewell here,' she said, already out of
his jacket. 'I wish you the very best on the Peninsula.'

'Let me escort you over to your friend.' Marcus was
even more sure now that Ella was a young lady of quality. Her friend reminded him of someone. Perhaps he'd
danced with her before he left town three weeks ago to
spend time with his parents before returning to London
today in advance of tomorrow's departure.

'Certainly not.' Ella smiled sunnily at him. And before he could in his turn wish her well, she very suddenly handed him his jacket and darted away from him.

He followed, so that he would know she was safe,
and nearly leapt forward at least three times to have a
stern word with men who looked far too interested in
her in that ridiculous gown. And then she reached the
side of her friend—whom he was sure he recognised—
and the friend, after a conversation lasting a few seconds and much gesticulation on both the ladies' parts,
took her domino off and put it round Ella's shoulders.

Ella pulled the ribbons of the domino tight and then looked in his direction for a long moment before raising her hand for a second and mouthing, 'Goodbye,' and then, as he raised his own hand and opened his mouth to bid her farewell in response, she turned away and disappeared into the crowd with her friend.

Marcus stood for a long time amidst the swirling horde, just staring after her, before turning and walking in the opposite direction.

Chapter Three

Eloise

Nine years later—London, July 1817

Eloise, Duchess of Rothshire, had almost forgotten how much she loved crowds and the attendant bustle and noise. As her friend Viscountess Bakewell, previously Lady Anne Crane, her closest confidante from her one London visit, nine years ago, leaned closer to her in order to regale Eloise with a particularly scandalous piece of gossip, she found herself almost beaming with happiness.

It was *wonderful* to be here. It wasn't that life in the country was boring; rather it was that there was something particularly invigorating about being surrounded by quantities of happy people, and she did miss that. And she missed balls and London theatres and shops and fashion. Now that her mourning period following the passing of her late husband, the old duke, was quite finished, perhaps she and her eight-year-old daughter, Amelia, would begin to spend more time in town.

A young buck jostled her as he pointed towards the

rapidly travelling balloon whose ascension they had all come to watch, and then apologised profusely. Eloise smiled at him and assured him that she didn't mind at all, before turning her attention back to Anne.

Noting the particularly fine fabric of her friend's gloves, she opened her mouth to compliment her and ask her where she had purchased them, when she was jostled again.

This time, the jostler was Amelia, back from a walk around the field with her nurse and a footman.

'Mama, Mama, I've met some friends.' Amelia gestured behind her at two little girls, both blonde and of a similar height to her, standing one at each side of a tall, immaculately attired man, presumably their father, each holding one of his hands. Eloise smiled at the girls and they both returned her smile.

'How do you do?' she said.

'Very well, thank you,' one of the girls said. 'I'm Lady Venetia Wright and this is my sister, Lady Maria, and we're twins.' Her earnestness was very endearing.

Eloise smiled more and said, 'I'm very pleased to meet you.'

'I see that I am going to have to introduce myself,' said their companion, laughing. 'I'm Malbrook. Good afternoon.'

'Good afternoon.' Eloise glanced away from the girls for a second to address him.

She looked back at Amelia and then found her eyes returning to the man. Something about him had struck a chord with her; she felt as though she recognised his voice, his smile, his height, his build.

Oddly, he reminded her very strongly of Marcus,

the man to whom she had made love at Vauxhall Gardens nine years ago.

It wasn't possible that it was him, though. He was dead. She was sure he was.

That evening at Vauxhall, she'd wanted to ask Anne his name—it had been obvious that he was a gentleman and the then Lady Anne would almost certainly have known him if so—but she hadn't wanted to confide in a soul about her…indiscretion. And so she hadn't asked. She'd perused the military news in the newspapers quite assiduously, and had read of the death of an officer named Marcus, and had presumed that he was *her* Marcus, and had suffered from very low spirits for a time as a result: reading of the deaths on the battlefield of so many healthy young men must always be an occasion for grief, but when you'd met one of them, and he'd seemed so nice and kind and had given you quite the best evening of your life, not to mention your daughter…

So she'd grieved for him, and she knew that this man couldn't be Marcus because Marcus was gone, and yet…as her gaze settled on him and she stared… she couldn't help beginning to think that it *was* him.

Alive.

Amelia's father.

He was greying a little at the temples and possibly even broader in the shoulders now, and there was something a little different about him, something intangible—a little more seriousness perhaps—but, yes, she was almost certain that it *was* him.

It was.

Definitely.

His eyes, crinkling now as he registered how very much she was staring at him, were just *his*.

He was alive. Alive!

Which was wonderful. *Wonderful.* It had been *awful* to think, believe, that such a vibrant, decent, energetic, strong young man had been killed.

Truly wonderful, so wonderful that she could barely even comprehend it.

But also... Good heavens.

It was terrifying.

He was standing right next to Amelia. Her, his— their—daughter.

What if he recognised Eloise? Said something and created some kind of scandal? Or, even worse, realised somehow that Amelia was his daughter and disclosed that knowledge publicly?

Having herself been effectively sold in marriage by her near-bankrupt father to the highest bidder, the then seventy-two-year-old late duke, Eloise was determined that if Amelia married when she was older it should be for love. If either she or Amelia were tainted by scandal, that might not be possible, especially since, while the duke had agreed not to disown Amelia, he had made little separate provision for her, so she would not have a large dowry.

She could not allow Marcus to recognise her or say anything. But what could she do?

She couldn't think. It was as though her brain was suddenly stuffed with cloth. And then her ears filled with a loud, hollow booming so that she couldn't hear anything else, and her surroundings seemed to shrink away from her, further and further away, fading into blackness, until she realised, as though from a great distance, that—for the first time in her life—she was fainting, and unable to do anything to stop herself.

Some time later—she had no idea whether it was seconds or minutes—she managed to drag her eyes open. The first thing she saw was Anne's concerned face, a few inches in front of her own.

'Oh, thank heaven,' Anne cried.

'Where is Amelia?' Eloise asked, struggling to stand upright from where she seemed to be lying in a diagonal manner in someone's—very strong and firm—arms.

'With her nurse,' Anne told her. 'Over there. We thought it best that she be distracted rather than worry about you.'

Eloise nodded and closed her eyes again for a moment. And… Oh, no. Whose arms was she in? Who was holding her? If she wasn't mistaken, they were masculine arms. Surely not? Surely she couldn't be lying in Marcus's arms? Surely it must be another man? There couldn't have been any shortage of chivalrous men in the vicinity, surely?

Also, who were the girls whose hands Marcus had been holding? Were they his daughters? That would make them Amelia's half-sisters.

Eyes still closed, she moved her head and shoulders very slightly. The person against whom she was lying was very solid, and large. Was it Marcus?

She opened her eyes again, very slowly, and looked at the arms encircling her. They were quite broad and were clad in a jacket of dark blue superfine and might belong to any man of fashion with a good build. The man's hands were…nice. Strong-looking. Quite big but not too big, with capable-looking, square-ended fingers, which were resting lightly on her forearms, supporting her.

Why was she suddenly feeling hot?

She tipped her head backwards and looked straight up into... Marcus's face. He was looking directly back at her, as though scrutinising her features. Did he recognise her? Or was he merely concerned for her because she had fainted?

Eloise was beginning to feel even hotter. Applying extreme self-control, she prevented herself from whipping her head round to see whether Amelia was in his line of vision. Which was ridiculous. Even if Amelia *was* there, he was hardly going to look at her and know by some supernatural power that she was his daughter, was he?

The far greater danger was that he would recognise Eloise and say something. Clearly, she needed to get away from him as quickly as possible.

'Thank you so much for your help.' She wriggled her arms a little to indicate that he should let go of her.

'Yes, thank you indeed, my lord,' Anne agreed. Eloise would be able to ask her later who Marcus was without arousing suspicion; it would be quite natural to enquire in this situation. He'd told her his name when he'd introduced himself but she hadn't really been paying attention and couldn't now remember what he'd said.

'I am quite recovered now.' Eloise wriggled her arms some more, and Marcus finally took her hint and assisted her to an upright position.

'Are you certain?' he asked, not quite letting go of her arm.

'Yes, indeed I am. I must, however, return home

now.' Eloise moved—tugged—her arm away and he let go.

'If you're quite sure. You will allow me to escort you to your carriage.' His words sounded like a command rather than a question. Eloise considered for a moment. What would she do if she'd fainted through genuine illness of some kind and he were a complete stranger? She would demur and then she would accept his help.

'That sounds eminently sensible to me,' interjected Lady Anne. 'I, together with your footmen and nurse, am very well able to escort the girls while you walk together.'

'Then if it isn't too much trouble for you, I thank you for your assistance,' Eloise told Marcus. She turned in the direction of her carriage; it would be best to get this over and done with as quickly as possible. The shorter the time they spent together, the lower the likelihood that he would recognise her.

As they began to walk, he said, 'I'm sure that you will not be the only lady to feel somewhat overcome today; it is markedly warm for standing still for long periods.'

'Indeed,' Eloise agreed. Normally, she wouldn't like to be thought weak, but on this occasion it was ideal that there was an obvious cause to which her faintness could be ascribed.

'Is this the first balloon ascension you have attended?' he asked.

'Yes, it is.' Eloise suppressed her natural instinct to reply more fully and to ask about Marcus's own experiences. The less conversation between them the better. And, really, if he thought her rude, it could only be a good thing; he would then be unlikely to wish to speak to her again should their paths ever cross in the future.

'I must confess that I had little interest in hot air balloons until my nieces begged me to escort them here. When I agreed, they bombarded me with so many dozens of questions that I was forced to read around the subject to avoid being thought the most dismal of uncles.' The girls were his *nieces*, not his daughters. That was a relief; Eloise didn't want to think that Amelia had half-sisters whom she would not be able to know as sisters. And, she realised, she'd very much liked Marcus when they met and would not have wanted to think that he had done *that* with her while being married, which he would have had to have been, because these girls were surely similar in age to Amelia. 'I now realise that the science behind them is quite fascinating. As is the mentality of those brave, or insane, enough to travel in them.'

Eloise laughed at his words, despite her whirring mind. 'I believe we must be grateful to those of such a curious or intrepid nature; without them we would probably still be living in medieval conditions.'

'Very true. I am, however, more interested in the steam locomotives on which much work is currently being done. Balloons seem to me a remarkably impractical mode of transport.'

'But what about the beauty of the scenery viewed from on high?'

'I am happy to view my scenery from ground level, to avoid freezing and then landing in a tree.'

'You are cynical, my lord.' She knew that Lady Anne had addressed him as *my lord*.

'Yes, apparently I am.' He grinned at her and seemingly of their own accord her lips widened into a smile in response.

There was a pause—which Eloise was certainly not going to fill, however much she was now remembering how much she'd enjoyed talking to him on the occasion they met—before he continued speaking.

'I believe that this weather is perfect for balloon travel.' Really, it was as though he *wanted* to create conversation; she was sure that he wasn't one of those people who *needed* to talk. Was it because he recognised her? No, surely not; she'd only been unmasked quite briefly when they'd met and it was nine years ago and he probably made love to women quite regularly and hadn't realised that she was a lady of quality, and from his perspective their encounter had not resulted in the birth of a child, so it would not have been the huge event for him that it had been for her. He was just engaging in polite small talk, as any man of fashion might do.

'Yes, I believe it is,' she said.

'Your daughter and my nieces seemed to make fast friends very quickly,' he continued. At the sound of the words *your daughter* on his—Amelia's father's—lips, Eloise nearly tripped, as though she had suddenly forgotten how to put one foot in front of the other.

'Are you quite all right?' Marcus's strong arm had prevented her from falling and he was now applying a little extra supportive pressure. 'You don't feel faint again?'

'Yes, thank you. The ground was a little uneven there.' Eloise nodded at the extremely even path along which they were treading. 'I never faint. That was my very first time and I'm sure it won't happen again. It must have been the heat.'

Marcus smiled at her and maintained his stronger grip on her arm and they continued the rest of the way to the chaise in silence, the rest of their little group a few yards behind them.

Eloise saw Marcus's eyes flicker to the crest on the side of the chaise before he made a small bow and said, 'I wish you very well, Your Grace.'

'Thank you again for your kindness.' She took the hand he was holding out to help herself into the chaise and nearly tripped *again* at the feel of the strength in his arm and the warmth of his bare skin through the thin fabric of her glove. She let go quickly and was then furious with herself when she caught a slight frown of perhaps surprise on Marcus's face. And then the rest of the group were gathered at the chaise, and he looked away.

Once she had exchanged adieux with Lady Anne, and Amelia and her nurse were also inside the chaise, Eloise had the door closed and the curtain pulled— ostensibly against the strong sun—as fast as she could, before sinking onto one of the chaise's well-upholstered benches.

As Amelia chattered about the balloon and her two new friends, Eloise took a couple of deep breaths to calm herself. Everything was all right. Marcus clearly hadn't recognised her, and, even if he had, he couldn't possibly have known that Amelia was his daughter. And even if he *did* know that she was his daughter, he might not comment or wish to be involved in her life in any way. After all, many men had by-blows whom they ignored.

He might not be one of those men, though, and Amelia was definitely Marcus's daughter. When Eloise had conceived Amelia, she hadn't been entirely sure of how babies were made, but she did know now, and Marcus was the only man with whom she'd ever made love. She and the duke had never consummated their marriage, as on the day of their wedding she had been with child and too ill from all-day morning sickness to do much beyond standing in the church and repeating her vows, and when she had stopped being constantly sick a few weeks later, she'd realised that she was in an interesting condition, and had had to admit that to the duke. He had informed her that he would have *liked* to have had their marriage annulled but his pride would not allow it, but that she should beware that he might at any moment choose to disown her and her baby. And then he had never spoken to her again—a great relief— and they had therefore never engaged in any intimacy.

As the coach began to move, Amelia pulled back the curtain at the window and began to wave at her new friends. Over her shoulder, Eloise got her first proper look at Marcus's nieces and nearly fell off her seat in horror.

They looked so similar to Amelia that the three of them could have been triplets.

If Eloise had felt faint before, she now felt truly sick.

The next afternoon, after re-entering her grandmother's house after a walk and game with Amelia in the garden in the centre of Berkeley Square, Eloise helped her daughter remove her pelisse and then took off her own, before giving Amelia a hug.

'I had a very good time, Mama,' Amelia told her. 'Can we play more battledore and shuttlecock tomorrow?'

'I hope so,' Eloise said, not completely truthfully. She was now fully recovered after her fainting episode, and while they'd been outside she'd been thinking and had decided that she and Amelia should return to the country as soon as possible, probably straight after breakfast tomorrow, to ensure that Eloise wouldn't encounter Marcus again.

Her grandmother would be disappointed as, in the last few days, since she had, thankfully, recovered from the illness that had been the cause of Eloise and Amelia's visit to London, she'd clearly been trying to make up for lost socialising time and had crammed into each day several visits with aristocratic ladies, at which she liked Eloise and on occasion Amelia to be in attendance. It seemed fortunate in hindsight that her grandmother had declared herself not yet ready for a return to full socialisation; it was possible that, if she had been, they might have met Marcus at a ball or similar event.

'Why don't you go up to the nursery with Lucy?' Eloise smiled at her maid and hugged Amelia tightly to her again for a moment. 'I'll come up to see you soon.'

'Your Grace.' Her grandmother's butler, Dawes, was holding out an envelope. 'This note has just been delivered to you from Viscountess Bakewell.'

'Thank you.' She took the note and smiled at Dawes. She wasn't going to open it while he was standing there.

She'd written to the viscountess as soon as she and Amelia had got home yesterday, to ask the name of the man who'd helped her when she fainted, on the pretext of wishing to thank him.

Dawes hesitated for a moment and then bowed infinitesimally and left her.

Dearest Eloise, the note read. *I hope that you are truly better. I was quite worried about you. The man who helped you was the Earl of Malbrook. I believe that he fought in the Peninsular and then Napoleonic Wars before returning home to take up his estates on his father's death. In haste, as I am now going shopping with Mama. Your good friend, Anne*

The Earl of Malbrook. Eloise's grandmother would almost certainly know him.

Eloise and Amelia did need to leave London soon.

When Eloise entered her grandmother's boudoir a minute or two later, she found her looking the picture of glowing health and seated at a side table looking through invitation cards.

'We're going to be extremely busy for the remainder of your stay,' she told Eloise in satisfied tones. 'We have a gratifyingly large number of invitations here and I believe myself finally to be back to full health. I'm just deciding which we will accept.'

'How lovely,' said Eloise, untruthfully; she really didn't want to, *couldn't,* go to any events at which the Earl of Malbrook might be present. 'What kind of invitations?'

'Balls, soirées, picnics, all the usual things,' her grandmother said, not looking up from her pile of cards. 'There will no doubt be all manner of impromptu outdoor breakfasts organised, with this wonderful weather we've been having.'

Eloise closed her eyes for a moment. It was such a shame because she didn't want to disappoint her grandmother and she'd been enjoying herself greatly, but until she'd had some time to think about the likelihood of Marcus's recognising her and acting on that recognition, she could *not* go to an engagement and risk seeing him again.

'Now that you are so much better, I feel that Amelia and I must return to the country very soon,' she said.

'But darling, I shall miss you if you leave now. Why not stay until the end of the Season, just another fortnight or so? And then perhaps I might accompany you to the country and spend some of the summer there with you?'

'That would be wonderful,' Eloise said. 'Your staying with us, I mean. We'd be delighted. I shall count on your coming and you will be most welcome as soon as you choose to arrive and for as long as you choose to stay. But I'm afraid I can't afford to spend any longer here. I have commitments at home with friends, tenants, discussions with the new duke about the estate. You know that I was very much in the way of assisting in the running of the estate when the old duke was alive, due to his ill health, and I have continued with many of those duties.'

'Can those things not wait? I must confess, my darling, that I should very much like to see you remarry, for love this time, and you are unlikely to meet a man in the country.'

'I have no intention of remarrying.' Eloise smiled at her grandmother to try to soften the harshness of her words.

'My own match was for love, as you know, and to be married to someone you love is truly wonderful.'

'But unattainable for many,' Eloise said. Her own

father had had very little interest in her, and her husband had treated her as someone of very little intelligence until he began to treat her with silent ice-fury once he'd discovered she was expecting another man's child. It was probably something about her; perhaps she just wasn't very loveable. In addition, if she were ever to meet someone with whom she might fall in love and who might also love her, there must always be a barrier between because she would never disclose the secret of Amelia's paternity to a living soul, and that could be no basis for a happy marriage.

The biggest thing, though, was that she had discovered that life as a widowed dowager duchess was vastly preferable to that as a daughter or wife subject to her father's or husband's every whim, and she had no intention of ever giving up her independence.

'Nonsense. It is just a question perhaps of having a little luck. Now.' Her grandmother tapped the gilt-edged card she was holding. 'The Featherhulmes' ball. Half the *ton* will be there. I shall accept on behalf of both of us.'

Eloise shook her head. 'I really do need to return home very soon, I'm afraid. I'm so sorry, but I don't think I will be able to accompany you to any of these engagements. I'm sure, though, that there will be local dinners and assemblies to which we can go together when you come to visit me in Sussex, and I should very much enjoy that and hope you will too.'

Their dispute was interrupted by a knock on the door and the entrance of Dawes.

'The Earl of Malbrook has called to see you, Your Grace.'

The two ladies replied at exactly the same time.

'Please tell him I'm not at home, Dawes,' said Eloise.

'We'd be delighted to receive him,' her grandmother said. 'Show him to the green saloon, Dawes.'

'I really don't…' Eloise, feeling a little sick again, was shaking her head.

'Why ever not?' Her grandmother rose to her feet and reached for the intricately carved stick that she'd recently taken to using. In Eloise's experience, she rarely leaned on it; its greatest use seemed to be for poking people. 'Now if ever there were a man who might make a suitable husband for you it is he.'

No, no, no.

Eloise made a huge effort and produced what she hoped looked like a nonchalant smile. 'If I were looking for a husband, I'm sure the earl would be more than suitable, but I have no intention whatsoever of relinquishing my independence.'

Her grandmother said something under her breath that sounded like, 'We'll see about that,' and held out her non-stick-holding arm for Eloise to take. 'Let us go. We will only entertain him for fifteen minutes and I will not leave you alone with him; we do not wish to appear desperate.'

Eloise stared at her grandmother's arm. She *couldn't* go and sit in the same room as Marcus for fifteen minutes. If he had already recognised her, he might say something. And if he hadn't, he'd have a *long* time in which to do so. 'Um…'

'Eloise?' Her grandmother had her painted eyebrows raised very high.

Eloise was going to have to plead illness; she couldn't think of any alternative.

'I feel quite faint,' Eloise said in a very low voice. She

didn't want to upset her grandmother, so she couldn't act *too* dramatically, but a swoon might be just the thing now. She glanced out of the corner of her eye at the chaise to her right. She could crumple slowly onto there without hurting herself.

She allowed herself to sway slightly and her grandmother screamed, 'Eloise!'

Eloise looked at her grandmother and saw that her face was suddenly very white, in stark contrast to her painted lips.

'I realise that I am actually not faint at all,' she said, alarmed. How could she have been so thoughtless and, just, *stupid*? She should have realised that her being ill would upset her grandmother.

Her grandmother had picked up some smelling salts from a side table and now waved them under Eloise's nose.

'Urgh.' Eloise took a step backwards. 'I really am already quite recovered. I think it was just a very momentary tiredness from the heat of the day.'

'You do look much better. Perhaps, though, you should rest in your bedchamber, while I speak to the earl.' Her grandmother put her head to one side with a pensive air. 'Perhaps that would be for the *best*, in fact. It would allow me to determine whether or not he might be a serious applicant for your hand.'

And it might allow the earl to tell her grandmother that he and Eloise had met before, without Eloise being there to turn the conversation.

'I am entirely recovered,' Eloise said. 'I will join you.'

'In that case, shall we go?'

'Certainly.' Eloise screamed internally, plastered a

smile onto her face and held her arm out for her grandmother to lean hers on.

'We must think tactically. He will have had his fill
of matchmaking mamas, I am sure, and will welcome
our seeming indifference.'

'Actual indifference,' Eloise said.

'We'll see.'

Good heavens.

In the space of four and twenty hours, Eloise had
gone from a happy, calm existence to *this*. Her beloved
grandmother was apparently trying to matchmake her
with the man with whom Eloise had made love nine
years before as an unmarried woman, and who was
Amelia's father, and the three of them were about to
sit down together in her grandmother's green saloon.

Chapter Four

Marcus

'Good morning, my lord.' Lady Kingsbridge swept into the room in a rustle of silks, ahead of her grand-daughter. She held her hand out to Marcus and he dutifully took it and bowed over it.

The Duchess of Rothshire, attired in a pale yellow dress, her thick curls framing her beautiful face, followed her in gracefully, and murmured, 'Good morning.' She did not offer her hand, and she only barely met Marcus's eye, for perhaps a quarter of a second, before transferring her gaze to the wall behind him.

Yesterday, she'd been quite composed once she'd recovered from her faintness, so it was odd that she was behaving in such a distant manner now. Perhaps she was embarrassed by her swoon.

'Good morning, Your Grace. I am come to enquire after your health. I trust that you are quite recovered after the events of yesterday?' He studied her as he spoke; he was certain he knew her very well from somewhere, but for the life of him could not work out where that might have been. If he was honest, that was really the reason that he'd come to call on her in person today rather than enquiring in writing after her health: curiosity. It was rare that one felt a burning sense that one *knew* someone, and a similarly strong feeling that one *had* to remember where one had met them.

'Recovered? Events of yesterday?' Lady Kingsbridge's head whipped round towards the duchess. 'What happened?'

'Oh, nothing, really. I found myself a little overcome by the heat at the balloon ascension. The earl was nearby and was kind enough to escort me back to my chaise. The slight faintness was quite momentary; I was recovered almost immediately.' Her voice was musical and charming and struck as much of a chord with him as her face. Almost more, strangely.

'Oh, Eloise.' The older lady put her hand on her granddaughter's arm. 'Are you quite sure that you are well? You also felt faint just as the earl arrived.'

'Certainly.' The duchess spoke in a particularly robust tone. 'I had already forgotten yesterday's lightheadedness.' She shot a very quick frowning glance at Marcus, and continued, 'That's why I didn't mention it.'

Marcus could very well understand her not wishing to worry her grandmother, so he smiled blandly and nodded.

'You do *seem* well.' Lady Kingsbridge looked her granddaughter up and down and then sat down majestically on a wide, gilt-finished, green silk–upholstered armchair to one side of the grand fireplace and pointed with her stick to indicate that the duchess and Marcus should sit in matching green velvet chairs one on each side of her. 'Now. We need sustenance.'

Her butler appeared at the room's door within seconds. 'Certainly, my lady.'

'It is beautiful weather today,' Marcus said into the brief silence that ensued.

'Indeed,' the duchess replied, after another brief pause.

'Her Grace resides in the country and enjoys the outdoors greatly,' Lady Kingsbridge told him. 'Although in moderation. Just the right amount, in fact.'

'I enjoy the outdoors just the right amount too,' Marcus said, his lips twitching. This call was seeming odder and odder. Why were *both* the ladies behaving strangely?

'I am pleased to hear it.' Lady Kingsbridge smiled at him. 'And I am pleased to see you. I knew your mother very well and I remember you as a baby. You had an excellent set of lungs. Very loud crying.'

Marcus laughed. 'I count myself fortunate in that my lungs seem still to be in excellent shape.'

'How are your sisters? You were quite spoilt of course, as a child; your parents were so relieved finally to have a son after producing so many daughters. How many girls was it? Six or seven?'

'Five. My parents might have spoilt me but my sisters did their best to do quite the opposite, and, frankly, still terrify me. They are all very well, and between them, together with my younger brother, have to date produced no fewer than nineteen nephews and nieces for me.' Thank the Lord: Marcus had no wish to marry—after witnessing so much death and misery on the battlefield, he had a horror of the idea of falling in love with someone and thus becoming vulnerable to grieving for them should anything happen to them—so it was ideal that he had so many heirs.

His extended family produced excellent conversational fodder for Lady Kingsbridge. Marcus laughed at her forthrightness and batted away her more outrageous questions, and while he was doing so kept trying to look at the duchess, who was holding a small, fixed smile and looking sometimes at her knees and sometimes at the wall above Marcus's left shoulder. Quite peculiar. Did she recognise him too? And not wish to acknowledge that? Why?

Halfway through a question from her grandmother about whether Marcus preferred to spend the majority of his time in London or the country, Marcus's gaze caught the duchess's. The two of them looked at each other for a long moment, and then colour rose to her cheeks and she coughed and looked away and twisted a little in her seat. Marcus found himself shaking his head very slightly. What had that *been*? For that moment he'd been unable to take his eyes from her.

'Are you quite all right, Eloise?' Lady Kingsbridge was staring at her.

'Yes, thank you.' The duchess's small smile reappeared and she resumed her study of the wall above Marcus's shoulder.

Two or three minutes later, Lady Kingsbridge said, 'Well, we must not detain you any longer, my lord; I am sure that you are very busy.'

Marcus took a surreptitious glance at his watch and was impressed by her timekeeping; the call had lasted exactly fifteen minutes.

'I have very much enjoyed seeing you today, and I know that Her Grace has too.' Lady Kingsbridge stood up and lurched alarmingly for a moment, before Marcus and the duchess simultaneously jumped forward and took an arm each. 'I should like your company at a musical soirée we are planning to hold tomorrow evening, at eight o'clock. Just a select gathering; you will very much enjoy it, I'm sure. Your dear mother would have loved you to join us. We will see you then. Her Grace very much enjoys music.'

The look of shock on Her Grace's face told Marcus that either she did not enjoy music or she had not until this moment known that her grandmother was planning to hold the soirée.

He hadn't felt this intrigued for a long time.

'I'd be delighted to attend.' He bowed over Lady Kingsbridge's hand. 'Thank you.'

As the door began to close behind him, he heard the duchess say, *'Grandmama.'*

Her grandmother hissed, 'Shh!' and then, irritatingly, the door closed.

Well. He would never have imagined it possible that he could look forward to a musical soirée as much as he was going to look forward to this one; but it was rare for one's curiosity to be piqued quite so much as his had been by the duchess.

Just under thirty-six hours later, Marcus was being shown by Lady Kingsbridge's butler into a saloon of mainly female musical soirée-goers. As Lady Kingsbridge bustled towards him with a wide smile on her face and a hand on the Duchess of Rothshire's arm, so that the duchess was forced also to move in his direction, he had a brief moment of wondering what on earth had possessed him when he'd thought it would be a good idea to come this evening.

The duchess's smile was as tight as her grandmother's was broad, and the room was busy.

He would like to have the opportunity to speak in private with the duchess to understand where he might have met her before. This was not the place, he now realised. But he could hardly turn tail and leave, so he was probably going to have to endure at least half an evening of music. He would just have to try hard to obtain a moment alone with the duchess, so that his musical misery was not for nothing.

'Good evening, Lord Malbrook.' Lady Kingsbridge's smile had widened even further. She held out a ring-laden hand for him to take. 'Her Grace and I are delighted that you were able to come.'

'Indeed,' murmured the duchess, looking particularly un-delighted.

'I trust that you remain in good health and have not suffered any further light-headedness?' he asked her.

'Yes, thank you; I am very well.'

'Eloise, why don't you ensure that Lord Malbrook is quite settled and has refreshments,' commanded Lady Kingsbridge, quite unnecessarily, as a footman had just handed him a glass of champagne. 'I must go and speak to dear Lady Morton.' And she moved away impressively swiftly for a woman of her years.

There was a brief pause, which Marcus determined not to fill; if she had to speak, he would be more likely to be able to work out who she was.

'I understand that my grandmother has an excellent repertoire lined up for us this evening,' she said unsmilingly after a second or two. 'I believe that we are to hear a soprano whose voice rivals that of Angelica Catalani.'

'That sounds wonderful.' The more he heard her speak, the more he *knew* that he knew her. 'A treat indeed for us all.'

'Yes; I am very much looking forward to it.' She scanned the room with her eyes for a moment. 'Allow me to introduce you to Miss Duxton.' She began to walk towards a young lady standing with an older woman, so that Marcus was obliged to follow her. 'Mrs Duxton, Miss Duxton, allow me to introduce the Earl of Malbrook to you. Lord Malbrook, Mrs Duxton, Miss Duxton. I believe that you have a love of soprano voices in common. Now, if you'll excuse me, I must go and see whether my grandmother requires any help.' And she disappeared from his side even faster than her grandmother had walked away a few minutes ago.

'My lord, I had no notion that you were as interested in music as Sofranella is.' Mrs Duxton nodded at her daughter. 'I declare I have far less expertise myself. You must not allow me to distract you from your discussions.' And off she went too, equally fast.

'Oh, my lord,' breathed Miss Duxton. 'You must call me Sofranella. I can see that we are going to be fast friends.'

A good five minutes later, Miss Duxton was still talking about sopranos—she'd been to a great number of musical recitals it seemed—and people were beginning to seat themselves for the start of the evening's entertainment.

'I'm afraid, my lord, that you and Sofranella will have to take a few minutes away from your conversation to listen to the music.' Mrs Duxton had appeared at his elbow and was ushering the two of them to seats on the edge of a grouping of chairs at one end of the room, clearly practised in the art of manoeuvring eligible men into spending entire evenings sitting next to her daughter.

Marcus smiled at her through somewhat gritted teeth and looked over to where the duchess was sitting down on the end of a row, next to Viscountess Bakewell, the lady with whom she had attended the balloon ascension, so that she was effectively protected from anyone—such as Marcus—who might wish to sit near or speak to her.

She glanced up and their gazes locked for a moment, before the duchess's slid to the Duxtons and Marcus caught a smile flit across her face. He found his own lips turning up in response and something within him just…chiming. He just… Well, he didn't know what.

'My lord?' Oh. Mrs Duxton was speaking to him and indicating a seat.

'Thank you,' he said, pulling his eyes from the duchess's profile, and sat down.

Marcus was not musical and he did not have a great interest in sopranos. He was fairly sure, though, from the wincing around him, that this particular soprano was not on course to rival anyone of renown or even just to sing in tune. He was fortunate in being seated at an angle that allowed him to study the duchess while appearing to watch the singer, so his time was not entirely wasted. By the end of the soprano's performance he had, however, made no progress beyond being *certain* that he knew the duchess and *certain* that he couldn't remember how and *certain* (he didn't know why) that he had to find out.

The extremely screechy cellist whose performance

followed that of the soprano caused him to wonder whether Lady Kingsbridge had perhaps put this performance together at very short notice. Either that or the world of music hated her.

Eventually, a mildly pleasant baroque quartet and a genuinely quite nice—in Marcus's untutored opinion anyway—harp duet later, a supper interval was called.

Marcus looked over—again—at the duchess, and caught her glancing in his direction before she whipped her head away so that she was staring straight ahead and all he could see again was her—very charming—profile and a slow tinge of red crossing her cheeks.

Perhaps he would have the opportunity to take her in to supper and talk to her there.

With great difficulty, he excused himself to the Duxtons and made his way over to her.

Lady Kingsbridge materialised at the duchess's side just as Marcus reached her.

'Perfect, my lord,' she beamed. 'You and Her Grace must go in to supper together.' Perfect indeed.

'That would have been delightful, but I have engaged to sit with Sir Edwin Pallon.' The duchess smiled in the direction of an elderly man who was making his way towards them with the aid of a stick. 'I wonder whether Miss Duxton has anyone to escort her.'

Enough was enough. Marcus did not want to sit through supper with the Duxtons and then more musical torture if he was not going to have an opportunity to speak to the duchess.

'I must unfortunately take my leave now,' he said. 'A prior engagement. Thank you very much, Lady Kingsbridge, for a most inspiring evening.' An idea occurred to him and he turned to the duchess. 'Your Grace, I wonder if you would like to accompany me for a drive in Hyde Park tomorrow.' He really could not have said why he was quite so eager to work out what connection he might have with her.

'I'm so sorry…' the duchess began.

'I'm sure that Her Grace would be delighted to accompany you,' her grandmother interrupted. 'I don't think we have any other engagements tomorrow afternoon.'

'I'm afraid that won't be possible.' The duchess's tone was steely. 'I will be returning to the country tomorrow.'

'In that case, I wonder if we might have a moment together now. I have a question to ask you.'

The duchess raised her eyebrows extremely haughtily and said, 'I'm afraid that I must go in to supper.' She turned to Sir Edwin, who was finally almost next to them.'

'I feel sure we have met before,' Marcus said. 'I wondered where that might have been.'

The duchess gave a tiny gasp, before clamping her lips together.

Lady Kingsbridge looked between the two of them, her eyebrows raised.

And then, to Marcus's surprise, the duchess said, 'Perhaps we have met before. I will be delighted to join you for a drive tomorrow.'

'I look forward to it. Shall we say four o'clock?' As Marcus spoke, he caught the merest hint of a frown on the duchess's face. And as he leaned forward in a small bow, he caught her scent, something delightfully summery, with just a hint of mystery in there, perhaps jasmine, and something quite unidentifiable but very attractive. And that chimed with him too. 'Good evening.'

He felt her eyes on him all the way to the door; he was sure she recognised him too. Why did he care so much, though? What was it about her?

As he drew up outside Lady Kingsbridge's mansion on the north side of Berkeley Square the next afternoon at exactly one minute before four, he was half expecting to be told that the duchess had already departed for the country after all. He really couldn't have said why—perhaps it was the enjoyment of attempting to solve a mystery—but he knew that he would be disappointed not to see her.

He was not to be disappointed, however: she was already ready for their drive, clad in a cream-coloured, flower-patterned dress that became her very well.

'Good afternoon, my lord.' Her touch on his arm was light as he handed her into the curricle, and for a moment, Marcus fancied that she was purposely trying not to touch him. Which was…odd.

'Good afternoon.' Once he had leapt up into the driver's seat on the other side of the curricle, he smiled at her. 'I trust that you're quite comfortable?'

'Yes, thank you.'

'Excellent.' He lifted his reins and encouraged his pair to move forward. 'I trust the second half of yesterday evening was as enjoyable as the first?'

'Yes, thank you. It was quite delightful. In fact, I think the standard of music was even higher than during the first half.' The note of sarcasm in her voice made Marcus smile.

'I was sorry to miss it,' he said politely, thinking

with satisfaction of the excellent dinner and drinks he had shared with some of his friends at his club after leaving Lady Kingsbridge's house. He had certainly made the right decision.

'Yes, I noticed that you dragged yourself away with extreme reluctance.' The duchess twirled her furled parasol as she spoke.

'Indeed.' Max steered his horses to the right to avoid a somewhat out-of-control-looking phaeton driven by a youthful dandy who looked to be still in his teens and who appeared unable—to the detriment of his driving—to turn his head more than an inch or two to the right or left due to the height of his shirt points. Turning his attention back to the duchess as they drove along Curzon Street, he said, 'The weather is beautiful today. Perfect for an afternoon drive in the park.' Well. That was a boring observation. The duchess would be in raptures to have agreed to accompany him.

'Yes. It is particularly pleasant to see the flowers in bloom in June.'

Marcus nodded. A suitably boring response.

'What do you enjoy most about driving in the park?' Good God. His conversation was that of a young sprig, unable to put two interesting words together in the presence of an attractive woman.

'The people, of course. Surely that is everyone's favourite thing about it? If one didn't wish to engage in seeing others and being seen, would one not prefer just to drive out to the country? Or not drive at all?'

'Very true. That was of course an inane question.'

'Indeed it was.' She turned a wide, sunny smile on him for a moment and suddenly Marcus was transported back in time, back to the night before he left for war. Back to dancing with a beautiful, entrancing, mischievous…shepherdess. Not a duchess.

He sat, staring at her, until she suddenly gave a small scream and pointed beyond him.

'That chaise, my lord.'

'Good God.' Marcus pulled his horses to the left just in time to avoid scraping an oncoming carriage. 'I must apologise,' he called to the chaise's driver. 'A lapse in attention.' He turned back to his companion. 'And I must apologise to you too. I don't think I've ever lost concentration like that before while driving.'

'I'm sure it happens to the best of us,' she said, as though to a small boy. 'I drive in the country, and while I count myself a competent driver, I'm sure that my concentration has failed on occasion. When did you learn to drive, my lord?' Was this self-possessed duchess *really* his shepherdess from that night—it must have been nine years ago?

'When I was barely out of leading strings,' he said, concentrating on driving *perfectly*, 'so I have absolutely no excuse.'

'The park is that way.' She indicated with a finger.

'Thank you; I know the way.'

'Oh, I'm sorry; I thought you might have suffered another lapse in concentration.' She bestowed another of her wide, faux-innocent beams on him. And in that moment he *knew* that it was her.

'Ella.' He glanced at her as he spoke and he caught the moment when she knew that he knew. She just froze: her entire body went completely still. He was sure then—he didn't know how—that she had already known that he was him.

Well, of course she had. When they'd met, she'd

been masked and wearing an outrageous shepherdess costume and her hair had been quite different, and yet he had still now recognised her. By contrast, he had been unmasked and dressed as himself. Of *course* she'd recognised him. Unless she'd done what they'd done then regularly with a lot of people. Which he was sure she hadn't. Unless he'd been the first of many. Because he *had*, he'd been quite certain, been the first.

Which was confusing, and something to think about later. Had it been before her marriage or after? Presumably before? Had her husband then realised?

'I am,' she said slowly, 'the Duchess of Rothshire.'

'Yes, Your Grace,' he said, as they passed through the gates of Hyde Park.

Ella did not reply.

Marcus glanced across at her. She was still staring rigidly ahead, stationary apart from the rapid rise and fall of her chest. Her profile was…beautiful.

'You were my shepherdess,' he stated. He knew from experience that his tiger, sitting behind them in the groom's seat, could not hear what he said unless he shouted.

'I am the Duchess of Rothshire,' she repeated. 'I would never…be a shepherdess.' She turned to look at him and he saw her draw a deep breath. 'I would…not.'

Marcus nodded. Obviously she would never want anyone to know.

'I, in my turn,' he said, 'would never tell anyone— *anyone*—about…that.' He wouldn't. He hadn't told anyone about it at the time, because there had been something special, almost magical about it, and at the same time he'd felt a little—ashamed, he supposed— because he'd thought that it was her first time and he'd wondered whether he should have stayed. He *couldn't* have stayed because he'd had to leave for war…and yet he'd worried that he should somehow have found a way to do so. Although he'd had no way of finding her.

He thought again of her husband.

'When did you…?' he began. No. He couldn't ask her when she got married.

They drove silently along until he became aware that the occupants of a carriage bearing down upon them in the opposite direction were waving at them.

Oh, God. It was his oldest sister and one of her best friends.

'Lucretia. Lady Bentley.' He nodded at both of them.

'I believe we have met before but I'm afraid that I cannot remember your name.' Lucretia was looking at Ella particularly haughtily.

'I beg your pardon.' He smiled at Ella and said, 'This is my sister, Lucretia, Lady Wright, and her great friend Lady Bentley. This is the Duchess of Rothshire.'

'Oh!' His sister must have imagined Ella to be a much less august person. Such as a shepherdess. To give her her due, Lucretia collected herself quickly, and said, 'How do you do? I believe that you are not often in London?'

'No, I'm not,' agreed Ella. 'I reside mainly in the country.' She moved slightly and her arm brushed Marcus's, and he almost jumped at the contact. 'Your brother very kindly asked me if I would like to accompany him for a drive as we have a shared interest in…' She looked around. 'Rhododendrons.'

'Rhododendrons?' Lucretia's look of scepticism was quite apt. Marcus knew nothing about flowers.

'Indeed,' he said. 'There are particularly fine examples in the park.'

'Where?' Lucretia tilted her head to one side. Marcus knew that look.

'Further along,' he said. 'How very nice to have seen you.' He smiled at Lucretia and Lady Bentley, and urged his horses forward.

'Rhododendrons?' he said, once they were out of earshot.

'I panicked,' Ella said, with dignity.

Marcus laughed. 'I had imagined you to be most competent in an emergency.'

'I am,' she told him. 'This was just an...unprecedented kind of emergency.'

'Unlike usual emergencies, which are entirely precedented.'

'Exactly.' She looked at him out of the corner of her eye and, damn, that look, it was pure Ella. Cheekiness and warmth and... *Damn.*

He applied pressure to his horses' reins to slow them and said, 'Would you perhaps like to walk?'

'No.' And there was another one of those sunny smiles, which just made him want to smile and smile too. 'Thank you.'

'We might perhaps have something to discuss?' he suggested.

'We have nothing to discuss.' Her hauteur was back. He didn't want to see a haughty duchess, he realised; he wanted to see Ella the shepherdess.

'Not even rhododendrons?' he said.

'Certainly not.' She was facing straight ahead again, but as he looked at her, she glanced at him out of the corner of her eye, and he caught just a little twinkle from her, which—somehow—took him right back to that night at the masquerade, when he'd seen her right at the beginning, at the window of her carriage.

Marcus did not wish to get married, but he was not averse to a little flirtation, and who better to flirt with than a widowed duchess. Especially one with whom he knew he had shared a—not inconsiderable—attraction.

'If you are not interested in the park's flowers,' he said, 'perhaps we might discuss their sheep, which I do believe you enjoy tending?'

'My lord!'

'My name is Marcus.'

Chapter Five

Eloise

Marcus's eyes were crinkling as he smiled at her. This was *not* a good situation, and yet Eloise found her own lips widening in response.

He slowed his horses even more and turned towards her.

He was so *large*. It seemed as though he filled almost the whole seat. She couldn't help noticing how his thick brown hair was just a shade longer than was fashionable and curled quite charmingly over his collar.

She felt quite short of breath.

Before he'd begun his outrageous flirting, he had suggested that they might have something to discuss. What if he had been referring to Amelia?

She pulled her eyes from Marcus's face and looked ahead at the horses and breathed carefully for a few moments.

She needed to find out whether he suspected anything.

If he did, then she would need to beg him never to betray her secret.

If he did not, then she would do everything she could to act in an unsuspicious manner and then leave for the country with Amelia as soon as she could without up-setting her grandmother. If he thought she was running away and linked her flight to their meeting and his re-alisation that she was the Ella of the masquerade, he would, she trusted, assume that that was because she was embarrassed at the memory of what they had done.

She turned her head a little in his direction and said, 'I should enjoy a short walk, my lord.'

'Certainly... Ella.'

'No one calls me Ella.'

'Really?' He turned his horses expertly down a side path. 'Were you Ella merely for that evening?'

'Perhaps.' There were—many—advantages to being a dowager duchess, and one of them was that no one at all, other than her grandmother, was ever impertinent or too forthright when they spoke to her. Marcus was being really quite...annoying.

'May I ask why?'

'No.' She smiled at him as he drew the horses to a halt and his tiger leapt down.

He laughed. 'Fair enough.'

Putting her hand into Marcus's as he helped her de-scend and feeling the strength in his arm as he guided her weight for a second caused her breath to catch again.

When she was on her feet on the ground and he held his arm out, she had the strongest desire not to take it; touching him at all was far too... Well, it was just...it reminded her too much of that night.

She must not act oddly, though.

She closed her eyes briefly to collect herself and

then placed her arm lightly on his and they began to walk down a path lined with flowering bushes.

'Perhaps these are rhododendrons,' Marcus said.

'They might indeed be,' she agreed.

'Your panic was quite adorable,' he said.

Eloise looked up at him. He was gazing at her in a way that suddenly made her feel very hot indeed. She was not accustomed to men like him flirting with her—very few men of her acquaintance would have the courage to do so—but she was sure that he *was* flirting. His gaze moved slowly from her eyes to her mouth to her chest and back again.

The bad thing about it all was that she was *so* tempted to pout and move a little closer and, yes, return the flirting.

The good thing, though, she realised, was that it was unlikely that he would be behaving like this if he suspected and cared that Amelia was his daughter.

'Thank you,' she said, as un-flirtatiously as she could, thinking fast.

Why had she agreed to this walk? What if someone saw them? She didn't want to cause any gossip and she could have carried on talking to him in the curricle to try to ascertain whether he suspected anything about Amelia.

'I realise that I need to return very soon,' she said. 'I had forgotten that I do not have time for a walk. I promised my daughter that I would spend some time with her before my grandmother and I go out this evening.' She glanced at him as she spoke the words *my daughter* and saw that he did not twitch. She almost stumbled at the feeling of quite immense relief that flooded through her; she was close to certain that he did not know or suspect anything. She should just make as sure as she could, though, if she could turn the conversation in that direction. 'My daughter is the most delightful companion.'

'I'm sure she is,' he said, again not reacting at all to the mention of Amelia, thank goodness. 'And of course; let us return to the curricle. Perhaps we might walk another day?'

'Certainly,' she said, smiling at him. Certainly not; she would be returning to the country as soon as she could.

They turned around to begin the short walk back to the curricle.

'May I ask where you and your grandmother are going this evening?' Marcus asked. 'The Featherhulmes' ball, perhaps? I might see you there?'

'Perhaps,' she said, with as much vagueness as she could summon.

'In that case might I have the first dance?'

Eloise almost wanted to stamp her foot in frustration. He seemed particularly eager to spend time with her. And she wasn't entirely sure that it was flattering. He couldn't possibly be contemplating marriage with her; eligible earls of perhaps three and thirty years did not marry dowager duchesses. So he must be contemplating a…flirtation. In which she would certainly not be joining him. No, now she thought about it, his interest was definitely not flattering. She was not to be dallied with.

She opened her mouth to refuse and then thought better of it. It was unlikely that she could avoid going to the ball without upsetting her grandmother, and if she did go Marcus was—going by his persistence now—

likely to ask her to dance once they were there. One dance couldn't hurt, and if she didn't dance at all her grandmother would be disappointed.

In order to avoid both suspicion and Marcus, she should probably dance with him at the beginning of the evening and then avoid him during the remainder of the ball, refuse any other social events where she might see him and return to the country soon.

'I'd be delighted,' she said unenthusiastically.

'Perfect.'

They had arrived back at the curricle and as Marcus handed her up she was again conscious of the strength in his arm and—shamefully—had to fight with herself not to feel almost…intoxicated by it. It was the memory of his hard body against her soft one all those years ago that was doing this to her. And the shock of his recognising her.

As he sat down next to her in the curricle, their legs and sides touched for a moment, and Eloise found herself saying *'Oh'* quite breathlessly.

'Oh?' enquired Marcus, settling into the seat, still very close to her.

'Oh…look at those…beautiful rhododendrons.'

The rumble of Marcus's laughter seemed to fill the curricle and…her body. And mind. All she could do was laugh with him.

And she almost didn't mind—well, in truth, she didn't mind at all, but she should—when he allowed his arm to rest against hers as he lifted the reins with his other hand.

The warmth from his body was spreading to hers and she was beginning to feel hot in places that only Marcus had ever…

No. What was *wrong* with her? Only a matter of minutes ago she had determined that she would certainly not be flirting, or anything else, with him.

She jerked herself away from him right to the end of the seat, and said, a little horrified at how breathless her voice sounded, 'You will wish to hold your reins with both hands, my lord.'

'Marcus. Yes, you're right: driving slowly around Hyde Park is a most treacherous activity; all manner of danger might befall us if I steer one-handed.'

'You are cynical, my lord.'

'Marcus. And, yes, I am, Ella.'

'Your Grace, my lord.'

He turned to look at her, one eyebrow raised, and then laughed.

'As you wish, *Your Grace.*'

They were prevented from further private conversation for the next few minutes by the constant stream of acquaintances, mainly Marcus's, whom they passed and who wished to speak with them.

The reaction of many of those people indicated that Eloise's drive with Marcus would be one of the day's *on-dits*, she reflected as they finally drove towards the gate to leave the park. Eloise did not wish to be the subject of gossip, but it could not matter on this occasion since she would be leaving London so soon, almost certainly never to see him again.

The extraordinary feeling of—was that *sadness*?— that followed that reflection was pierced by Marcus saying, 'I have enjoyed our drive together.'

Eloise nodded. 'It has been most enjoyable.' That wasn't true. She had been shocked, she had been worried and she had been tempted to flirt with the one man in the world she needed to avoid. None of those emotions were pleasant.

'Really?' Marcus asked rhetorically a moment later when a young man driving his phaeton far too fast nearly crashed into a gig full of vegetables. The young man fought to get his horses under control, succeeding just in time. Marcus shook his head. 'I think he needs a few more lessons.'

He was entirely right, but Eloise couldn't resist saying, 'Hmm, I seem to remember an incident involving...*you* earlier?'

Marcus laughed. 'Perhaps a bit hypocritical on my part but in my defence I was distracted for the first and only time in fifteen years of *extremely* competent driving.'

Eloise was saved—mercifully, because she could feel herself descending into flirtation again—from having to respond by their arrival in front of the steps of her grandmother's house.

Marcus—obviously—within seconds of halting the horses had himself out of the curricle and round on her side to help her down. As she looked down into his face she saw... Well, she saw the face that had haunted her dreams for years, older now and even more handsome. And she saw Amelia. Facially, Amelia was an exact little girl version of Marcus; she had nothing of Eloise.

'Ella? Your Grace?' He was regarding her quizzically.

Oh. She'd been staring for...a while.

She shook her head. 'Yes, of course. Thank you.' She took his arm and stepped down from the carriage.

When she was steady on her feet, still holding on to his arm—she really ought not still to be holding it but it seemed that she didn't want to let go—he put his free hand over hers for a moment. His hand was large and warm—but not unpleasantly hot or sticky, just the right amount of warmth—and covered her smaller one entirely. She could feel her heart beating stupidly fast. When she looked up at him, she saw that he was watching her with a small smile.

'I look forward to seeing you this evening at the ball.' He accompanied his words with a small squeeze of her hand, which, oddly, made her feel almost *protected*. And as though she wanted to experience more, a lot more, of his touch.

It was as though she was under some kind of spell; she couldn't move, and she couldn't think of anything to say.

'Your Grace?' The voice of her grandmother's butler came to her from afar—well, from the top of the steps to the house, she realised when she had collected herself enough to look in his direction—and she pulled her hand from Marcus's arm.

'Good afternoon,' she bade him, and walked forward up the steps, sure that he was watching her the entire way.

When she reached the door, she turned slightly, against her better judgment, and, yes, he was watching her, still with that small, intimate smile. She felt something stir inside her, which was not at all right, and whisked herself straight inside.

Four hours later, she was being helped into one of the ball gowns her grandmother had insisted on having made for her last week. Despite Eloise's protestations that it was unnecessary, the modiste had said that for dear Lady Kingsbridge she would willingly work through the night, and had produced a number of quite exquisite gowns very quickly.

And it *was* lovely to have such carefully, luxuriously made clothes.

The late duke had allowed her a certain amount of pin money, but he had not been generous in his provision, and she had had Amelia to provide for and in addition had wished to maintain to the world the pretence of a reasonably happy alliance, so she had been careful with her pennies, and had made do with a small number of gowns made by the dressmaker in the local village from quite everyday fabrics.

She had been able to spend more since the duke's death, as the new duke was considerably more generous in providing for his dependants, but a dowager duchess in mourning did not have great occasion to wear excitingly lovely gowns.

As she smoothed her intricately sewn skirts and looked at her image in the looking glass in the corner of her bedchamber, she reflected that this really was the nicest gown she had ever owned.

And tonight was going to be the grandest ball she had ever attended.

She had once, while married, intended to go to a ball in Brighton with some female friends. As she had descended the castle's grand staircase in her village shop-made gown, the duke's butler had brought her a note from her husband. In it he had asked her if she was dressed like that in order to bed a rake like the trollop she was. Those were the first words he had addressed to her in any way for months. She had told the butler that she had changed her mind about the evening ahead and gone to the nursery to hug Amelia, terrified that the duke's ire would lead him to disown her, and then—after burning the note and poking around in the embers to make sure it was entirely destroyed—she'd cried herself to sleep that evening.

She *loved* being a widow. She was *never* going to remarry.

Just over an hour after surveying herself in the looking glass, Eloise was in the middle of quite the most crowded ballroom she'd ever been in. It was hot from the bodies around her and the extraordinary profusion of candles above, it was a little smelly—again from the bodies and the candles—and it was very noisy. She *loved* it.

A tall, broad-shouldered man passed close to her and she looked up to check whether he was Marcus. She brushed aside the disappointment she felt when she saw that it was another man—one who did not cause her heart to beat at all differently—and smiled at her grandmother next to her. She must not spend the evening looking for Marcus. He might not even come. And if he did, did she really wish to speak to him, dance with him?

Well…maybe. Because he really did seem to have absolutely no idea about Amelia and they would very soon be leaving for the country, and nothing scandalous could possibly happen in such crowded and yet most proper surroundings, so she would like to—*love* to—just enjoy herself this evening. And talking to Marcus was…enjoyable.

Another tall and broad man appeared close to them and she lifted her head, feeling herself begin to smile and…no, not Marcus. Which did not matter. She could certainly enjoy herself even if he didn't come. Really, she could.

'Perhaps we might find seats,' her grandmother said in her ear.

'Of course.' Eloise should *not* have been thinking about Marcus; she should have been trying to make her grandmother comfortable. Arm in arm, the two of them began to make their way slowly through the throng towards the side of the room.

'Good evening.' A deep voice from just behind them made Eloise jump and her heart begin to beat a little faster.

'Good evening, my lord.' She turned to greet Marcus and couldn't help just *basking* in the particularly warm smile he directed at her. There couldn't be any harm in amusing herself a little this evening, she told herself; this would after all probably be the last time she would see him.

'Malbrook.' Her grandmother gave him her hand. 'You may escort us to the side of the room so that we might be seated. We shall otherwise feel faint in this crush.'

'Certainly.' Marcus's broad shoulders and sheer presence parted the crowds most effectively and they were soon at the side of the room, ensconced all three of them in chairs.

'Her Grace and I are delighted to see you,' her grandmother told him. 'Will you dance together?'

'I have already been granted the honour of the first dance with Her Grace.'

'Excellent.' Her grandmother smiled at the two of them and nodded, as though she had arranged that dance herself. 'Oh, there is the music. You must stand up together immediately. I shall sit with some of my friends.' She signalled to two other ladies and then almost pulled Marcus and Eloise together, a hand on each of their arms. 'Go.'

'Lady Kingsbridge is certainly eager for us to dance together,' Marcus said, laughing, as they walked away from her, Eloise holding his arm.

'My grandmother has a particular liking for, erm, punctuality,' Eloise lied. What she clearly actually liked was the thought of her granddaughter marrying Marcus. To which Eloise would never agree and which in any case she was certain was not Marcus's intention in spending time with her now.

'For dances?' he queried, still laughing.

'Exactly.'

'And are you a punctual person?' he asked as they took their places.

'Of course.' She shook her skirts out and smiled at him.

'Because you possess every virtue?'

'I think I must do.' She smiled at him over her shoulder as she turned for the dance. 'I certainly have not recently nearly driven into anything.'

'Indeed. And you also possess excellent knowledge of rhododendrons.'

'I do.' Eloise nodded. 'And what is important beyond punctuality, driving and rhododendrons?' The sensation of flirting like this—safely—was quite intoxicating. This would never happen again because she would never see Marcus again, and she just knew that no other man would inspire this kind of, well, *naughti-*

ness in her, but just now it was really quite deliciously enjoyable.

'What is important beyond those?' Marcus spun her just a little faster than was necessary, which served to increase her heart rate even further. He leaned in so that his breath as he spoke skimmed her ear, and said, 'Why, *pleasure*.'

'My lord,' Eloise squeaked.

'Yes, Your *Grace*?'

'You are…you are…'

'Correct?'

'No. I was going to say you are bold.'

'I am not correct? Pleasure is not important?' He was speaking far too loudly and he was chuckling far too much.

'No, of course it…' She stopped talking and wrinkled her face at him. 'I believe that I nearly fell into a little trap there.'

'Nearly?' His smile was only for her and she could have looked at it forever. The next steps of the dance caused them to move very close to each other again and Marcus said, 'I am finding this evening very…*pleasurable*,' which caused Eloise to shiver, most…*pleasurably*.

She took a moment to catch her breath and then said in her primmest manner, 'I am so pleased for you,' which made Marcus laugh a lot.

The dance—quite the best one of her life—came to an end far too soon, and with its end it was as though the entire evening had finished for her, because she certainly wouldn't dance with Marcus again—she must never allow herself to be considered a fast widow—and she realised that there was no one else here this evening with whom she would particularly like to dance; and she did like dancing. And having danced with Marcus, she would have to dance with anyone else—within reason—who asked her, or she would look remarkably rude.

Two dances later, as she laughed in genuine amusement at the wicked anecdote that the wealthy and apparently confirmed bachelor Mr Deuchars had just told her, she reflected that she was enjoying herself very well dancing with other men.

She caught a glimpse of Marcus over Mr Deuchars's shoulder and wondered what the young lady with whom he was dancing could possibly have said to make him laugh so; indeed he was laughing almost too much. Surely nothing could be that amusing.

Mr Deuchars, by contrast, certainly was amusing, and Eloise was excessively diverted by his conversation; she really was.

They passed close to Marcus and his companion and just at the moment they crossed each other, Marcus leaned into her and said into her ear, 'Really? He's genuinely that funny?'

Eloise tried to ignore him but couldn't help smiling.

The second the dance finished, Marcus was somehow by her side, and saying, 'You look rather faint, Your Grace. Allow me to escort you somewhere cooler.'

'Her Grace is taken for this dance.' Eloise's next partner, Viscount Marsh, was at her elbow and drawing himself up to his full height.

'I understand that Her Grace is unfortunately feeling a little faint.' Marcus tucked Eloise's hand into his arm.

Eloise looked up at him. She would very much like to give him a set-down at this point; he was *so* sure of himself. Then she looked at the eager young viscount. Why was he quite so keen to dance with her, an older, widowed woman, though? Did *everyone* think youthful widows—*any* widows—were fast?

Well, she didn't know but she had already decided that she wouldn't attend any more balls before she left London, so she might as well enjoy this one.

'I do feel a little faint,' she told the viscount.

'Then I…' he began, but Marcus was already escorting her away, at a far faster pace than someone who did not feel well would probably wish to move.

He directed her towards the opposite end of the room from where they had entered, straight towards some doors opening onto what looked like an outdoor terrace.

'This is outside!' she said, as they reached the doorway.

'Your powers of observation are most impressive.' He smiled at her and stepped through the doors. 'Would you care to join me in the fresh air? Given that you feel faint?'

Looking at the half smiling, half mocking expression on his face illuminated by the lanterns clustered around the doorway, Eloise was reminded again of the night at the masquerade.

Thinking about that night, yes, of course she *wanted* to go outside. But looking around and reflecting on the fact that tonight, unlike that night, she was unmasked and visible to half the *ton*, she was certainly not going to do anything at all that could be construed as scandalous.

'I discover that I do not feel at all faint,' she said. 'And therefore I have no need to take any air. I should like to remain inside the ballroom.'

'Certainly.' Marcus immediately stepped back inside. If he was disappointed, there was no trace of it in his expression.

'Perhaps you would like to sit down?' he suggested.

Eloise looked around. She really didn't know exactly what Society's rules were for dowager duchesses.

'I believe that I should return to my grandmother,' she said. 'Perhaps I might see you in the supper room later.'

'I will accompany you,' Marcus said immediately. 'I very much enjoy talking to Lady Kingsbridge also.' As they began to cross the room, he continued, 'Perhaps we might drive out somewhere together soon, somewhere where we might be less...*visible*. Have you visited Richmond Park? It is particularly attractive at this time of year.'

Eloise knew that she would almost certainly enjoy a drive out to Richmond Park with Marcus; he had already proved himself to be extremely diverting company. She also knew that she was certainly not going to accompany him there, or anywhere else. There must always be a risk of scandal in so doing, and in addition the less time she spent with him the better, to minimise any risk of him finding out about Amelia.

'Perhaps next week,' she told him. She would have left London by then.

When they reached her grandmother's side, she moved to hold her hand out, expecting that he would leave and perhaps ask her if he might escort her in to supper. But no, he pulled up a chair and sat down next to the two of them.

And her grandmother beamed at them both and said,

'Eloise, Malbrook, entertain me. Malbrook, you must have some gossip for me.'

'Let me think,' he said, laughing. 'Have you heard about Lord Salvin's latest horse purchase?'

'No, I have not. Tell me all. That man wouldn't be able to tell a thoroughbred from a jobbing gig horse.'

'Exactly.' Marcus leaned in, and so did Eloise's grandmother, and Eloise watched—unsure whether she was more impressed or slightly terrified—as he wound her grandmother around his little finger.

They talked until it was supper time and then the three of them ate together, until her grandmother declared herself both sated and ready to go home.

'Allow me to accompany you to your carriage,' Marcus said.

'Anyone would think you had developed a tendre for me.' Her grandmother faux batted her eyelashes, chuckling at her own joke.

'Lady Kingsbridge, there can be no man alive who would not fall very quickly under your spell.' As he spoke, Marcus looked right into Eloise's eyes, as though his words were almost serious and meant for her.

Eloise suppressed a shiver and rolled her own eyes at him, and said, 'Goodnight, my lord. We must not take advantage any further of your kindness. I believe that a footman will be more than able to accompany us.'

As he bowed and they moved away, she had to admit to herself that she had very much enjoyed this evening. Perhaps she might even permit herself a small flirtation in a few years' time.

Not with Marcus, though. That would just be too... dangerous.

Chapter Six

Marcus

'I did not realise that you were well acquainted with the Duchess of Rothshire,' Marcus's sister Lucretia told him the next morning the second he entered her carriage, when she picked him up so that he could escort her to the Royal Academy to see Lawrence's latest exhibition.

He should have walked.

'A recent acquaintance.' He busied himself sitting down on the bench opposite her. A man did not wish to discuss with his sister the woman with whom he would most like to pursue a flirtation.

'I'm not sure that a dalliance with a dowager duchess will enhance your chances of marriage to a suitable young lady.' Lucretia tapped the roof of the carriage with the tip of her parasol and the vehicle began to lumber forward.

'There is no dalliance,' Marcus said shortly. Lucretia's attempts to interfere in his affairs never ceased to annoy him. 'And I have no wish to marry.'

'A number of my acquaintance have remarked upon your drive with the duchess and your dance and conversation with her last night.'

'The duchess and I are old friends and we enjoyed seeing each other again. I doubt we shall meet again, however.' He felt a flash of disappointment as he spoke, because what he had said was true. He *had* very much liked Ella's company, but she had clearly been right about the likelihood of gossip if they spent too much time together and, for her sake, she was probably also right that there should be no dalliance between them. So he would not call on her again.

'I am confused. You just said that the duchess was a recent acquaintance.' Lucretia did not look confused; she looked delighted at her own cleverness.

Marcus sighed. 'I meant a recent reacquaintance.'

'I see.' She looked out of the window for a few moments and then said, 'You *should* marry.'

'There is no need for me to do so. Our brother and my many nephews see me better equipped for heirs than the most paranoid of kings might aspire to being.' Marcus was on much safer ground here.

'Nonetheless.'

Marcus smiled at her blandly and she glared at him. She opened her mouth to continue but was thwarted by their horses halting as they arrived outside Somerset House, the site of the exhibition.

Half the world seemed to be here, which was ideal in preventing Lucretia from having the opportunity to continue this conversation. He must remember to walk home or perhaps on to White's afterwards to avoid a return carriage journey with his sibling.

* * *

As soon as they arrived inside the gallery, Lucretia abandoned him for a gossip with a chance-met friend, which was a great relief.

After about fifteen minutes of gazing with some interest and a fair amount of boredom at pictures of persons he did not know over the heads of shorter people, he realised that a particularly firm voice that he could hear on the periphery of his awareness was that of Lady Kingsbridge. He turned to his left to look in the direction of her voice, and saw that she was seated in an upright chair, with Ella standing next to her. Lady Kingsbridge was poking with her stick at the people in front of her and remonstrating with them for having the temerity to stand in her way, and Ella was visibly trying not to laugh.

Marcus—with no thought; it was just the obvious thing to do—made his way through the crowd until he was standing next to them.

'Good morning.' He dipped his head to both the ladies.

Ella gasped. 'Oh!'

'Good morning, my lord.' Lady Kingsbridge smiled broadly at him.

'Good morning,' Ella murmured.

Lady Kingsbridge aimed another poke at a gentleman in front of her, who turned round with the openings of an expostulation before seeing the elderly lady on the end of the stick and closing his mouth and moving out of her way.

'Perhaps I might find you a better viewing position?' Marcus suggested.

'That would be wonderful,' Ella said. 'I feel that

Grandmama might otherwise cause someone quite a serious injury with her stick.'

'These people are causing quite serious injury to my ability to see the paintings,' Lady Kingsbridge said, and aimed some further stick pokes at more people in front of her.

Marcus laughed. 'Allow me.'

He had Lady Kingsbridge on her feet and installed in a much better position quite quickly.

'Thank you,' she said. 'Now, go, the pair of you. I should like a rest here in order to study these marvellous portraits, but I believe that Her Grace would enjoy looking at the other rooms, and you are just the person to escort her, my lord.'

'We must not trespass on the earl's kindness,' Ella said.

'It is not a trespass,' he told her, truthfully, and held out his arm to her. This would be a much more enjoyable way of spending the morning than viewing art with Lucretia would have been.

She gave him the slightest of glares, before taking his arm extremely lightly and saying to her grandmother, 'We shall be back very shortly, Grandmama.'

'There is no need to hurry,' Lady Kingsbridge said, leaning back and closing her eyes, looking for all the world as though she was preparing for a nap.

Marcus was sure he saw Ella frown before she asked, 'Are you a fan of Lawrence?' as they moved through the room.

'He is certainly most gifted, and I do enjoy seeing the remarkable likenesses he paints of people. He painted my mother last year, and she was most gratified by the portrait.'

'Oh, that's wonderful.'

'Indeed. Have you sat for a portrait?' Marcus suddenly had a vision of Ella seated in a chair wearing one of her beautiful smiles, and spending hours on end with the painter, and frowned. Everyone knew that artists and their muses often engaged in flirtations and more.

'No, I haven't, but I wonder whether I should, for my daughter. I do have two portraits of her.' She suddenly coughed, and clutched harder at his arm for support as her whole body was wracked for a second.

'Are you all right? Can I get you some water?'

'No, I thank you.' She cleared her throat and released her grasp on his arm. 'Have you sat for a portrait, my lord?'

'Yes, when I was younger. My mother commissioned portraits of my siblings and me on more than one occasion. A doting mother, like you.' He smiled at her.

Her return smile looked a little forced and she didn't meet his eye.

There was a strange pause, and then she said, 'What other art do you enjoy, my lord?'

He talked a little about the works of Turner and Constable, and then the conversation moved on to some of the art he had been privileged to see in Europe during his Grand Tour, and Ella's expressed hope to travel to Europe one day, and soon the strangeness in her manner had completely disappeared. Perhaps he'd imagined it, he thought, as he noted the charming dimple that appeared on Ella's left cheek when she laughed.

'I should return to my grandmother,' she said after a few more minutes.

Marcus immediately felt bereft, which was ludicrous, because this was hardly the most exciting conversation he'd ever had. It was *nice*, though. They'd barely flirted; they were just talking, like friends. Not *entirely* like friends, though, he thought as he looked down at her and saw the way her lips parted slightly as she returned his gaze, and her chest rose and fell, and he felt his own breathing quicken a little.

'I should like to see you again soon,' he said, on impulse. Surely there could be nothing amiss in a *friend-ship* between a mature man and a widow.

'Oh, I don't think so.' She was still gazing at him in that way, and now she sounded somewhat breathless. From the way she was looking at him, anyone would think that she had just said, *Yes, I should very much like to make wild love to you*. She lifted a hand and then dropped it again and Marcus had to fight hard with himself not to take it.

He said nothing, and she repeated, 'We... I... I am afraid we cannot meet.' Her voice was low and he had to strain to hear the words.

'Of course,' he said. Why did he feel so...almost deflated? There were other women with whom he might pursue dalliances.

'Goodbye, then.' She suddenly turned and hurried away from him, her slight form swallowed by the crowds around them very quickly.

A man next to him bent and picked up something from the floor and handed a pair of gloves to him.

'I believe the lady dropped these,' the man told him.

'Thank you.'

He should send them back to her via a footman.

Perhaps, however, he would take them in person, have one more opportunity to speak with her...

* * *

He went to see an Italian opera that evening with some of his closest friends. A few minutes after his arrival, he thought he saw Ella in a box opposite his. He half rose to leave his own and walk round to hers before realising that that would of course occasion comment about which she would not be pleased.

Perhaps he would somehow see her during the interval instead.

Oh. On closer inspection, it seemed that the lady was not Ella after all.

The play was not particularly engrossing, he found, and while he did very much enjoy his friends' company, he clearly had no urge to flirt with any of them.

Really, he realised, the evening was marred by Ella's not being present.

He would definitely return the gloves to her in person.

Late morning the next day, he was striding up the east side of Berkeley Square, Ella's gloves in his pocket. As he turned the corner onto the north side, where Lady Kingsbridge's mansion was, he saw a grand travelling chaise coming towards him. Was it Ella's? It was certainly reminiscent of the one in which he'd seen her at the ascension.

As it passed him, he saw first that, yes, it was her crest on the side of the carriage.

And secondly, he saw her face at the window.

And next to her face, as the carriage paused next to him for the coachman to turn it, he saw her daughter's face.

And he couldn't believe that he hadn't looked at

her properly at the ascension when she'd been playing with his nieces.

The little girl's face contained nothing of Ella's features. She looked entirely like…his nieces. Who, everyone always said, looked exactly like…him.

He stood staring after the carriage for a long time after it had disappeared from sight.

He felt as though the image of Ella's dropped jaw and the little girl's smile would be imprinted into his memory forever.

His nieces were nine and seven. Ella's daughter had seemed to be between them in size, so she was probably eight. He knew that it was just over nine years since he'd left for war. And a pregnancy took nine months.

Was she? Could she be?

She had to be.

His daughter.

And did Ella know that? Or had she had relations with her husband at a similar time and assumed that her child was his?

Marcus was eventually roused from his thoughts by another vehicle clattering over the cobbles next to him.

What should he do?

He should speak to Ella.

He would go and call for her now using the gloves as a pretext, and hope that Lady Kingsbridge would tell him when Ella would return.

'I am delighted to see you,' Lady Kingsbridge informed him a few minutes later. 'Her Grace has left for the country and I am already missing her and Amelia.'

Left?

'You may entertain me instead for the time being.'

'I…was not aware that Her Grace was intending to leave so soon,' Marcus said, not caring whether or not his implied assumption that he should have known about Ella's plans indicated anything that she would not wish to have indicated.

'Nor I. She decided quite suddenly.'

'Indeed?' Marcus hardly knew what he was saying. That implied perhaps that Amelia was certainly his daughter and that Ella *knew* that. Why had she gone for the drive in the park with him, though?

'Her Grace invited me to go and visit her for several weeks over the summer, and I believe that I will go. I think I might perhaps prevail upon the new duke to host a house party while I am there.'

Marcus had met the new Duke of Rothshire once or twice and was quite sure that he would *not* happily have his house filled with a party of Lady Kingsbridge's cronies.

'We should very much like you to join the party,' Lady Kingsbridge continued.

He blinked. Was she…*matchmaking*? Between him and her dowager duchess granddaughter? Did she really think that a rich, unmarried earl would wed a widow with a child? Even if he wished to marry, he would only ever consider a flirtation with such a lady.

If he *did* wish to ask Ella about Amelia, Lady Kingsbridge's matchmaking could however be very useful in allowing him to visit her without occasioning comment, so he could not complain.

'Thank you. I will wait to hear from you as to whether you will go ahead with the party, and will check whether my engagements allow me to attend.'

He continued the conversation with more difficulty than he usually experienced while making small talk, until he was able to take his leave a few minutes later.

After an unsatisfactory evening at a card party, he left early and walked home, before failing to sleep well that night. He awoke with a feeling of frustration, irritation, confusion, which a crack-of-dawn, hell-for-leather gallop along Rotten Row was unable to dispel, and as he ploughed his way through a less-hearty-than-usual breakfast, all he could think about was Ella and Amelia.

He didn't want a daughter. He didn't want any complications in his life at all.

As he so often did, he'd woken drenched in sweat in the early hours of this morning after yet another terrible dream. Until he stopped having nightmares about the horrors of the battlefield and could stop thinking about the friends he'd lost and the ones who'd been maimed, he would not want to marry or have children. He didn't want any more people in his life to love and about whom he would worry. He already worried far too much about his nephews and nieces and his siblings. Fortunately, he had his younger brother and eight nephews, and the state of his finances was excellent, so he had no reason to marry for either heirs or money.

The girl, Amelia, seemed to be well-loved and well-cared-for by her mother and her nurse; there was no need for him to enquire after her.

And that should be the end of it.

It was probably a blessing that Ella had decided to leave.

He really didn't need to think any further about either Ella or Amelia. Really.

He put down his cutlery and picked up his tankard to take a final swill of ale. Then he pushed back his chair and stood up. He'd survived war, both physically and mentally, and, if the mental survival was harder than the physical, he was trying hard to ignore that fact, and he was not going to let a memory of a woman, and the knowledge that he had perhaps—probably—sired a daughter disturb his equilibrium.

Many men had children whom they did not know, after all.

He was going to go to Jackson's saloon and engage in some boxing practice; physical exercise was always very helpful in preventing one from being able to think. And then he was going to continue with his day as though he'd never seen Ella since the masquerade nine years ago.

Questions about Ella and her daughter intruded far too often into Marcus's thoughts over the next two days.

He failed entirely to follow the plot of the Drury Lane play he attended, he agreed without realising what he was saying to attend a luncheon with all five of his sisters and no one else, which was blatantly going to involve them interrogating him about the marriage plans they thought he should have, and he couldn't concentrate on the conversation of his friends during what should have been a hugely enjoyable reunion with some fellow army officers during an evening at White's.

'Marcus?' His old friend Hugo was peering at him. 'Is something troubling you?'

'No.' Marcus shook his head. 'No. Certainly not.' He wished that he could confide in Hugo, but for Ella and Amelia's sake he couldn't mention this to anyone.

He was still extremely torn about what he should do.

He did not wish to complicate his life by seeing either Ella or Amelia again.

Except…did Amelia have any kind of father figure in her life? Images of his own childhood with both his very loving parents and all his siblings flashed into his mind. He was sure that his sisters had benefited from spending time with their father. Of course, amongst the *ton* it was quite fashionable for parents to be distant from their children, but that didn't mean it was a good thing.

But he didn't want to cause any scandal, for Ella or for the girl, and he didn't want to be a father, certainly not now, and perhaps not ever. But if he was already a father…

Damn these circular thoughts.

'Marcus?' Hugo was staring at him again, as though he'd grown a second head. 'Another round?'

Marcus looked at the table in front of them. Oh, yes, piquet.

No. He needed some fresh air, to clear his head.

'Another time,' he said, standing up.

'It's still early.' Hugo was still looking at him as though he didn't recognise him.

'I'm tired,' Marcus told him. 'Goodnight.'

The next morning, after further boxing practice following another night tossing and turning, he returned home to an invitation from Lady Kingsbridge to an 'impromptu house party' to be hosted by the new Duke of Rothshire.

Holding the card in his hand, he realised that it was as though his shoulders had lightened. His decision was made. He was going to visit Ella and ask her about Amelia; it was the right thing to do, he was sure, whether or not he wanted to be a father, and doing the wrong thing would not sit well with him.

God, though.

Yes, his shoulders had lightened because he no longer had a decision to make, but now he could feel himself tensing at the thought of definitely seeing Ella again.

If she'd recognised him, why had she not told him the truth? The more he thought about that, the angrier he felt. And then, despite that anger, he was, he realised, looking forward to seeing her again, just because… well, just because. She was *her*. Ella.

Three days later, Marcus was standing in the great hall of the new Duke of Rothshire's castle, his back to an enormous fireplace and hearth, beneath some huge stag heads, surveying the assembled company.

It was testament to Lady Kingsbridge's standing in Society, and of course the allure of a stay in a ducal castle, that she had managed to rustle up such a large number of house guests so quickly.

His attention was caught by a little commotion at the grand double doors on the opposite side of the room, and then he saw over the other guests' heads Lady Kingsbridge herself and the dowager duchess making their way into the room arm in arm.

Ella was dressed in a blue gown in the current fashion, with a high waistline and low neckline, which suited her lovely figure very well. He observed her smiling and laughing with the guests she spoke to as she and her grandmother made their way into the room, standing at an angle that allowed him to see the line of her slim, graceful throat and profile, and felt his pulse quicken. He reminded himself that he was certainly not here to engage in anything of *that* nature again; he just wanted to satisfy himself as to whether Amelia was indeed his daughter, and do his duty by her if she was.

Lady Kingsbridge was glancing around the room, from face to face. She paused when she saw Marcus, very much as though she'd been looking for him, and then began to walk towards him, causing Ella to go with her.

The two ladies were conversing as they moved in stately fashion towards him, arm in arm, and it was a few moments before Ella's gaze alit on Marcus. The moment at which she saw him properly and realised that it was him was very obvious; her step faltered, which caused her grandmother nearly to trip beside her, and her face noticeably whitened.

Her grandmother turned to her and said something, before shaking her head at Ella's response, and tugging at her arm a little. Ella visibly collected herself, straightening her shoulders, her chest lifting with the deep breath she'd taken, and they continued in his direction.

A few seconds later, they were in front of him.

'Good afternoon, Lord Malbrook.' Lady Kingsbridge was now wreathed in smiles and holding out a ring-laden hand for him to take. 'Eloise and I are delighted that you were able to come.'

'Indeed,' murmured Ella, her eyes not meeting his.

'I trust that you are both in good health?' he asked.

'Yes, thank you, we are both very well.' Ella's eyes rested momentarily on his face as she gave him a small smile before she returned her gaze to somewhere just beyond his left ear.

'Eloise, why don't you describe to Lord Malbrook the entertainment we have planned for our guests over the next few days,' commanded Lady Kingsbridge. 'I must go and speak to dear Lady Morton.' And she moved away impressively swiftly for a lady of her years.

Ella looked at him for a moment and then cleared her throat. 'I believe that you will be well entertained here, my lord. The estate provides good hunting and fishing, and the duke's chef is renowned amongst our local acquaintance.'

'That sounds wonderful.' Marcus did not wish to stand here and talk to Ella surrounded by people any more than she seemed to wish to talk to him. He wanted to be alone with her so that he could ask her immediately about Amelia.

After a few long seconds, Ella said, 'Allow me to introduce you to Miss Heatherington.' She began to walk towards a young lady standing with an older woman, so that Marcus was obliged to follow her. 'Mrs Heatherington, Miss Heatherington, allow me to introduce the Earl of Malbrook to you. Lord Malbrook, Mrs Heatherington, Miss Heatherington. I believe that you have a love of, um, travel in common. Now if you'll excuse me, I must go and welcome our other guests.' And she walked off as quickly as had her grandmother a few minutes ago.

'My lord, Hermione is quite the expert on geography.' Mrs Heatherington nodded at her daughter. 'I declare I am only a novice by comparison. You must not allow me to interrupt your conversation.' And off she went too.

'Oh, my lord,' breathed Miss Heatherington. She began a long discourse on the subject of all the counties of England she had thus far been privileged to visit, while Marcus followed Ella's progress around the room out of the corner of his eye.

She was doing an excellent imitation of being the consummate hostess, but every so often he caught her glancing in his direction. There was nothing remotely flirtatious in her manner; it seemed to him that her reason for looking over at him was anxiety. Which implied, he thought, that she knew that he was Amelia's father and was worried by his proximity to her.

Miss Heatherington's monologue was interrupted—thank God—by Lady Kingsbridge's announcing that she should like to escort the ladies around the rose garden, while the gentlemen were to be shown around the stables if they so desired.

Marcus did not so desire. He desired to speak to Ella, alone, at the earliest opportunity.

He bowed deeply over Miss Heatherington's hand and said, 'How very interesting. Allow me now to return you to your mother so that you may visit the rose gardens together.' From the slightly sulky moue that Miss Heatherington made, he suspected that he might have cut her off mid-sentence—he really hadn't been listening—and while he didn't like to be rude, it would be a good thing if she did not regard him as a potential suitor, so he made no effort to apologise.

Having reunited Miss Heatherington with her mother as efficiently as he could, enduring only a few sentences of gushing from Mrs Heatherington, he managed to manoeuvre himself next to Ella as the company began to chatter their way out of the room.

Looking around to be sure that no one else would hear his words, he said to her in a low voice, 'I should very much like to walk with you in the grounds at your earliest convenience. Perhaps now?'

Ella gave the tiniest of gasps, before beginning, 'I'm so sorry…'

'I'm sure that Eloise would be delighted to accompany you.' Her grandmother had again shown great speed for someone of her years, to appear at their sides from several feet away. 'There is no need to feel concern for me, my dear. I am very well able to show the ladies the rose gardens without your assistance.'

'I couldn't possibly leave you, Grandmama.' Ella's tone was steely. 'I shall perhaps be able to walk with the earl another time.'

'I have a question to ask you.' Marcus really didn't care how that might be interpreted.

'A question?' A smile was beginning to spread across Lady Kingsbridge's face. 'I'm certain that my granddaughter can be spared for a walk.' Her tone was even steelier than Ella's had been.

Ella was looking very pallid again. Soon, she'd probably be looking even paler. Marcus almost felt sorry for her, except he did not like people lying to him, and he was quite sure now that she had kept a very important piece of information from him.

'Of course,' she said, unsmilingly. 'Let us go now.'

She slipped through the group of guests towards the castle entrance, and Marcus followed her.

He held out his arm to her as they descended the steps below the front door, but she ignored it.

'This way.' She led him round the side of the castle and into a wooded area.

They moved in silence for perhaps two or three minutes, until Ella stopped under a large oak tree, turned to face him and said, 'You had a question, my lord?'

'Yes.'

Unlike when they'd spoken inside the castle, she was looking him directly in the eye, her head tilted just a little to one side. She was expressionless, and if it hadn't been for the way she had her hands clasped so tightly in front of her that her knuckles were whitening, and the slight tension he could see in her shoulders, Marcus might even have thought she was quite happy to speak to him.

He'd thought he wanted to ask the question because he needed to *know*. But now he was here... Perhaps he should after all say nothing. He could just enjoy a carefree day or two of shooting and fishing, and then leave, perhaps spend a few days in Brighton before returning to London and then to his own estate. Complication free.

But, no, he did need to know. He would wonder forever otherwise.

The words suddenly rushed out. 'Is Amelia my daughter?'

Chapter Seven

Eloise

Marcus looked like a stranger.

He was standing, large and handsome, and forbidding, a few feet away from her, clad in a dark coat that emphasised the width of his shoulders. Inside, he'd seemed to dominate the entire great hall of the castle just by his presence, and even out here against broad-trunked, centuries-old trees he seemed huge.

The look on his face was...horrifying. All traces of the smile he habitually wore had been wiped away; she could never have imagined he'd look so stern.

He knew.

Eloise closed her eyes briefly, and then reached for the tree behind her for support for a moment while she gathered herself.

What if he wished to claim Amelia? Told people? Created scandal, so that Amelia and she became outcasts? How would Amelia then be able to have a good life, be happy?

She opened her eyes to see Marcus looking hard at her.

'I…' What could she say? Could she lie somehow? Say that she didn't know whether Amelia's father was Marcus or the duke? Would that be better for Amelia? Lying to Marcus about his daughter would feel terrible, but she had to consider Amelia above all.

She shifted her gaze away from Marcus's. She couldn't look him in the eye when she was considering prevarication.

Thank heavens that Amelia was safely in the dower house with her nurse and that they'd already been out for a long walk today, so there was no possibility that she and Marcus would come across each other in the grounds by chance.

'You can't look me in the eye.' Marcus's voice was raspy.

Eloise immediately forced herself to look straight at him.

'Is Amelia my daughter?' he repeated.

Eloise opened her mouth and then closed it. She shook her head. She couldn't lie to him. She would just have to trust him. From what she'd seen of him he was a kind and courteous man, albeit a little rakish. Please God she'd been right in her assessment of him.

'Are you denying it?'

She shook her head again and found her voice. 'No.'

'No, you aren't denying it, or no, she is not my daughter?' He was still completely unsmiling.

'I am not denying it.' Eloise kept her gaze steady. 'She is your daughter.' It was hard to believe she'd just said the words out loud after all these years of keeping the secret.

'Are you…certain?' Marcus's voice was hoarse.

'Yes. I…' She was going to have to utter more words

that she'd never expected to say out loud. 'I did not engage in marital relations with my late husband. Ever.'

'You…?'

'Just one time. At the masquerade.' More and more things she'd never have expected to say.

'I see.' Marcus visibly swallowed. 'So she is my daughter.'

'Yes. There can be no question.'

Marcus nodded but didn't speak. Perhaps he was thinking about what to do next.

'Please don't create a scandal,' Eloise said. 'For her sake.'

'Of course I won't create a scandal.' He was frowning at her and shaking his head a little. 'How could I wish her any harm?' His words sounded sincere.

'Thank you.'

He acknowledged her thanks with a very slight nod, and then said, 'You lied.'

'I what?'

'You lied,' he repeated.

'I did not lie.' There was something very annoying about being accused of something you'd thought about doing but had not in the end done.

'You did. You could have told me about Amelia any time last week. You could have told me immediately when I asked. But instead you shook your head.' His voice was low and fierce.

Eloise stared at his handsome face, his strong cheekbones and jaw, his perfectly proportioned mouth, his thick hair. She'd had probably the best evening of her life with him and had then dreamt about him far too many times. She'd grieved him when she thought he was dead. And, knowing how dangerous it could be, she had still allowed herself to flirt with him in London.

She had *not* lied to him. Had she even shaken her head? Perhaps she had, but she hadn't *said* no out loud.

And suddenly, she was *furious*, so much so that she was actually *hot* with anger. She touched her hands to her cheeks. Yes, hot.

Men. Their lives were so much more straightforward than women's.

Why had it been acceptable for her late husband, the duke, to have been a renowned rake in his younger days when it would obviously be deemed completely unacceptable by Society if anyone were to find out that she had committed her indiscretion with Marcus?

Why had Marcus thought it acceptable to attempt the kind of flirtation with a widow that no debutante could risk having with a widower?

And why, actually, should Marcus be able to make love to someone and disappear off to war without a backward glance, *knowing* what he must have known about how babies were made?

'You asked me a question,' she stated, suddenly ice cold now, rather than hot. 'I have one for you. When it is women who bear all the consequences of love-making, from being ostracised by Society to having babies, why should men be able to dictate anything at all in the kind of situation in which we now find ourselves? Why should I *not* conceal the truth from you if I so choose? I *cannot* have any scandal surrounding my daughter, or she, like I, will have no choice but to marry the highest bidder—should there be one at all—for her hand, as I did.'

'*Our* daughter,' Marcus interjected.

Eloise ignored him. 'Of what possible benefit could it be to Amelia for either of you to know that you are her father? Why *should* I have told you?'

'Because…'

'There's no good reason that I should tell you. It should be up to me.' Eloise's voice was rising and she didn't care. 'You—men—should not be able to dictate to women. Why do men dictate *every*thing?'

'That is the way of the world, Ella.' Marcus seemed calmer now, but Eloise was still *angry*.

'I do not like the way of the world. I do not like the way men treat women.'

'Not all men are the same.'

'Indeed?' Eloise had her hands on her hips now. If she had been a man, she'd probably be squaring up to Marcus now with her fists raised.

'Indeed. There are many honourable men.'

'And yet.' She tilted her head to one side and injected as much false sweetness as she could into her tone. 'And yet, you made love to a lady of quality, impregnated her and left.'

Marcus visibly took a deep breath. 'I did not know who you were or that you would become with child.'

'And if you had known?' she asked, eyebrows raised, hands still on hips.

'I…'

'You…?'

'I… I hope I would have stayed and done my duty.'

'You *hope* you would have done?'

'I was young.' Marcus's brow was furrowed and his jaw clenched.

'And so was I. And I would not have walked away from my duty.'

'My duty then was to go to war. And my duty now was to ask you if Amelia is my daughter.'

Eloise sighed, long and loud, not caring at all if it sounded rude. 'Ridiculous.' She wasn't even sure what it was that was ridiculous. His words? This situation? *Everything?*

'Ella.' He reached a hand out towards her. She ignored the hand and after a moment he dropped it.

'Please don't call me Ella. It is not my name.'

'I see. It was part of your disguise that evening.'

'I suppose so.' She shrugged.

'Because you didn't want anyone to know what you were doing?'

'Of course I didn't. I'd have been ruined. Whereas you would not.'

'I would have been deemed a cad had anyone known that I had ruined *you*.'

'Briefly being considered a cad can hardly compare to being ruined for life.' Eloise moved her hands from her hips to cross her arms across her chest.

After a pause, Marcus said, 'That…is true.' He gave her a half-smile. 'Ella…'

She raised her eyebrows.

'Eloise. Your Grace,' he said.

Eloise inclined her head a little, her arms still clasped round herself.

'Could we cry truce?' Marcus held his hand out. 'I believe we now have a common purpose: the welfare of our daughter.'

Eloise took his hand gingerly.

His fingers were strong, and firm, and just the right temperature. And touching him was… It was making her hot and reminding her of not just her dreams about him, but the reality of what they'd done when they'd conceived Amelia. She looked up at him, at the strong line of his neck, into his eyes, and swallowed, hard.

He was looking into her eyes intently, in a way that made her stomach almost turn over.

She licked her lips and his gaze shifted to her mouth. His own lips parted very slightly and he moved his head a little towards hers.

Their breaths were almost mingling now, they were so close to each other. It was as though the very air between them had thickened with some strange tension.

He moved even closer to her and she in her turn inched towards him. Their chests were almost touching now, she felt the pressure of his fingers on hers, she couldn't wait... They were going to...

No.

What were they going to do? What *was* this?

It was as though she'd fallen under some ridiculous spell. It had to be the shock of finally disclosing the truth about Amelia, and to Marcus of all people, followed by their argument.

But she was Amelia's mother and she was a duchess.

And if she was quite honest she'd been about to kiss someone in the woods.

She snatched her hand away from Marcus's and took a step backwards.

'I thank you—very much—for your assurance that you will not create any kind of scandal with regard to Amelia.' She turned to begin to walk back immediately towards the castle, to escape this situation.

And then his voice rang out behind her. 'I should like to meet her properly.'

Eloise stopped dead, her back to Marcus, and then turned around slowly.

'You said that you wouldn't cause a scandal,' she said.

'And I will not. But I should like to meet her. I presume that it will be possible for her to meet guests on the estate.'

'I'm afraid that I don't think it will be possible. You have already seen her, at the ascension. Is that not enough?'

Marcus frowned and Eloise tensed further, sure that he was about to start arguing with her again.

And then he said, in a much softer voice than he had been using, 'Please?' He accompanied his plea with a small smile.

Eloise closed her eyes. She really wanted to say no to him. She opened her eyes again. The little smile was still there. It was an uncertain smile, it made Marcus look several years younger, almost as young as he had when they first met, and it was a smile to which it was difficult to say no.

'I'm not sure,' she began, and the smile shrank a little, and she immediately felt guilty.

'Maybe a short walk,' she said. 'Tomorrow morning. With me. And Amelia's nurse. There can of course be no question of our telling Amelia anything. And we must both of course continue to behave entirely as though we are mere acquaintances.'

'Certainly,' Marcus agreed. 'Thank you. I'm very grateful.'

'Not at all. Let's meet at the copse immediately to the west of the lake that you can see from the terrace at the back of the house. At half past ten tomorrow morning.'

'I will look forward to it.'

Eloise didn't return the wider smile Marcus was now directing at her.

Should she have agreed to his request to meet Amelia? She wasn't sure, but she suspected that she should not have done.

She had nothing more to say now, so she turned again to begin to walk back to the castle, and this time Marcus accompanied her. They walked next to each other but three or four feet apart, and in silence.

For most of the short walk, Eloise was bursting to break into a very unladylike run, so that she could get away from Marcus as soon as possible. She felt as though she needed to be alone to cry, or scream, or perhaps just *punch* something. Too much had happened in the past few days. Marcus was alive. Marcus had been flirting with her. Marcus knew about Amelia. Marcus was going to *meet* Amelia. And Marcus was even more attractive now than he had been nine years ago, and for a moment under that tree they had almost kissed, which was madness. Unlike when she'd first met him, she wasn't in disguise and she was in the grounds of her own home, and a large number of her acquaintance were also in the grounds.

'I must…go,' she told Marcus, as soon as they reached the castle. 'I am sure Fenton, the duke's butler, will be able to assist you.'

And then she walked off at a great pace towards the dower house, without looking back.

When she got there, she went straight to the little nursery she'd had set up on the attic floor for Amelia, and hugged her so tightly that Amelia very soon squeaked and asked to be let go.

'Would you like to play a game or read a book?' she asked her daughter, still hugging her. 'Anything?'

They played shuttlecock and battledore for significantly longer than Eloise could usually happily manage. She just didn't want to leave her daughter. What if, somehow, everything changed tomorrow when she met her father, even if she didn't know that's who he was?

Finally, after another long hug with Amelia, she went to her chamber to change for dinner up at the castle. She considered for a moment feigning illness again, but then thought of how anxious about her health her grandmother had been when she arrived in Sussex. She couldn't worry her further. And her grandmother had very kindly—matchmaking ulterior motive or not—insisted on undertaking all the hostess duties herself. Well, by directing the duke's servants in a somewhat high-handed manner. And Eloise couldn't let her down by not attending any of the meals or excursions she'd planned.

She was going to have to go to the dinner, avoid Marcus—because she'd experienced enough emotion for one day—and hope that the guests were tired enough from their travels that day to cause the evening to end early.

She wished for a moment that she had a close friend there for support, Anne, Viscountess Bakewell, for example—who had not been able to attend as she was increasing heavily—but then realised that there was of course no one in whom she would ever be able to confide about her situation with Marcus.

* * *

After much thought, she dressed for dinner in one of her most demure dresses, one of lilac-grey shot silk, and teamed it with pearls. Her moment of insanity with Marcus in the woods—really, she had definitely nearly kissed him and that would have been *such* a stupid thing to have done—could not be repeated, and she wanted both to signal to him that she wasn't dressing to attract him and *not* to attract him.

'What are you *wearing*?' her grandmother asked as soon as she walked into the dower house sitting room. 'I declare you could pass for thirty.'

'Well, I'm twenty-eight, so that wouldn't be surprising.'

'But normally you don't look a day older than three and twenty. You'll have to change.'

'But there's nothing wrong with my looking thirty.'

'There are a number of eligible young men here, including, for example, the Earl of Malbrook, and the other women will be dressed in their finest.'

Eloise tried not to roll her eyes. 'I have no interest in eligible young men.'

'Nonetheless.'

'I love you, Grandmama, but *honestly*.'

'I love you too, and that's why I'm insisting that you change *now*.'

So when Eloise entered the grand ducal dining hall with her grandmother, she was wearing a pale green evening dress that her grandmother had told her went particularly well with her creamy skin, red-gold hair and blue eyes, twinned with a sapphire earring and necklace set.

Marcus was standing very close to the door and she almost bumped into him as she entered. From the momentary flash of appreciation she read in his eyes, she could see that both she and her grandmother had been right. This gown became her well enough that Marcus had noticed. So she should not have worn it.

She felt the little glint in his eye and his slow smile almost to her very core, which just made her feel quite cross. She was a mature woman now, and she really shouldn't be affected by a handsome man's smile.

'Good evening.' Marcus bowed slightly and she smiled at him as blandly as she could, hoping that he couldn't possibly have known how his smile had affected her.

'Good evening.'

'I trust you were able to rest before dinner? My mother has always said that it's quite exhausting hosting parties.' He was the picture of the perfect guest.

'I am fortunate in that my grandmother is a most enthusiastic hostess, and has retained great strength and vigour,' Eloise said. She was beginning to relax a little; of course he wasn't going to refer to anything he shouldn't.

'And of course we will all be staying in the main house while you, I understand, reside in the dower house. The perfect way to host a party.' He twinkled at her for all the world as though they barely knew each other and were engaging in small talk. Eloise was impressed despite herself.

'It is indeed the perfect way to host a party,' she replied. 'If any of our guests should annoy me—which of course none of them will; this is purely hypothetical— I will be able to retreat to my house. In addition, we have many country pursuits, such as shooting and fishing, and riding of course, available for the men, so you should be very well occupied with little endeavour on the part of your hosts.' She was interrupted by her grandmother clapping her hands together and announcing that dinner was ready.

Eloise looked around and then realised that, as her grandmother was on the duke's arm, it would be Marcus, as the highest ranked man present, who escorted her, as the highest ranked woman of the party, into dinner. He was already holding his arm out for her to take. She glanced over at her grandmother, who was looking at her with a definite hint of a smirk. Really. Incorrigible. Well, she would catch cold at any matchmaking plan. Eloise would not be marrying ever again.

She turned back to Marcus and caught him looking between her and her grandmother. She was fairly sure that she saw his shoulders shake, just very slightly. Perhaps he also suspected a matchmaking plot. She supposed it was a good thing if he found it amusing.

'You were about to enumerate, I think, the many sporting pursuits available on the estate,' the earl said as they walked.

'I must not monopolise the conversation. Tell me about your own estate, my lord.'

He did have a very nice voice, Eloise thought as he talked and she half listened around thoughts about Amelia and their walk with Marcus tomorrow, veering between slight panic and almost relief that something she'd feared so much had come to pass and was proving— thus far—better than she'd expected.

She'd always liked deep voices like Marcus's. The

late duke's voice had been quite high, particularly when he was annoyed.

'You must be very pleased that your grandmother was well enough to come and stay with you,' Marcus said after a few minutes, clearly having decided it was time to turn the conversation back in Eloise's direction.

'Yes, it's wonderful to have her company. Even if…' She stopped.

'Even if she's blatantly trying to matchmake you with people with whom you do not wish to be matched?'

Eloise looked at him from under her eyelashes. 'You are blunt, my lord.'

'Yes. My apologies?'

Despite everything, Eloise found herself laughing.

The duke, seated on her other side, laughed extremely loudly at something someone across the table had just said. Eloise caught Marcus's eye and they shared a tiny smile.

'So we were saying that, while your grandmother is a wonderful woman, you do not appreciate her match-making?' Marcus said.

'No, we were not saying that.'

He raised an eyebrow.

'*You* were saying that,' Eloise said. 'It might be true, but I would not say it.'

'What *would* you say?'

'I would say that I adore my grandmother. I would also say that I am very happy with my life as it is and that I have no desire whatsoever to remarry.'

Marcus nodded. 'Because as you were saying earlier you find the difference between the lot of men and that of women particularly annoying?'

Eloise immediately looked over her shoulder to her

right to check that the duke wouldn't have heard Marcus's words, and then turned back, to glare at him. 'Shh!'

'Apologies,' he said, not looking at all contrite. 'Why, though, do you not wish to remarry?'

Eloise choked on her mouthful of buttered turbot and Marcus passed her wine glass to her.

'Are you all right?' He lifted his hand as though to pat her on the back. 'Can I help?'

'Yes,' she spluttered. 'By talking about something else.'

'I'm so sorry. I understand that the duke has a splendid collection of butterfly specimens. Have you seen it?' He accompanied his abrupt subject change by a wide-eyed look of enquiry, which made Eloise, recovered now from her choking, laugh.

'Are you interested in preserved insects, my lord?'

'No.' He smiled at her blandly and she couldn't help laughing again.

'Some butterflies are remarkably pretty.' She cut off a small piece of turbot. 'I like butterflies very much.' She was not going to allow the conversation to turn back to any awkward topic.

'Which are your favourite?'

'White ones. And also other coloured ones.'

'You sound most knowledgeable on the subject. Preserved ones or live ones?'

'My preference would be for live ones, but preserved specimens must always be instructive.'

'Indeed.' Marcus laughed out loud and she narrowed her eyes at him.

'I remember you telling me that you were particularly interested in the development of steam locomotives?' she asked, having nothing further to say about butterflies but determined to keep the conversation on mundane topics.

'Well, *quite* interested. In truth I wouldn't be able to hold a *long* conversation on the subject but I do think they seem more viable as a mode of popular transport than balloons.'

'Have you ever seen one? I must confess I am very interested in them myself.'

'Really? What do you know about them?' His lips were twitching again.

'They are long and they run on rails and they transport things,' Eloise said, in her haughtiest duchess tones. 'And they employ steam. Do try some of this swan dish, my lord. I believe that you will be impressed by the duke's chef.'

Marcus laughed again before saying that he'd be delighted to try any dish at all that she recommended.

And, somehow, astonishingly, Eloise was enjoying herself just as much as she had done last week before he'd found about Amelia.

Indeed, when her grandmother rose and stated that the ladies would be withdrawing, she was almost disappointed to leave Marcus. Sitting in the ducal drawing room with the other ladies, listening with half her mind to the chatter and gossip while also reflecting on their dinner conversation, she realised that her shoulders felt significantly lighter than they had since the moment she had discovered that Marcus was part of her grandmother's house party. From his behaviour so far, it seemed that he really did not intend to cause any gossip or scandal.

It might nonetheless be wise to retire now to bed to avoid further conversation with him this evening.

She looked over at her grandmother, who was looking a little drawn.

'Are you tired, Grandmama? Might it be wise to retire early given your recent illness? I will accompany you.'

'I saw you enjoying a comfortable coze with the earl,' her grandmother said as they walked through the ducal park a few minutes later.

Eloise rolled her eyes in the dark. 'He's very nice, but I have no wish to form any kind of attachment to a gentleman.'

'Hmm.'

Her grandmother could *hmm* all she liked; Eloise would not be remarrying—to Marcus or any other man—and she was safe in the knowledge that Marcus had no interest in her in that way either.

Chapter Eight

Marcus

Eight hours later, Marcus was awake with the larks.

He rejected the first three shirts and first five cravats laid out by his valet, Norris, because, well, they just weren't quite right.

And then he had to discard the first three cravats that he attempted to tie because they weren't falling as he desired.

As Marcus smoothed his jacket to get rid of a couple of small wrinkles, Norris said, 'May I ask if this is a particularly important day, my lord?'

This was the downside of asking your army batman to be your valet. He was a tremendous companion and extremely efficient—Marcus could never ask for a better valet, or friend—but he was too perceptive.

'Just that you normally wear the first shirt and cravat that I put out and I'm fussier about the tying of your cravat than you are,' Norris continued.

'Lady Kingsbridge and the duke seem to have gone to a great deal of trouble to ensure that we all enjoy the house party,' Marcus improvised, 'and from my side it seems only right to ensure that I am well dressed for it.'

'I see. Highly plausible.'

Marcus glared at Norris while the man smirked.

'Your new boots, I assume, then?' Norris asked.

'Yes, please.' Although, when he thought about it, he'd never worn them before, and on the small off chance that they weren't immediately comfortable he should perhaps wear his second newest pair, given that he would be walking with Ella and Amelia. 'No, the black ones that Hoby delivered last month, please.'

'Are you planning to walk or ride, then, today?' Norris cocked his head to one side and waggled his eyebrows and Marcus had to laugh at his blatant curiosity. He so very obviously wished to ask if it was the desire to impress a lady that had caused Marcus's unusual sartorial care.

He was right. It was indeed the desire to impress a lady, but a considerably younger one than Norris might imagine, and one who would almost certainly not in fact notice whether his cravat was perfectly tied or his close-fitting boots and jacket quite smooth. Her mother might notice, of course, but despite how much he enjoyed her company his thoughts at this moment were filled with his daughter and only her. His *daughter*. God.

He would never be able to tell anyone, including Norris, that Amelia was his daughter, for her sake and Ella's.

Strange how now that they were home from the battlefield he'd begun to have secrets from Norris.

When they were in the army together there was little that he wouldn't have shared with him, but he couldn't

tell him about the nightmares, because it was shame-
ful, embarrassing to be experiencing them. So many
of his friends had perished or been awfully injured; he
couldn't forget about them, and he could never complain either, including about his dreams.

And now, this secret—about Amelia—was huge,
and a second thing on top of his nightmares that he
couldn't talk about with anyone, including Norris.

'I'm not sure what entertainment Lady Kingsbridge
has planned for us today,' he said. 'I might take a stroll
around the grounds this morning, and presume that we
will do something active this afternoon.'

'Well, I hope you have a good day.' Norris had obviously given up trying to get information out of him.

'Thank you. I hope you do too.'

Odd how no one else other than Ella was aware of
how big a day this was for Marcus. Not just big; it was
terrifying. He didn't want another person to care about,
worry about, worry that they might die or be maimed
like his fellow soldiers.

Part of him almost wanted to pack up and leave now
and pretend that he'd never found out about Amelia.
She would never know, after all.

Most of him, though, was desperate to meet her
properly.

As he checked his cravat in the oak-framed looking
glass in the chamber he'd been allotted, he reflected
that there was something quite earth-shattering about
the knowledge that one had a child, that one had helped
to create another living being.

Breakfast felt like one of the longest meals he'd ever
experienced, filled with inane and uninteresting conversation with his fellow guests and the duke—a par-

ticularly unenthusiastic host. Marcus had to fight the inclination to look frequently at his watch. When he did eventually give in to the temptation, he found that time had passed even more slowly than he had thought, and it was still well over an hour before he was due to be meeting Ella and Amelia.

The meal was followed by newspaper reading on the part of the male guests. Marcus usually found much to interest him in current affairs, particularly in reference to the army and the political situation in Europe, but today he found all that he read extremely dull.

He began to pace the room, and then realised that he must be annoying his companions, so he sat down and just waited for the time to pass.

Finally, after what felt like many hours later, the clock hands had reached fifteen minutes before the allotted hour for his walk with Ella—Eloise, Her Grace—and Amelia, and he stood up to make his way down to the area of the parkland in which Ella had suggested they meet.

Eloise, not Ella.

It only took about five minutes for him to get there, so when Ella—Eloise—and Amelia, accompanied by another woman, presumably a nurse or maid, appeared in the distance, he was waiting, and able to watch them walk over to him.

Amelia was holding Eloise's hand, bouncing up and down as she walked, smiling and giggling at things Eloise said. She had blondish-auburn curls and looked happy and healthy and as though she was very much enjoying the company of her mother.

And Eloise looked…beautiful. Or maybe that was

the wrong description. It was perhaps too basic a word; she was more complicated than that. It wasn't just her lovely face that drew you to her, it was her liveliness, her smile, her mannerisms. Her pout all those years ago. And now…the way she was looking at her daughter, her focus on her, her tender smile, the way they seemed to mirror each other's gestures unconsciously.

Amelia suddenly stopped and pulled on Eloise's hand and pointed at something.

Eloise bent towards Amelia and put her finger to her lips, but Amelia clapped, so loudly that Marcus heard the clap.

Whatever creature she'd been pointing at must have run off at the noise, and she began to run after it, while Eloise stood and laughed.

When Amelia returned to her mother, she threw her arms around Eloise's middle and Eloise hugged her to her, and Marcus felt a wave of an emotion he couldn't name.

After a few seconds, Eloise and Amelia began to walk again, and some minutes later reached the spot where Marcus was standing at the edge of the copse.

'Oh, good morning, my lord. I remember your saying that you enjoyed walking.' Eloise's fake nonchalance was very well done; Marcus almost believed himself that they'd come upon each other quite by chance. He smiled at her. He would of course fall in with her pretence.

The woman standing a few feet away from them was presumably Amelia's nurse. Marcus would have preferred to have met without her, so that his conversation with Eloise might have been freer, but he appreciated her desire for full propriety, and no one would think that a widow, who did not need to take a chaperone on a morning walk with her daughter, would engage in anything clandestine in front of her child's nurse.

'Good morning,' he replied. 'Yes, it's a very pleasant day for a stroll.' He gestured at the cloudless sky. 'Would you care to take a turn around the grounds together?'

'Certainly; we'd be delighted. This is my daughter, Lady Amelia. Amelia, this is an old friend of mine and of Grandmama's. The Earl of Malbrook.'

'You may call me Marcus.' He smiled down at the little girl—his daughter—as she skipped on the spot. Her features were strikingly similar to those of his nieces, but her smile was all her mother's, accompanied by the same dimple.

'How do you do, Marcus? We just saw some rabbits.' Amelia pointed back down the hill.

'Which you scared away by your clapping,' Eloise said, laughing. She turned her attention to Marcus. 'I trust that you passed a comfortable night, my lord, and enjoyed your breakfast?'

Amelia tugged on her mother's hand and said, 'Mama, shall we go?'

Eloise shook her head at her daughter, although with a smile. 'Amelia, my darling, try for a little patience and indeed politeness. I just asked the earl a question.'

Marcus laughed. 'I slept very well, thank you—' not true; he'd had another of his dreams '—and hope you did too. I remember well as a young child the frustration of having to listen to adults talk. Where would you like to walk, Amelia?'

Amelia glanced at Eloise, who gave her a little nod, and said, 'I like walking around the lake. It's this way.'

As they set off together, Amelia between Eloise and Marcus, she continued, 'I am not a young child any more. I am eight.'

'I apologise,' Marcus said. 'What I meant was that you are young compared to me. When is your birthday?' He was sure that he was going to seem quite ridiculous if he gave in to his inclination to question her about every aspect of her life, but he was also sure that he was going to do the questioning anyway. He wanted to know everything he could to find out about the eight years of her life that he'd missed. He couldn't quite believe the depth of emotion it was possible to feel on first meeting someone. How did other men discover they had children and blithely carry on with their lives without making any effort even to meet them, let alone spend time with them?

'The ninth of April. This year, because Mama was out of mourning after a very long time, we had a tea party on my birthday with my friends.'

'That sounds wonderful. What are your favourite party treats?'

As Amelia chattered and they walked, Marcus drank in her words, her mannerisms, her laugh. He could happily listen to her all day.

They stopped at the lake to look at the moorhens and coots.

'What do you love most about them?' Marcus asked Amelia.

'I like the colours. I like the moorhens' beaks and the way all the blackness of their feathers looks all shimmery.'

'I like the colours too. Have you ever seen a peacock?'

'I don't know.'

'I don't think you have,' Eloise said. 'You might have seen pictures of them in books.'

'They're big birds, nearly as big as swans, and they have the most extraordinary green and blue plumage that they unfurl behind them like a huge and very beautiful fan,' Marcus explained.

'Do they live in England?'

'Yes. I have several on my estate and I believe that there are many other groups of them in the country. A group of them is called an ostentation or a pride, because the male birds like showing off so much. For which you can't blame them, because they are a wonderful spectacle. I think they were introduced to England from India, several hundred years ago now.' He wished very much that he could show his own land and birds to Amelia.

'Mama, do you think the duke would get a peacock?'

'Maybe,' said Eloise, scrunching up her face. 'But probably not.'

Marcus wasn't surprised; the new duke seemed particularly set in his ways for a relatively young man.

Eloise looked at a watch that she had pulled from a pocket in her dress and then around at Amelia's nurse, who was sitting placidly on a bench a few yards away from them.

'Lucy, I wonder if you would be able to take Amelia back to the house now? She needs to eat luncheon in time for her lessons this afternoon. I will follow in a minute or two; the earl wished me to direct him towards some areas of interest on the estate for him.' She was very good at prevarication.

Amelia demurred briefly, before capitulating in the face of an impressively strict look from Eloise.

Marcus didn't want her to leave but he could hardly beg that she stay.

He watched her skip off with Lucy until they were out of sight, and then turned to Eloise. The two of them just stood and stared at each other for a long moment.

Marcus had so many thoughts fighting for prominence that he had no idea what to say, which was quite an odd sensation.

Apparently Eloise was also speechless.

Eventually, he said, 'She's adorable.'

'Yes.'

'I should thank you for...' For what? What should he say? 'For looking after her so well.' He was, he realised, deeply impressed by the bond Eloise and Amelia seemed to share and by how happy Amelia seemed to be. 'Thank you also for allowing me to meet her.' Although the meeting had of course been under duress on Eloise's side. 'Would you ever have told me about her?' He wasn't sure of his motive in asking the question.

Eloise shook her head and replied immediately. 'No! Of course not. Until very recently, I didn't know who you were, other than a soldier named Marcus. Indeed, I thought you were dead. And once I knew that you were alive, still no, of course not. I have to put Amelia first and I would always wish to avoid any scandal for her sake. I had no idea how you would react had I told you about her.'

Marcus nodded, slowly. He could not, in all fairness, be in any way angry with her for not having told him.

'Does she have a governess?' he asked. He hoped that Eloise wouldn't think that his question implied that he would wish to interfere in Amelia's upbringing—although he would certainly like to be involved now—but he was interested in all the details of her life.

'Yes, she does. I originally thought that I would instruct her myself, based on my own reading, but my sad lack of education combined, I have to be honest, with my lack of aptitude in certain areas such as the sciences means that I am unable to give her the instruction that I should like her to have. Without of course wishing for her to be a bluestocking—unless she would like to be one—I hope that she will be as well-educated as any man of her acquaintance when she is older.'

'That sounds very wise.' Marcus hadn't before devoted any thought to the education of girls, other than to ensure that all his tenants' children, boys and girls, had access to schooling, but he now realised that of course his daughter should be educated as well as any aristocratic boy might be.

He had also realised, at some point during their walk, or maybe even the second he had laid eyes again on Amelia, that, as he was certain his sisters had done, she would benefit from having a paternal influence as well as a maternal one in her life.

'Thank you.' Eloise was regarding him with one eyebrow raised. 'I am delighted to receive your approbation.'

'I apologise if I sounded patronising,' Marcus told her. 'I genuinely do think it sounds very wise. And I genuinely think that not everyone is that wise.' Although while that decision of Eloise's had been good, could any one person make the right decisions for a child every time? Amelia would surely benefit from spending time with Marcus, and from Marcus being involved in future discussions about her education, her coming out, really anything of import in her life.

Eloise relaxed her stance and laughed. 'Thank you.'

'Thank you again for allowing me to meet Amelia properly.' He needed to talk to Eloise for longer. They needed to make a plan for the future. 'Would you care to promenade a little further? Perhaps a circuit of the lake?'

'I…' She hesitated for a few moments and then looked around, perhaps to see if anyone else was in sight, and then said, 'I have time for a short walk but must then return to the house.'

'Excellent.'

As they set off in a clockwise fashion under willow trees, Marcus said, 'Amelia is…wonderful. I count myself fortunate beyond words to have chanced upon you both at the ascension.'

'Indeed.' Eloise had her head held straight and facing forward as she spoke, so he was unable to see her face beneath her bonnet, but her tone did not indicate enthusiasm.

'I should like to spend time regularly with her,' Marcus persisted. 'I believe that that must benefit her.'

'With respect—' Eloise continued to walk without looking at him '—and without wishing to sound rude, I wonder whether the benefit would rather be on your side. I understand that you might wish to see her but I am not sure whether she would in fact benefit from meetings with you.'

'I believe that she would.' Marcus followed a large dragonfly with his eyes for a moment while marshalling all his powers of persuasion. 'I believe that girls, as well as boys, benefit greatly from time spent with their fathers. My own father devoted unfashionably large amounts of time to his family, and I believe that my five sisters, as well as my brother and I, benefited very considerably from his influence.'

'I am happy for you that you enjoyed such a positive experience with your father. My childhood experience was quite the reverse. I am, however, happy now, and trust that I am a good mother to Amelia, and therefore I do not believe that I have suffered in that lack of paternal contact.' Her words served the precise opposite purpose of what she must have intended; she had just provided Marcus with further ammunition.

'With advance apologies for my frankness, I must tell you that your father giving your hand in marriage to a man more than fifty years older than you does not indicate a lack of suffering.' He could not go so far as to refer to the lack of marital intimacy that she had mentioned, but she must be aware that that did not demonstrate a happy marriage.

Eloise stopped walking. Marcus stopped too.

'Frankness indeed.' She tipped her head back to look up at him. 'Obviously, I do not discuss my marriage or my late husband. I will reiterate, though, that I am very happy now. I will also say that as Amelia's sole parent and guardian, I would never give her hand in marriage to a man to whom she did not wish to be wed. Your argument is therefore poor.'

'I remain convinced that Amelia would benefit from spending time with me, for so many reasons: skills I might be able to teach her, introductions to certain members of Society that might be advantageous to her.' *Surely* there must be an argument he could produce that would convince Eloise. 'And it must be a huge responsibility for you to have her entire care in your hands.'

'Responsibility, yes; burden, no. We are very happy as we are.'

'Eloise. Ella. I... I wish to help to enrich Amelia's life.'

Eloise began to walk again, really quite quickly. 'You will be welcome to visit perhaps once a year, in an unobtrusive fashion. Perhaps you might strike up a friendship with the duke and be invited to hunt and fish with him.'

'I would like to visit more frequently.' Marcus already knew that he wished to spend as much time as possible with Amelia.

Eloise increased her walking speed. 'That will not be possible, I'm afraid. Your visiting us regularly must I am sure occasion comment, which would almost certainly be to our detriment.'

'I do not wish to cause any scandal.'

'Thank you.' Eloise spoke as though that was the end of the matter.

It must not be, though.

It felt really as though it was Marcus's *duty* to be a part of Amelia's childhood, life.

Thinking about the word *duty* reminded him of the conversation he'd had with Eloise yesterday, when she'd challenged him on that subject. And, Good God, he'd been so caught up in his reaction to the knowledge that Amelia was indeed his daughter that he'd failed to think of the most obvious thing.

Knowing that Eloise had become with child as a result of their lovemaking, there was only one thing he could do.

And while he hadn't wished to marry, he also hadn't wished to become a father. He *was* a father, however. And duty was duty. Given the choice, he certainly wouldn't marry, because he didn't wish to care too much about anyone, but perhaps even without marriage he would in any case care quite deeply about Eloise, because she was Amelia's mother. And he enjoyed her company, and certainly it would be no hardship to engage in further intimacy with her, so it could be worse.

'Could we perhaps sit down for a few moments?' he suggested, indicating a bench a few dozen yards ahead of them.

'I would prefer to continue to walk,' she replied with no hesitation. 'I feel that sitting together on a bench is even more compromising than taking a walk together.'

If she agreed to his proposition, such a thing would no longer be an issue. He couldn't *make* her sit down with him, though.

'Of course,' he said.

'How long do you intend to stay here?' She had moved so that she was walking right on the edge of her side of the path, holding herself several feet away from him. Certainly, no one seeing them from a distance would be able to suggest that they looked remotely amorous at this point.

'As long as the other male guests remain.' He could cancel or postpone the other engagements he had in town and in the country, where he'd been planning to go for the summer months. Perhaps he might take a house in Brighton for the remainder of the summer instead. And after that he would perhaps be living with Eloise and Amelia permanently.

'Then you will be able to see Amelia once or twice more.'

'Ella. Eloise.' This conversation would be better had while they could see each other's faces, so he stopped walking.

Eloise continued to walk.

Marcus began to walk again. 'In reference to your conversation the other day, I must apologise.'

'I'm sure you should,' she agreed sunnily, still walking.

Marcus laughed. Clearly, she wasn't going to ask for what specific thing he ought to apologise. If she were a man, she would make an excellent adversary in a court of law.

'The thing for which I must specifically apologise is that, since I became aware of your identity and Amelia's existence, I have failed to do my duty.'

'I understood from you that you believed your duty to be to visit her, and you have done that. I must, with reluctance—' she tilted her head to look sideways at him and shoot him a little smile '—absolve you of the necessity to apologise.'

'My duty was clearly not merely to visit her. I am deeply sorry for not having asked you immediately; we must marry.'

Eloise stopped stock-still and turned to look at him. 'We must what?'

'Marry.'

She stared at him. 'You do not *look* as though you are funning.'

'I am not funning.'

'*What?*' She was shaking her head, her eyebrows raised, her lips pressed together in a straight line.

'I must apologise again.' Really, from the moment he'd met her, he'd behaved badly in her presence. 'I worded my question poorly. Would you do me the honour of becoming my wife?'

Chapter Nine

Eloise

Marcus *looked* as though he was entirely serious.

He couldn't be.

Except…he had his eyebrows raised a tiny bit, there was no hint of the quirk to his lips that Eloise knew was evident when he was joking, and he was just standing there…waiting. Apparently for an answer.

So maybe he *had* meant his extraordinary proposal.

Well, whether he'd meant it or not, her answer would always be the same.

'No,' she told him. 'Thank you.'

Marcus blinked, as though he was surprised. 'We should discuss this,' he said.

Well. It really did seem as though he *had* posed the question in all seriousness. Madness. Eloise had been forced to make one marriage to a man she didn't know at all; she certainly wouldn't be making a second marriage to a near stranger. Or to anyone, in fact.

'I'm very sorry but I'm afraid there is nothing *to* discuss. I will not be remarrying.' She began to walk again, fast.

She was happier now, as a wealthy widow, than she'd ever been before, and she had no desire to change her situation.

Why would *any* woman wish to give up her independence if she didn't have to do so? Being her father's possession to be sold into marriage and then at her husband's mercy, with the constant fear that he might disown Amelia, had been awful. Eloise was infinitely happier as a widow and could not contemplate relinquishing control over her life and that of her daughter.

Before Marcus had found out about Amelia, she had worried that he might make the secret public if he ever found it out, but now she was somehow sure that he wouldn't.

And given that Amelia looked so much like him, people might add two and two and make four if she married him and they were seen together.

And so she had absolutely nothing to consider; her answer would always be no.

'May I ask your reasons?'

She shook her head. 'I'm sorry, but no.' It was remarkably satisfying being in a position to be as assertive as she liked towards a man.

Marcus gave a half laugh. 'That is of course your prerogative. May I explain my own reasons?'

She was quite sure that she knew his reasons: he felt a retrospective sense of duty having discovered to whom he had made love that night and what the outcome had been, and he wished to spend time with Amelia. There was therefore little point in him telling her. But he was looking at her with such an air of entreaty, which sat quite incongruously on him—he was so big, handsome and confident that you did not expect to see any vulnerability about him—that she couldn't bring herself to deny him the opportunity.

'You may, of course, although I must tell you that I only have a very short time left for this walk because I need to go back to the house to ensure that Amelia is eating now and will be ready for her afternoon lessons, and then to escort my grandmother up to the castle to luncheon with our guests.'

The difference between being a young, entirely de-fenceless and dependent nineteen-year-old girl and a mature, independently wealthy dowager duchess was vast. Almost infinite. If *only* Eloise had been able to say no to her father when he had told her she had to marry the duke.

Although of course then she would not have felt so desperate for a glimpse of happiness that evening at Vauxhall and would not have allowed herself to make love to Marcus and she would not have Amelia, so she could have no regrets.

Marcus cleared his throat. 'My first point,' he began.

'I'm so sorry.' Eloise almost *did* feel sorry for him because he looked quite discomfited, and from what she'd seen of Marcus he was a man who was usually in command of every situation in which he found himself. 'The hour is quite advanced and this path here—' she pointed between trees to their left '—takes me back to the house. I really must return to my grandmother. I imagine that I shall see you with the other guests later on. Good afternoon.' She nodded to him before taking the path and not looking back.

She was sure she could feel his eyes on her back as she walked but she wasn't going to turn round to check.

What would it be like to be married to Marcus? It

would certainly be different from being married to the duke.

Marcus would, she was sure, speak to his wife and he would perhaps wish to make love to her. At that thought, Eloise shivered under the hot sun as she emerged from the tree-lined path onto open grass.

She must not think about how attractive he was. Knowing that one had once enjoyed making love with someone, as complete strangers, many years ago was not a good reason for considering even for one second giving up one's independence and placing one's happiness and, far more importantly, one's daughter's happiness in that person's hands.

In addition, and now that she'd thought of this, she couldn't believe it hadn't occurred to her before— shock had clearly addled her brain—his proposition had been, frankly, quite *rude*. He was suggesting *marriage* out of a sense of duty and clearly also because he wanted to spend time with Amelia. He was suggesting that Eloise give up her independence because *he* wanted to salve his conscience and have an excuse to see his daughter. And he'd seemed quite astonished when she'd dismissed his offer out of hand, as though all he had to do was propose and she would jump at the idea.

Extremely rude.

It was a good thing that she'd had to cut him short to return to the dower house because hearing him set out his reasons for the proposal could only have annoyed her further.

She would have to make sure that she wasn't alone with him again, so that they could have no further conversation of a personal nature.

* * *

There was in fact no opportunity for Eloise to spend very much time with Amelia when she got back to the house, because her grandmother had already departed for the castle, assisted by a footman, and had left word that Eloise should follow her as soon as she could.

As she neared the castle, she discovered that her grandmother had decided that, as it was such a beautiful day, the company would take their luncheon on the lawns below the castle's rear terrace, so the duke's servants had the misfortune to have to run backwards and forwards in the heat to set up tables and chairs under large parasols and tent-like structures that Fenton, the duke's butler, had remembered were kept in the depths of the castle's cellars.

As Eloise stared at the chaos before her, a maid appeared to swoon in the heat. Eloise ran forward to assist her into shade and to help her take a cooling drink when she was recovered sufficiently to do so.

As the maid assured Eloise that she was now fully recovered, the duke's housekeeper, Mrs Smith, who had worked at the castle for over thirty years and whom Eloise knew very well, marched towards her and announced that she would resign if Lady Kingsbridge made any further unreasonable demands.

Eventually, Mrs Smith was calmed, peace was restored throughout, and Eloise had instructed all the servants to spend a few minutes cooling down in the freshness of the lower rooms of the thick-walled castle, just as the guests began to sit down for their meal.

Eloise had been so busy that she was now almost as hot and bothered as the servants had been, and wasn't thinking as clearly as usual, so she did not think tactically when she seated herself.

It was only when she looked up and saw Marcus making for the seat to her right that she realised that she'd made the great strategic error of placing herself on a chair next but one to the end in a little grouping with the end chair vacant. Whoever sat in the end chair—Marcus—might very easily begin a private conversation with her.

'Good afternoon, Your Grace.' He smiled blandly at her as he settled into the seat. The chairs were delicate ones made from wrought iron, not really intended it seemed for large men, and Marcus looked quite ridiculous on his, like an adult sitting on a child's chair.

'Good afternoon, my lord.' Eloise inched her own chair round a little, to try to draw someone—anyone—else into their conversation. 'I trust that you passed the morning pleasantly.' That should indicate to anyone who *did* overhear them that they had certainly not been for a walk around the lake together this morning.

'I had a splendid morning, thank you,' he told her, 'except for the final part, which was a little frustrating.'

'I'm so sorry to hear that.' Eloise tried hard not to glare at him and instead fixed a smile on her face, before looking round again to see if there were anyone nearby whom she could draw into their conversation.

'Fortunately,' Marcus continued, 'it seems that I might have the opportunity to recover now from that frustration.'

Eloise's smile was so fake and fixed that she could feel it eating into her cheeks. She was *not* going to glare at Marcus, though, because that might occasion comment. She was going to continue to smile with her head tilted just so, for all the world as though they were conversing about the weather. In fact...

'It is quite beautiful weather today, is it not, my lord?' she said. 'Although perhaps a little warm. I am very glad of these parasols.'

'Quite lovely, yes.' Marcus scanned the area behind her with his eyes before continuing in a low voice. 'If I may, I would like to continue our conversation from this morning. I am not sure that we entirely finished it.'

'I think that we did finish it.' Eloise smiled politely at him as she would if he were a very new acquaintance and they were still discussing the weather. 'I have nothing further to say on the subject and there is nothing you can say that would make me change my mind.' She altered her smile and the angle of her head slightly as though she was considering something quite mundane. Really, she might make a very fine actress upon the stage. 'I would not like to feel that I was causing you to waste your time.' She cleared her throat and raised her voice a little as Marcus opened his mouth. 'I should be very grateful for a glass of the lemonade I see over there, my lord.'

Marcus looked at her for a long moment, and then produced an extremely polite smile of his own. 'Certainly, Your Grace.'

While Marcus was procuring the lemonade, Eloise did her best to catch the eye of *any*one else, succeeding very quickly in smiling at and indicating to Mrs and Miss Heatherington, who immediately came over to her. Despite her antipathy towards her late husband, Eloise did have to own that being a duchess had its advantages, and one of them was that lesser-titled people were often eager to be seen in the company of someone deemed by Society to be so much more illustrious than they, and so on any occasion where she wished to talk to someone, she was never short of candidates for the position.

'Thank you.' Eloise bestowed a wide smile on Marcus when he returned with her lemonade. 'I believe that Mrs Heatherington and Hermione are both quite parched as well and would also very much like some lemonade.'

'Of course.' Marcus gave small bows to all three of them and turned back in the direction of the lemonade table.

Eloise invited her companions to be seated and moved her chair, so that the three of them were in a small circle, and began a conversation about the local countryside.

When Marcus returned with the lemonade, he handed glasses to Mrs Heatherington and Hermione and then addressed Eloise. 'I wonder whether you would care to take a walk down to the lake to cool down.'

Eloise looked slightly away from him as he spoke and began her response—a definite *no*.

At the same time, Mrs Heatherington gave Hermione a quite tremendous nudge, and Hermione said, 'Why, yes, my lord, I should like that above all things.'

'Excellent,' Marcus said, with the merest twitch of eye-narrowing at Eloise over Hermione's shoulder for a moment, before holding his arm out to the other woman.

Eloise really should have felt a lot more victorious than she did as she watched them stroll towards the lake together. There was, however, something quite annoying about the way Hermione hung on Marcus's arm as they walked, and something even more annoying about the fact that as he leaned down to listen to her words he looked perfectly happy to be walking with her. Given that he'd *proposed* to Eloise this morning—clearly just out of duty, but even so—he could at least have the decency not to look as though he was enjoying talking to another lady only a short number of hours later.

It was nothing to her, of course, she thought as she followed them with her eyes as they took the path to the left of the lake; she really did not mind what Marcus did. In fact, should he choose to marry someone else, she would be pleased for him that he was happy and she would be pleased that he might have less inclination and less opportunity to visit Amelia too often.

She really couldn't imagine him being happy with Hermione though. From the time she'd spent with him, she knew that he possessed a lively and sarcastic sense of humour, and, from what she'd seen, Hermione had a more literal turn of mind.

Hermione was very beautiful of course. And looking *very* proprietorial over Marcus as she leaned into him.

Well. It was Marcus's choice of course whether or not he fell in love with someone else.

It was nothing to Eloise.

'It is a most beautiful day, is it not, Your Grace?' One of the older guests, Sir Walter Amies, sat down next to Eloise.

'Indeed,' she murmured, forcing her attention away from Marcus and Hermione. Were they really going to walk all the way round the lake and at such low speed? That would take a very long time. People would certainly talk about them. And they would have a very long time to talk to each other.

'Your grandmother tells me that there is to be dancing this evening after dinner. I should like to ask to have the first dance with you.'

'I…' She couldn't refuse but it felt a little odd that Sir Walter was quite so eager to dance with her. 'Yes, of course.'

'Wonderful.' He beamed at her and she tried not to blink at the blackness of his teeth. Perhaps he was particularly fond of sweet food. 'Would you care to take a walk with me down to the lake now? I have a particular question to ask you.'

What? Surely he couldn't…

Eloise did not wish to find out.

'I'm so sorry but I see that my grandmother just indicated that she would like to speak to me,' she lied.

Sir Walter leaned closer. 'I must tell you that my question relates to marriage.' He showered her face with spit on the word *marriage*, which felt quite apt really. Eloise leaned backwards and fought with herself not to wipe her face with her hand. 'I would be honoured if you would agree to be my wife,' he continued.

'I am so sorry but I do not intend to remarry.' Eloise stood up as fast as she could. 'I must go and speak to my grandmother.'

What on *earth* was happening today? Two ridiculous marriage proposals? One from Marcus, who was doing what he thought to be his duty nine years too late, and the other from Sir Walter, who… Well, who knew? But no, a thousand times no. She'd rather…well, she'd rather marry Marcus than marry Sir Walter. But she'd rather not marry anyone.

She turned to make her way across to her grand-mother and bumped straight into Marcus.

'Oh. I thought you were walking with Miss Heather-ington.' Why did she suddenly feel breathless? It must be the heat or delayed shock from the hideous Sir Wal-ter proposal.

'I did not wish to keep Miss Heatherington too long from her mother.' He smiled at her. 'Since you are now on your feet, perhaps you would now like to take a stroll.'

'I cannot, I'm afraid. I just told Sir Walter that I was unable to walk with him because I was going to speak to my grandmother, and therefore I must go over to her.' She wished she could tell Marcus about Sir Walter's proposal; she was sure that it would make him laugh as much as she now felt that she wished to laugh about it. She couldn't and wouldn't tell him, of course. She would just have to content herself with telling her grandmother about it. She would have some satisfactorily strong words to say on the subject, Eloise was sure; her grandmother would certainly not hold her tongue if she thought there was the slightest possibility of Eloise entering into a second marriage with a man whom she did not think an appropriate match for her.

'Why do we not go and speak to Lady Kingsbridge together and then take a stroll?' Marcus's smile was so much more attractive than Sir Walter's. 'Please?'

Oh, why not? She knew what he was going to say, but she could allow him to say it and then repeat her refusal of his proposal and then that would be the end of it. And if it looked to Sir Walter as though she had been a little rude, that could only serve to underline the emphatic nature of her refusal of his proposal.

Perhaps she should also tell Sir Walter that someone had reminded her that she had promised the first dance to them? Or that she wasn't going to dance at all? Not dancing at all would be better; otherwise he would just ask her to dance later on.

'Perhaps a short stroll,' she told Marcus. 'After we have spoken to Grandmama.'

Her grandmother was sitting at a table with Lady Morton, whom Eloise knew was a close friend of hers of long standing. They were eating small sandwiches and sipping their drinks, their heads close together, talking earnestly.

'My lord. Eloise.' Her grandmother smiled at them both and raised her painted eyebrows. 'How nice to see you together.' Eloise really wished she could roll her eyes. She smiled politely instead.

'I just wanted to make sure that you're quite comfortable before we take a short walk down to the lake.' As her grandmother's smile widened, Eloise hurried into a fake explanation. 'The earl is particularly interested in birds. He was greatly excited to hear that we have an extremely rare type of coot here. He has requested that I take him to see the coot for himself.'

'Indeed.' Her grandmother stared at them both for a long second. 'Enjoy your ornithology. Off you go.' She waggled her fingers at them and then turned back to Lady Morton.

'I very much like your grandmother,' Marcus told Eloise as they began to walk in the direction of the lake.

'Me too,' Eloise agreed. Although her blatant matchmaking endeavours could become very annoying.

'We were in the middle of a conversation,' Marcus said as their distance from the rest of the company increased. 'When you unfortunately had to leave.'

'I'm not sure that we actually were. From my perspective we'd finished talking, but it seems that you have something to say and that you're going to feel frustrated until you've said it.'

'And so you're going to humour me and listen?'

'I suppose, as a good hostess, I must.' Eloise gave an exaggerated fake sigh and then smiled at him; there was something about Marcus that made it impossible to be annoyed with him for long.

He laughed. 'Thank you for your extreme kindness.'

They walked a little way in silence. Eloise certainly had no desire to engage in what should be private conversation within earshot of any third party, and she supposed that Marcus must feel the same way.

When they were several yards away from the nearest person, Marcus cleared his throat and said, 'Thank you for agreeing to speak to me again.'

'My pleasure,' said Eloise, not meaning it.

'Obviously you don't mean that. And obviously you don't intend to be easily swayed by my arguments. But I should be grateful if you would listen with an open mind.'

'Certainly.' Open or closed mind, Eloise knew that there was nothing he could say that could cause her to consider even for a second agreeing to his proposal.

'Excellent.' Marcus held his arm out for her to take and then gently directed her left of the trees that lined the lake, so that they would be visible to the rest of the party, although out of earshot.

'Very well done.' Eloise nodded approvingly. 'Very

gentlemanly. There can be no possibility of your compromising my reputation in any way if we remain in sight throughout our promenade.'

'Exactly. Just one more reason that I would make a splendid husband.'

'Firstly, your humility is most impressive. And secondly, should a husband rather not *wish* to compromise his wife?'

Oh! No! She'd sounded as though she was *flirting* with him, which could not be the right way to behave immediately before she turned down his marriage proposal for a second time. Which she was definitely going to do.

Apparently, though, having a little to-and-fro repartee with him was irresistible. She couldn't help directing a little twinkle in his direction.

'Should you agree to marry me, I will more than happily compromise you.' Marcus's pace had slowed, and Eloise slowed with him. She glanced up at him and saw that he was looking down at her intently. She swallowed, suddenly unnerved.

'That—' his eyes travelled from hers to her lips, before he returned his gaze to hers '—is just one of the many points I had to make in favour of our marriage.'

'Points?' Eloise couldn't move her eyes from his face. A tiny smile was playing at his lips now. He stopped walking entirely and she did too, unable to continue because their arms were still linked. He moved a little closer to her, and then lowered his voice slightly, his eyes on hers the entire time. Standing so close to him, she could see a shadow of beard growth already beginning even though it was barely the afternoon. She wondered briefly how it would feel if she placed her hand against it.

'If we were to be married—' somehow the lowness of his voice was igniting all her senses and fuddling her wits '—I would happily compromise you.'

'Oh.' Eloise couldn't find any real words, because Marcus's eyes were travelling to the décolletage of her gown and she could feel herself growing extremely warm under his gaze.

Her arm was still through his and suddenly she could feel every inch of where their arms met, her bare skin against his jacket sleeve, the strength of his forearm evident beneath her touch.

She was unable to prevent herself from taking a deep breath, conscious as she did so that his eyes were still on her chest.

He smiled a little more widely as her chest rose and fell, and then returned his gaze to her face. Eloise immediately had to take another big breath when he looked into her eyes again.

Marcus lifted his free hand and Eloise felt her heart beat faster. Was he going to touch her face? Was he…? And then he brushed something with the back of his hand very close to her cheek, so that she almost felt his touch.

'A money spider,' he told her, his voice so husky that she shivered from that almost as much as from the near touch.

She took another shuddering breath. What was *happening* to her?

This was *not* how this conversation was supposed to be going. She'd just intended a little…joke, she supposed.

'I apologise,' she began. 'For implying that I might...' Might what? Wish to flirt with him?

How was it that this—standing here together like this—felt like so much more than flirting, almost as though it were a prelude to, to...? To something *much* more.

She really needed to gather her wits, very fast.

Because...good heavens. What if the rest of the party could see what was happening between them? They were in full view of them.

Although...*was* anything happening between them? Or was she imagining things? Perhaps all this *warmth* was from her side only.

'No apology necessary.' Marcus applied a tiny bit of pressure to her arm and somehow they were walking again, very slowly. 'The point that I was trying to make was that—to be explicit—we already know that it is likely that we would both find the intimate side of marriage together enjoyable.'

'My lord!' Eloise's voice had emerged as a high-pitched squeak.

'Yes?' He sounded as though he wanted to laugh.

If she was honest—which she certainly wasn't going to be with anyone except herself—Eloise had sometimes over the years—fairly often at times—relived in her mind her night with Marcus, but only when she was alone. She *certainly* didn't want to think about it right now, when she was *with* him.

It was difficult not to do so, though. The strong arm on which her own was resting, his deep voice, his strong profile when she stole a look up at him, the half serious, half laughing look with which he now regarded her, *and* his words... All combined to remind her very forcibly of what she'd dreamt of all these years. Except, in the flesh he was *more* seductive.

No. This would not do at all.

Ignoring the fact that her heart was now galloping faster than her horse might go, she made a great effort to gather herself and decided not to dignify his words with any kind of response.

'I do not wish to remarry, my lord.'

'I understand that you had not *planned* to remarry. Would you not, however, for Amelia's sake, reconsider?'

'Is that not perhaps a somewhat low blow?' Eloise was delighted to have recovered her wits and her ability to form coherent sentences. 'I do of course always attempt to put Amelia first. I do not believe that a marriage founded on nothing but duty would be likely to make either of us happy, and if that were the case, I know that Amelia would not be happy either.'

'And based on the time we spent together when she was conceived, I believe that our marriage would have a greater foundation than mere duty.'

'As we are speaking plainly, I have to say that I do not believe that duty coupled with carnal desire would be a much better start to a marriage than mere duty.'

'Well, it would certainly make the marriage more enjoyable, at night if not during the day.'

'For all we know—' Eloise pressed her lips together so that she wouldn't laugh in response to the big smile Marcus was now wearing, apparently in response to his own audacity '—we might no longer be compatible in that way.'

'Really?' His look was incredulous.

Eloise shook her head. It didn't seem very wise to continue this topic.

'There can be no further reason to continue this conversation,' she said. 'I do not wish to remarry and I will not change my mind.'

Chapter Ten

Marcus

As they passed under a particularly fine weeping willow, Marcus gently—but as firmly as he could—guided Eloise so that they would continue round the lake rather than turning up a much shorter path to walk directly back across the lawns to the remainder of the party. He had a lot more to say and the conversation had run in an entirely different direction from where he had intended it to go.

In fact, he had no idea what had happened. One moment he'd been putting forward sensible arguments as to why he and Eloise ought to marry—for Amelia's sake and for duty—and the next he'd been standing almost mute next to her unable to take his eyes from her face and form. The Ella to whom he had made love that night when they were young had been saucy and pouty and light-hearted. From what he'd seen, Eloise, the Duchess of Rothshire, the mother of his daughter, was for the most part dignified and organised and mature.

And then Eloise had joked with him and twinkled

at him and had reminded him again of her Ella sauciness, and he'd been lost. Lost in a ridiculous conversation where he'd tried to convince her that they *should*
get married because they knew that they were physically compatible.

For a moment he'd even believed his own words.

He shouldn't, though; that was *not* why they should
get married. They should get married because of their
daughter. He did not wish to care for any more people
and if it weren't for Amelia he certainly wouldn't be
wishing to marry Ella. But he did want to be able to
spend time with his daughter. And at least he and Ella
were physically compatible.

And there he went again, getting himself confused.

'I believe that Amelia would benefit greatly from
my presence in her life,' he said firmly. As he spoke, a
large white butterfly fluttered directly in front of them
and he saw Eloise follow the path of its flight with her
eyes. He was quite sure that she did so to give herself
time to formulate a response to him.

'Everything I do, I do for Amelia.' She was still looking in the direction of the butterfly.

'Yes.' He nodded. He was quite sure that she was a
devoted mother beyond reproach. He was sure too that
she was a very sensible woman.

'I appreciate—' she paused as though searching for
words '—that knowing a decent, honourable man as
a father must be in the interests of a child *if* both the
child's parents are happy. But I do not believe marriage
to be a happy institution for women. In addition, if
people see the two of you together, they might realise
that you are her father, which would tarnish her repu-

tation. I remain deeply relieved that my late husband did not disown her.'

Marcus shook his head. 'Even if people suspect her birth, they would never dare say so to the very respectable Earl and Countess of Malbrook. And the parentage of many aristocrats is known to be dubious, but those people are received everywhere as long as their father owns them.'

'I'm sorry, but no.'

'Would Amelia not benefit from having siblings?' Despite how very much they annoyed him at times, he really could not imagine life without his older sisters and younger brother. Or, he realised, without being able to see his daughter regularly. And how could he see her without causing gossip if he didn't marry Ella?

'I…' She stopped walking and he came to a halt too. She took her arm from his and took a step backwards and looked up at him very seriously. 'My lord. Marcus. There can be no benefit to either of us in prolonging this conversation. I do not have siblings. My father effectively sold me to the late duke, which exactly demonstrated his feelings for me. I do have a wonderful grandmother, as you know. I no longer have my parents but am very happy as I am with neither siblings nor parents in my life. Amelia is very happy now. I am certainly not going to contemplate marrying you in order perhaps—but not definitely—for her to gain a much younger sibling with whom she might or might not be lifelong friends. I have nothing further to say on the subject. Could I direct your attention to the island in the middle of the lake? If you look carefully now you will see some of the young coots to which Amelia referred during our walk.' She pointed at the island

and turned a little away from him so that he could see only her profile. If it hadn't been for the way her chest rose and fell quite so rapidly, he might think that she was fully composed.

'The coots are certainly delightful,' he said, not looking at them. 'I apologise for pressing you so hard in regard to the marriage issue.'

Eloise—still looking intently in the direction of the island—inclined her head.

'I should be very grateful if you would allow me to see Amelia as much as possible,' he continued.

Eloise didn't move.

Marcus could feel his shoulders and neck tighten.

'I will do what I can.' She finally turned to look at him. 'That sounded ungracious; I'm sorry. It is what I mean, though: I will do everything that I can to allow you to see her as regularly as possible, for example for walks during your stay here, but we must be careful to ensure that there can be no suspicion of any impropriety between us.'

'Thank you. And I do fully understand and agree. I emphatically do not wish to hurt either Amelia or you in any way.' He looked round. They were perhaps two thirds of the way around the lake now. 'On which note, I believe that we should make reasonable haste to return.' It would be silly to invite any suggestion of impropriety on their part if they were not going to marry.

'We should indeed.' Eloise accepted the arm that he put out for her to take again, and they began to stroll again. 'Otherwise—apart from anything else— my grandmother will become quite insufferable in her matchmaking attempts.'

Marcus laughed. 'She certainly seemed enthusiastic about my suggestion that we walk together.' He couldn't remember now quite why it was that he had thought that an eligible man would not choose to marry a widow. Not that he would wish to marry Eloise if it weren't for that fact that he felt he *had* to, to do his duty and to see Amelia.

'She wishes me to achieve the marital felicity that she shared with my late grandfather. Which is very kind of her, but, as I have explained, not something that I intend to pursue.'

'She is a redoubtable woman.'

'As am I.' Eloise was twinkling at him again. And Marcus couldn't help laughing again. She pointed ahead at the castle. 'Let me tell you a little about the history of the house. It's genuinely quite fascinating.' And it genuinely was, particularly when narrated by Eloise.

She touched on not just the formal history, but the mundane.

'The late duke's cousin Augusta firmly believed that the terrace was haunted by a dog,' she told him as they emerged from the trees that bordered the lake. 'She was ecstatic finally to see it, only for it to relieve itself against the butler's leg.'

'I have always had it on great authority that ghost dogs do not relieve themselves.'

'Exactly.' Eloise smiled at him, and then said, her voice a little lowered, 'I would just like to reiterate that I truly will do all I can to enable you to spend regular time with Amelia over the years.'

'Thank you. I truly am grateful.'

They finished their walk actually smiling at each other, before they both nearly tripped over the elderly

Sir Walter Amies, who glared at them far more than was warranted, especially given how profusely they had both apologised.

As they walked away from him back towards Lady Kingsbridge, Marcus glanced back over his shoulder to see Sir Walter staring after Eloise. Could it be possible that the old man was *interested* in her? Disgusting. Truly disgusting. The man had to be forty years her senior and was deaf to boot. Really. How dare he even think of her in that way? *Any* much younger woman of course, not just Eloise. But Eloise in particular: how utterly ridiculous. Really. If she *were* to remarry, it should be to someone who deserved her.

'Eloise.' Lady Kingswood was holding her hands out to them. 'And Marcus; I do not stand on ceremony with you any longer, my lord. Firstly, as you know, I held you as a baby. Indeed, you quite ruined a dress of mine returning some milk after being brought from the nursery too soon after a feed. And secondly, I now feel that we are quite friends. So I will call you Marcus.'

He smiled at her as they reached her side. 'I am honoured at your use of my Christian name. And I must apologise for the ruined dress, Lady Kingsbridge.'

'I forgave you immediately,' she said.

'Perhaps you should no longer torment His Lordship with the memory, in that case,' Eloise said, laughing.

'I said forgave, not forgot. I never forget anything. Now, how was your walk?'

'Very enjoyable,' he said. Which was somewhat true. There had been the extraordinary few moments they'd shared where he'd, frankly, wanted to gather her into his arms and kiss her quite passionately. And then she—the mother of his child—had turned down his marriage proposal most thoroughly.

He wasn't sure how he felt about that. He would of course never have proposed to her—or anyone—if she hadn't been the mother of his daughter. Conceptually, he still did not wish to marry. But it seemed that his aversion to the idea was not as strong as his desire to live under the same roof as his daughter. And the intimate side of marriage to Ella would he knew be no hardship.

Perhaps he should attempt to woo her.

'It was quite lovely.' Eloise didn't look at him as she spoke. 'The earl is particularly interested in coots and was extremely pleased to see the chicks.'

'Oh, yes, your mutual interest in bird fancying.' Lady Kingsbridge rolled her eyes a little.

'Grandmama, your glass is empty. Perhaps the earl might be so kind as to procure more ratafia for you.'

'Certainly.' Marcus bowed slightly and then turned on his heel, chuckling internally. It seemed as though Lady Kingsbridge was a woman who would not easily give up an ambition.

When he returned to the ladies, Eloise immediately said, 'Thank you very much, my lord. I note that the duke is standing alone and remember that you said you had a particular desire to discuss fishing with him.'

Marcus was impressed by her combining acting on improving his acquaintance with the duke with avoiding further awkward three-way conversation with her grandmother.

'Indeed I did. Thank you.' He nodded a bow at both the ladies and moved away towards the duke. He had never been able to see the attraction of fishing—there was too much standing still involved—but if Ella would not marry him and it would enable him to see Amelia reasonably regularly, he would very happily adopt the sport.

Fifteen minutes later, the duke—usually a monosyllabic conversationalist in Marcus's experience—was still holding forth extremely enthusiastically on all things piscine, requiring nothing more from Marcus, it seemed, than the occasional *ah* or *certainly*.

Marcus's attention had been wandering for several minutes and he couldn't help looking over to see what Eloise might be doing. He knew that she'd been talking to her grandmother for a while, but now Sir Walter was making his slow way over to her. Marcus frowned. And then smiled when his close friend Sir Richard Elliott—whom he had been very pleased to see here when they'd arrived—sat down beside Eloise, beating Sir Walter to it.

And then began to frown again when Eloise and Sir Richard bent their heads together and began to talk with great animation. Really, what on earth could they have to say to each other? Apparently they were finding each other's company very amusing. Too amusing, some might say; if they continued like that, Lady Kingsbridge would begin to suspect that there might be some understanding developing between them.

'My lord?' The duke was looking at him with his head cocked to one side and his eyebrows raised. He had obviously just asked a question.

'Certainly,' Marcus said, stabbing in the dark.

'Excellent. I suggest we meet in the great hall at

six o'clock in the morning. My servants will provide you with any fishing attire that you are lacking.' Good God. Apparently they were going fishing together tomorrow. Which was of course ideal.

'Splendid,' he said.

The duke left his guests shortly afterwards, citing estate affairs to which he needed to attend, so there was at least no danger of Marcus having to join him in further fishing conversation for the time being. But Eloise was still busy talking to Sir Richard, and also now to a man Marcus knew less well, Viscount Stockall, and they had their chairs arranged in a little group in such a way that it would be difficult for anyone else to join them. Marcus eyed them for a moment and decided that he could not possibly push his way into their conversation without occasioning comment.

Well, he would just have to chat to some of the other guests. He could usually find enjoyment in conversation with most people.

Today, though, sitting next to Ladies Kingsbridge and Morton, he did not find it easy to concentrate on the heart-to-heart that Lady Kingsbridge seemed intent on having with him. Time passed very slowly, in fact, and he found it remarkably difficult not to look over his shoulder at Eloise to see what she was doing. Eventually, he moved his chair so that he could look at her out of the corner of his eye without being too obvious.

'You are now in the full glare of the sun, Marcus,' Lady Kingsbridge said. 'You must move yourself into the shade or you will feel ill quite quickly from heat, however invincible you young men believe yourselves to be.'

'I'm quite all right, I assure you.'

'Nonsense. Move yourself over here.' She rapped him on the knuckles with her fan before vigorously airing herself with it. 'It is remarkably warm.'

Marcus moved his chair. 'Thank you for your concern.'

'Not at all.' She prodded him in the ribs with the fan and leaned closer to him. 'Many would think, from your inattention to our conversation and the way in which you moved your chair to get a better view, that you had eyes only for my granddaughter.' If she imagined that she had lowered her voice, she was wrong. If anything, it was even more ear-splittingly loud than usual.

'Her Grace is an excellent hostess and I enjoyed our walk,' Marcus replied, aware that half the company were now listening to their conversation. He looked directly over at Eloise and smiled blandly. She returned his smile with a small one of her own before inclining her head back in the direction of her companions.

'I am pleased that you enjoyed it. Now tell me more about yourself. How do you spend your time?' Lady Kingsbridge was definitely sizing him up as a potential husband for Eloise.

The rest of luncheon did not pass quickly and he was heartily relieved when Lady Kingsbridge—possibly bored almost to a stupor by his monologue on the subject of his estates in answer to her question—announced that it was too hot to remain seated on the lawns, even in the shade, and that she would accompany the ladies inside before returning to the dower house to rest for an hour or two, while the gentlemen partook of any number of diversions.

* * *

After a short stroll with a number of the other men, Marcus took himself off to his chamber to look through his correspondence and write to his man of business. He found himself yawning as he wrote, a direct result of very little sleep the night before. He'd woken from one of his habitual nightmares—the horrors of the battlefield portrayed vividly in his mind—and then been even less able to get back to sleep than usual, for thinking about Amelia.

He became aware some time later that Norris was standing in front of him, and that he had a painful crick in his neck from where he'd obviously nodded off in his chair.

'You seem tired. Are you all right?' The obvious concern in Norris's eyes was heart-warming, and yet Marcus could not admit to him that he no longer slept well.

'It must be the Sussex air,' he said, and produced what he felt was a convincing laugh.

Norris nodded. 'I believe that the ladies and gentlemen are now all assembling to visit the duke's maze.'

'Thank you.' Marcus rolled his neck, blinked another couple of times and then stood up. Sprang up, almost, refreshed after his snooze. Thank God for his army-honed ability to sleep any time, anywhere. Even if that same army experience had caused his current sleep problems.

Having joined the others in the hall, he walked down to the maze with Sir Richard and Viscount Stockall. Eloise was ahead, walking with her grandmother, who had a stick upon which she occasionally remembered to lean heavily, but which seemed to be redundant most of the time.

'The first maze on this site was created with hornbeam trees in the middle of the last century, during the late duke's childhood,' Eloise informed them all when they reached the maze's entrance. Marcus found himself frowning at the reminder that her husband had been so much older than her.

'His father, the twelfth duke, had visited the one at Hampton Court Palace and much admired it,' she continued. 'The maze then fell into disrepair towards the end of the century, and the new duke had a new maze constructed on the site of the old one, with yew trees. It was finished only last year and is now the largest maze in England. If you find your way to the middle in under half an hour, you may count yourself quite victorious. Only one person to my knowledge has succeeded in doing it in under thirty minutes.'

'What is the longest anyone has ever been lost in there?' Sir Richard asked, to laughter from the group.

'Oh, some people went in there over six months ago and have not yet emerged. We throw food to them from time to time.' Eloise smiled as the laughter continued. 'No, in all seriousness we have on occasion quite lost people and had to go in to rescue them after two or three hours.'

'I think we will need a prize for the winner,' Lady Kingsbridge said. 'I shall seat myself here—' she pointed with her stick at a shaded bench '—while the rest of you go into the maze and think of a suitable reward.'

'We quite count on you to guide us,' Mrs Heatherington said to Marcus, including her daughter, Miss Heatherington, in her *we*.

'And I shall request the honour of guiding Her Grace.' Sir Walter Amies bowed—quite horribly—in Eloise's direction.

Good God. Twice over. Marcus had never really considered before to what extent a maze must give rise to the possibility of innocent people being unwittingly compromised.

He opened his mouth to say something to try to rescue both himself and Eloise, who was looking a little wild-eyed, when Lady Kingsbridge said, 'I am afraid that I shall require Her Grace to remain here with me in case I need to send her in to rescue anyone still lost at dusk. And I shall have to ask His Lordship—' she pointed with her stick in Marcus's direction '—to remain here also to help, as the tallest gentleman present, as he will be able to see over the hedges.' The hedges were at least eight feet high and Marcus measured no more than six feet and one inch, but he was certainly not going to quibble.

'My height is at your disposal.' He bowed in Lady Kingsbridge's direction.

Eloise's eyes had swivelled between Sir Walter, her grandmother and Marcus, and she murmured, 'Certainly,' clearly having decided that Marcus was the lesser of two evils.

'Lord Stockall, you must accompany us,' Mrs Heatherington trilled, apparently accepting defeat, for the time being at least. 'Hermione and I are sadly lacking in knowledge of mazes.'

Once Lady Kingsbridge had dispatched the rest of the group into the maze in twos and threes, she settled back on her bench with Lady Morton, and said, 'Perhaps the two of you would like to take a promenade for a few minutes; I don't think anyone will immediately need your assistance.'

'I am quite happy to remain here, Grandmama.' Eloise sat down on a bench on the other side of the maze entrance.

'I would also be very happy to wait here,' said Marcus, hoping not to annoy either lady too much.

'Certainly, if you wish.' Lady Kingsbridge pointed from Marcus to Eloise's bench and turned slightly in the direction of Lady Morton, so that she was angled away from Eloise and Marcus, and said, 'We were interrupted earlier when you began to tell me about your delightful grandchildren. Do continue.'

She angled herself even further as Lady Morton embarked upon a description of what sounded like an extremely large family, and Marcus couldn't help smiling as he obediently sat down on the same bench as Eloise, but at the other end of it.

He looked at her and saw her eyes dancing.

'My grandmother is a very determined woman,' she said in a low voice. 'And always loving and caring but at times misguided.' It was clear that she was referring to her grandmother's blatant matchmaking. 'I suppose that it is useful, though, for the time being. A disguise as it were for your spending some time with Amelia. As long as neither of our reputations suffers.'

'Your reputation is of course important. I have no great regard for my own. My friends know and respect me, I hope, and I doubt that anything that people might say about a few walks with you could reduce the allure of an earldom to matchmaking mamas, but if it does, all to the good; I have no wish to marry any of the debutantes paraded in the direction of eligible men.'

'Although you did of course mean your earlier proposal *quite* heartfeltly.' Eloise's eyes were dancing even more now.

Marcus laughed, because he couldn't help it, and then said, 'I did mean that proposal very seriously. It is the only one I have ever made. I would like to marry you. I am not intending to make any other proposals.'

'I am almost tempted to thank you for the compliment in making your first and only proposal to me. I would be particularly honoured if it had not been made entirely out of a sense of duty.' She softened her words with a smile and then tilted her head to one side, her brow a little furrowed. 'You do not wish for heirs, my lord?'

'I have a younger brother and nephews. I am well-equipped in that regard. And…' He stopped short. He'd been on the brink of explaining to her that after the difficulties of war, he craved a calm existence. What was wrong with him? Heat stroke? The shock of learning that he was a father? Or was it something about Eloise that caused him to say strange things, as he had this morning when he'd proposed and gone off on a tangent talking about physical intimacy?

'And?' Eloise prompted.

'And I wonder how the others are doing inside the maze,' he said.

She looked at him for a moment, as though trying to work something out, and then gave an almost imperceptible nod and said, 'Unless they are very lucky they will be getting quite lost.'

'Is there not a well-known easy way to the middle

of any maze?' He'd heard many years ago that all one had to do was put one's hand on the hedge to one's right and keep walking, and that one couldn't then fail to find the middle, and on the few occasions he'd been in a maze it had worked very well.

'No.' Eloise shook her head. 'Modern mazes are much more cunningly designed.'

'Interesting. How?'

'You'll have to wait and see. I'm quite sure that Grandmama will design to send us in quite soon.'

And Eloise was proved right within a small number of minutes, when Lady Kingsbridge interrupted their conversation about the parts of England to which they would both like to travel—Marcus wasn't entirely sure how they'd got on to that topic but he'd been enjoying himself—to say, 'I am concerned that some of our guests might be feeling hopelessly lost. Could you perhaps go and look for them, Eloise and Marcus?'

'I'm not sure they have been in there for *that* long,' Eloise said.

'Yes, they have.' Her grandmother looked at her pointedly.

Eloise stood up and said, 'I am of course very happy to go in to offer any necessary assistance.'

'She's incorrigible,' she whispered to Marcus as they entered together.

Marcus laughed but said nothing. Lady Kingsbridge *was* incorrigible but he liked her and she was Eloise's grandmother, and he was not going to criticise her.

The maze was immediately impressive. The hedges were tall and thick and it was impossible to see through from their passage to the adjacent ones.

'Do you know your way to the centre?' he asked.

'No, although I believe that one knows once one is close to the centre. I've only been in here three times. I came with Amelia the third time and fortunately had the foresight to ask a footman to accompany us with water, because we became extremely lost and spent nearly an hour and a half in here. Amelia was quite delighted, of course, and was hoping that we would have to spend the night in the maze.'

Marcus suddenly wondered what it would be like to spend the night in the maze with Eloise, just the two of them.

Perhaps she was wondering the same thing; she stopped talking quite suddenly, visibly swallowed and then said, 'I don't hear any sounds of distress. We can either stay here next to the entrance and listen, or we can attempt to get to the centre.'

'We should certainly make our way towards the centre. I feel from what you told us that it's a challenge I cannot turn down. I believe you said that only one person has arrived there in under half an hour?'

'Yes, that is correct. I think you'll be very lucky to be the second one.'

'For all you know, I am fiendishly gifted in regard to maze navigation.'

Eloise laughed. 'I look forward to witnessing your fiendish gift.'

Marcus listened for a moment, and then said, 'This way.'

'Are you basing your decision on the direction from which the sounds of chatter are coming?'

'Not at all,' Marcus lied, and headed off, fast, in the opposite direction from the voices. If the others were all together, and there were no exclamations of victory, they must all have gone the wrong way.

'You're walking particularly fast,' Eloise said after a minute or two.

'Am I?' Of course he was. The faster they walked, the more ground they could cover in half an hour. 'I have to say I'm feeling quite confident.' They'd gone left and he was just going to keep on going left at every opportunity. Although... 'What cunning ploy do modern hedge designers use?'

'No, no.' Eloise shook her head. 'I'd be ruining your enjoyment if I told you that. You're going to have to work it out for yourself.' She shot him a teasing glance over her shoulder, and in that moment reminded him so much of herself as Ella nine years ago that he was hard pushed not to put his arms around her waist from behind and pull her into him for a kiss.

'All right,' he said, wishing that his voice wasn't suddenly so hoarse, 'off we go.'

He wasn't sure what he even wanted right now. Well, he was sure. He wanted to make love to Eloise. What he couldn't work out was whether doing so would be a good thing or a bad thing.

If they did make love, they would *have* to get married, and he would be able to see Amelia all the time and would have done his duty.

But he didn't want Ella to feel that she'd been forced into marrying him. The thought of marriage was still terrifying—it made you so much more vulnerable if you cared about your wife—but he was halfway there already, with this love he felt for his daughter.

It was all so damned confusing.

Chapter Eleven

Eloise

Eloise shivered, feeling Marcus's gaze on her skin almost as though he was touching her with his fingers.

This was quite ridiculous. She didn't *want* to be made to feel like this by him.

She needed to pull herself together. What had they been talking about? The maze.

'You lead and I'll follow,' she said.

Marcus laughed. 'Why, certainly.'

'Strictly with regard to this maze,' she said. 'Until we're quite lost, when I will be forced to rescue us.' She looked at him over her shoulder and wondered if she was *pouting* at him. She'd run quite mad.

'There is *no* possibility of our becoming lost.' Marcus raised his eyebrows and smiled at her and she felt butterflies deep in her stomach. 'This way.'

'I will not think you ungentlemanly if you walk ahead of me,' Eloise told him. On the contrary, it would be to her benefit for him to be ahead of her. He wouldn't be able to see the effect this proximity was having on her, and obviously—because who wouldn't?—she would enjoy the opportunity to watch him walk. His broad shoulders, encased to perfection in his jacket, his narrow hips and strong legs all came together in the most delightful fashion.

'This way.' Marcus turned left again. He was obviously going to keep on going left until eventually he realised that his method wouldn't work.

After a few minutes of walking behind him at too fast a pace for real enjoyment, Eloise said, 'Are you still quite sure that you're going to find the centre like this?'

'Certain. We might slow our pace a little, though; it is very warm.'

'I also am too hot. And I assure you that a reduced speed will not make any difference.'

'To my imminent success?'

'To your imminent realisation that today's maze designers are cleverer than those of yore.'

'Oh, my God.' Marcus stopped so suddenly that Eloise walked straight into him.

'Are you all right?' he asked when they had untangled themselves from each other.

'Yes, thank you.' She was all right apart from a *ludicrously* fast-beating heart, and the effort of preventing herself from having stayed where she was right up against his back and wrapping her arms around his firm body. She took another step away from him. 'Are *you* all right? Why did you stop?'

'I had a realisation.' He looked *so* handsome when his eyes were crinkling as they were now.

'That you are not as clever as you think you are?'

'In essence, on this one occasion, yes.'

'In what way?'

'I *think* that if the maze designer were to put islands of hedge within the maze, the always going to the left or right wouldn't work.'

'I think you might be right.'

'So we've just been going in pointless circles?'

'Yes.' Eloise beamed at him and Marcus rolled his eyes. 'Sadly, I don't think you're the maze aficionado you thought yourself to be.'

'There must be other ways of working it out.'

'Like…hedge recognition?' Eloise suggested, her head on one side, faux interested.

'Exactly. To name but one method.'

'Are you good at recognising hedges?'

'Certainly I am.'

'Would you say we've seen this particular hedge here before?' Eloise pointed in front of them.

Marcus looked at the hedge for a long moment and then said, 'No, definitely not.'

'And you know that because…?'

'The leaves here are particularly distinctive.' They all looked exactly the same as everywhere else in the maze. 'And also because we've been going left the entire time and we haven't passed the entrance so we can't have done a full circle. I think.' He looked up and down the path. 'How difficult can it be? We're going to be in the centre very soon. Come on.'

Eloise adored Amelia, but if she was being entirely truthful she hadn't enjoyed her lengthy maze experience with her as much as she was enjoying this one.

Amelia had got tired and Eloise—somewhat tired herself, because walking slowly was particularly draining—had had to carry her for quite a long time, and their conversation had dwindled to a running commentary on the—identical—hedges that surrounded them.

Marcus did not seem to be at all tired and he kept Eloise laughing almost the entire time. And when she wasn't laughing, she couldn't help enjoying the intimacy of the moment; it was as though they were in their own little hedge cocoon. They could hear the others at times, and once or twice they caught glimpses of other pairs or little groups of guests—some looking happier than others—but in the main they were on their own.

Eventually, they heard a commotion from somewhere over to their left and looked up to see Mrs and Miss Heatherington and Viscount Stockall's heads above them.

'There's a viewing platform in the centre,' Eloise explained. 'It makes getting out of the maze much easier. And it's extremely satisfying to get a good look at it all from up there.'

'I look forward to getting there. One day.'

'Oh, look.' Eloise stared at the platform. Sir Walter had just joined the other three and was standing remarkably close to Mrs Heatherington. *Very* close. Perhaps he liked widows and perhaps—if Eloise was lucky—he had transferred his attentions to a somewhat older widow. 'I see that we—you—have been beaten by Sir Walter as well as the others.' Two more heads popped up. 'And by Sir Richard and Mr Forrest. Some might regard you as having failed.'

'Let's keep walking.' Marcus began to shepherd her along the path again. 'No time to stand gawping at other competitors. I should point out that we did start quite a long time after the others. At this point we have certainly not lost the maze battle.'

Quite a long time—perhaps fifteen minutes—later, Marcus was still searching in vain for the centre.

'Would you perhaps care to take a short rest here?' He indicated a wrought iron bench in a little clearing.

'Certainly.' Eloise sat down and sighed. 'My feet are surprisingly tired after so much circular walking. And it is quite warm.'

'It is indeed.' Marcus inspected their surroundings. 'We definitely haven't been here before. I would have noticed the bench. We have seen one or two other benches, but not this one, I'm certain.'

'Definitely not this one.' Maybe she should point out to him the clue in the back of the bench. At this rate, they would still be here by dusk, if not nightfall. Or maybe she wouldn't; she was enjoying herself and he'd been *far* too confident in his own maze-solving abilities. 'If we continue like this, the others will have to throw food and drink in for us,' she said.

'I presume our getting lost was your grandmother's intention.' Marcus stretched his long legs out in front of them and leaned back, while Eloise tried hard not to be too aware of quite how nicely solid his thighs looked and just how *tall* he was. And broad.

When she thought about it, it was very rare for her to spend so much time alone with a man. That was probably why she was quite so affected by the physical proximity to him.

'I think this probably *was* her intention, but even she, with the most optimistic matchmaking designs in the world, cannot have imagined that you would fail quite so spectacularly to make any progress towards the centre.'

'It does seem that I have not succeeded *particularly* well.' He grinned at her and Eloise felt her insides practically *melt*. He had a *lovely* smile. She was sure he could get away with all sorts of misdemeanours if he just used that smile. And for her, something that made it even more attractive was that it reminded her of Amelia. To whom she could never say no when she smiled like that.

'Would you like to give up?' she asked, knowing that he would refuse.

'Certainly not.'

Perhaps ten or fifteen minutes later, they sat down on another wrought iron bench in another clearing, on Marcus's suggestion.

'I cannot comprehend how it is possible that this feels almost as tiring as a day of hard riding and boxing practice, or indeed a day's marching with an army,' he said as he settled onto the bench. 'We have essentially done nothing.'

Eloise nodded. 'I have often noted that walking very slowly is particularly tiring. A day's shopping, while quite delightful if one is fortunate enough to purchase what one needs or desires, or attendance at an art gallery looking very carefully at each picture, can both make one quite exhausted. I cannot believe, though, that they can compare to a day's marching.'

'They are certainly very different activities.'

'It must be…' She always wondered how men managed to return to daily life in England after living through battles. The contrast had to be enormous. It felt intrusive to ask too much, though. 'It must be difficult, perhaps, at times, to return home after war.'

'Indeed.' The word sounded harsh, a shocking change from the tones he normally used.

'I apologise; that was intrusive.'

'Not at all; it is more that I... That, yes, you are right; it is difficult.'

'I'm sorry. And of course grateful. So many of you sacrificed so much for us at home.'

'My sacrifice was nothing compared to those of many.' His voice was still harsh. 'Look at me.' He held his arms wide. 'Unscathed. The only thing...'

Eloise waited, and then said, 'The only thing?'

'I have nightmares,' he said after a long pause. 'The memories. So much death, so much suffering. I just...' He shook his head. 'But it's nothing. I'm very lucky. I should never complain.'

'Oh, Marcus.' Eloise couldn't help reaching out and putting her hand on his arm. 'That must be awful. Yes, you're lucky that you returned physically unhurt, but that wasn't your *fault*.' The look on his face and the tension she sensed in his arm made her desperate to find some words to help. 'You aren't lucky that you have nightmares. You have every right to complain.'

He shook his head. 'No. I don't.'

Eloise looked at his profile. Somewhere during the course of the past week, it had become extremely familiar to her. He was staring straight ahead, his expression sombre. She wanted him to laugh again. Maybe, if they spoke of this on another occasion, she might find some words to help him, but now she sensed that he needed lightness.

'I'm sorry,' she said. 'Now, I wonder whether we

should continue to the centre. Unless you'd like to stop now?'

'Thank you.' He relaxed his features and turned and smiled at her. 'And, yes, we should continue because no I am not giving up.'

'In a few minutes' time I'm going to give you a clue,' Eloise said.

'How can you give me a clue? How can you possibly remember the way? It's huge and a hedge is a hedge.'

'You'll see.'

'Hmm.' He narrowed his eyes and then laughed as she smiled blandly at him.

They stopped again, in front of a third bench, a few minutes later.

'I'm not sure we should sit down this time,' Marcus said. 'We should keep…' He stopped talking and moved closer to the bench. 'Why are the designs of the backs all different?' He stared hard at the bench and then turned to her. '*Eloise.* There are *clues* written into them, aren't there? You wretch.'

She smirked. '*I* didn't write the clues.'

'But you knew.'

'But don't you feel a lot better knowing that you worked it out yourself?'

He'd moved closer to her in his mock outrage and was standing looking down at her. As he looked, the laughter in his eyes died and turned to something more…serious. Eloise moistened her lips. She could hardly bear to hold his gaze; the intensity of it felt almost burning. Equally, though, she could hardly bear to look away.

'Eloise.' He reached one hand up and traced the line of her cheekbone, very gently, with his finger.

'Mmhmm?' Her voice was shaky, as shaky as her whole body now felt.

Marcus took a step closer. Eloise didn't move. She wasn't sure that her legs even worked any more.

He lifted his other hand and placed it on her waist and pulled her a little closer to him. Eloise's hands went to his—hard—chest, and she turned her face up towards his, unable to do anything else.

Slowly, very slowly, he began to lean down towards her. Their lips were less than an inch apart now. She could feel his breath whispering across hers, and under her fingers she felt the muscles in his chest flex as he moved his arms to hold her.

Marcus brushed her lips with his and Eloise sighed deep inside her and…

'Will you marry me, Mrs Heatherington?' Sir Walter Amies's voice came loudly from only feet away.

'Eek,' Eloise squeaked against Marcus, before they as one sprang apart, as though Sir Walter was right next to them.

'Who is that?' Marcus whispered.

'Sir Walter. Shh.' Eloise leaned her ear towards the hedge.

'Oh, Sir Walter,' said Mrs Heatherington in throbbing tones. 'I am most honoured. Could I make so bold as to ask the size of your fortune?'

'No!' Eloise mouthed as Marcus put his hand over his mouth, stifling a laugh.

'I am thinking of my daughter,' Mrs Heatherington added, her voice sounding soulful.

'Of course you are, my dear, and I understand. I

have ten thousand a year and a wonderful estate in Hampshire.'

'Sir *Walter*.' Mrs Heatherington's tones were throbbing even more now; she could easily pass for an opera singer. And then they heard the sounds of…

'Is that…? Are they…?' Marcus's eyes were round.

'Yes.' Eloise nodded. 'I think they are.' Which was more than she and Marcus were now doing, she couldn't help thinking.

'Well.' Marcus was still whispering. 'I feel that we can't speak out loud because—obviously—if we can hear them they can hear us. Although they are of course distracted.'

Eloise nodded, trying not to giggle.

'So. The clue.' He looked at the bench. 'Back the way we came? In the direction of the second bench?'

Eloise nodded again and Marcus shook his head.

'My *darling*.' Sir Walter's tones rang out through the hedge again. Eloise's eyes automatically went to Marcus's. Like her, he was pressing his lips together, clearly trying hard not to laugh out loud.

And then there was a loud cracking sound, followed by an *Ow*.

'Was that a *slap*?' whispered Eloise.

'I think so.'

'There will be *no* such liberties until we are married,' Mrs Heatherington pronounced loudly.

Sir Walter moaned, 'Ow,' again as Eloise and Marcus both dissolved in silent laughter.

'We should go,' Eloise whispered when she could speak. 'It feels *bad* that we're listening.'

Marcus nodded, wiping his eyes, and they walked away to the sound of raised voices behind them.

'Goodness me,' Eloise said when they were out of earshot.

'Indeed. I had no idea that an afternoon exploring a maze would involve so much drama.'

Or so much tension, Eloise thought. She'd expected to be mildly entertained walking around the maze with some of the other ladies, but instead had been extremely diverted by Marcus as well as by Sir Walter and Mrs Heatherington.

As they walked side by side, their arms occasionally touching, she reflected that it felt as though they were now friends. She had female friends but she did not have male friends. She'd never had a male friend in fact. She had no brothers and had not really known any boys when she was growing up, she had never had a close relationship with her father, she'd had very few conversations with her late husband, and there was no man of her acquaintance whom she would count as a friend. The only men she knew remotely well were the new duke—and he was taciturn, and they did not share the same tastes in conversation—and some of the male servants.

This felt…nice.

'I still can't believe that happened,' Marcus said as they approached the second bench, to which they'd returned. 'Oh, yes, the clue's there in the back. On we go. So, yes, it has to be rare to be privy—through no fault of one's own—to someone else's marriage proposal.'

'And *such* a proposal.' Eloise suddenly really wanted to tell Marcus about her own conversation with Sir Walter. And, really, it couldn't hurt to tell him. 'I am still quite stunned. And quite relieved.'

'I did see Sir Walter pursuing conversation with you quite assiduously during luncheon.'

'Yes. In fact, without wishing to blow my own trumpet, I have received *two* marriage proposals in the past four and twenty hours.'

'Good Lord. You mean that Sir Walter has therefore *made* two marriage proposals in that time?'

'Indeed. In less than that time. My own proposal was just before luncheon, while you were walking with Miss Heatherington. Goodness.' Eloise had been struck by another thought. 'Perhaps he has made *more* than two proposals today. Perhaps he made one at breakfast time.'

Marcus gave a snort of laughter. 'Enterprising.' He stopped for a moment and she looked up at him and saw that his face had become serious. 'I should not laugh. I hope that you weren't too distressed by his proposal.'

'I must own that I was not *pleased*. But I was surrounded by people so I did not feel at all alarmed, just…unenthusiastic.'

'Perhaps someone a little closer to you in age.'

'*If* I were going to remarry, which, as we have discussed, I am not, it would certainly be to someone younger than Sir Walter.'

'What other attributes would this putative husband-to-be have?' He was smiling at her, definitely flirting.

Eloise found herself smiling back. Also flirting, if she was honest.

'I have not considered the matter,' she told him, truthfully. 'Given that I truly do not intend ever to marry again.'

'If you *were* considering it?' They had just reached the first bench. Marcus walked over to it and indicated with a nod of his head accompanied by raised eyebrows that they should perhaps be seated.

And somehow, Eloise found herself sitting down next to him and saying, utterly ridiculously, 'Well, if I *were* considering it, which I certainly am not—' she really wasn't '—I suppose he would have to be someone with whom I could enjoy talking. And laughing. I would like to be friends with my husband.' That must have occurred to her because she'd been thinking about friendships with men just now. 'Should I remarry, which I won't.'

'What else?' The way Marcus was looking at her was making her feel quite breathless and, frankly, addling her wits.

'He would have to...' No, she couldn't say what had come to her mind; she didn't even want to articulate those words to herself. 'He would have to be decent and honest and kind.' There was *no* need to think about physical attributes.

'And would he...' Marcus put his arm along the back of the bench so that if Eloise leaned back even an inch he would effectively be encircling her shoulders. 'Would he be someone with whom you would enjoy...' He leaned his head down so that his lips were close to her ear, and spoke in a low voice. 'Intimate relations?'

Eloise fought with herself and did not lean back against his arm or answer him with the kind of—frankly—risqué response that sprang to mind. Instead, she turned so that she was facing him, with the intention of saying something brisk and sensible to disperse the—she didn't know what it was—the *tension* she could feel between them, the thing that meant that if she *had* leaned back against his arm, spoken in the low, husky voice she was tempted to use, he would, she was almost certain, have kissed her.

'I imagine,' she began her brisk and sensible response, and then she looked at his mouth, his perfectly shaped lips, the way they were turning up just a little at the corners. And then the only thing she could imagine was kissing him, feeling those lips against hers. Properly this time.

She couldn't stop looking at his lips. Until she moved her gaze to his strong jaw, and the shadow of beard growth, now even stronger than it had been earlier in the day. And then she allowed her eyes to travel down his face, to look at his strong neck, his shoulders, the way she could see—even through his jacket—how his muscles moved when he turned his arm a little. And then she looked back up at his eyes.

And *he* was looking at *her*. He was looking at her as though he was a wild animal and she was his prey. And, Lord help her, she very much liked it. And she was beginning to think that she was going to give in to that liking. They were alone. They'd already been in the maze together for a long time. And she was feeling things deep inside her that she hadn't felt for a very long time. Since that night with Marcus in fact.

'You imagine?' His voice was hoarse.

'I…' Eloise tried to gather her thoughts and then shook her head. 'I can't remember.'

'I can.' He put one finger under her chin and gently tilted her head up to his. 'We began like this.' He grazed her lips with his own. 'And then—' he was almost whispering again '—we did this.' He kissed her properly now. His lips were firm and warm and perfect against hers, as she remembered them. And then he teased hers

open with his tongue, and Eloise found herself respond-
ing, sinking deeper and deeper into the kiss.

He pulled her closer against him with the arm that
had been almost around her shoulders, and pushed his
other hand into her hair, so that his fingers were cup-
ping the back of her neck.

They kissed and kissed for a long time—Eloise had
no idea exactly how long—until suddenly Marcus drew
back and took his hand from where it had been cradling
her head, which immediately—ridiculously—felt cold.

She stared at him, hardly able to focus. He was swal-
lowing, looking as dazed as she felt.

'We…' He pointed somewhere behind her. 'Voices.'

'Oh.' Eloise looked around and then wriggled a little
against his arm. He let go of her immediately, and she
moved along the bench away from him. 'We should
go.' She stood up, without looking at him.

'Eloise…'

'Your Grace, Malbrook.' It was Sir Richard and Mr
Forrest.

'We came into the maze on my grandmother's instruction to ensure that no one became distressingly
lost,' Eloise said.

'And then the only person who became distressingly lost was, in fact, I,' Marcus said. 'We have not
yet attained the centre, but I have finally realised that
there are clues, and so I expect to reach it very soon.'

Both the other men laughed and they continued in
the opposite direction from them, to a chorus of *Good
luck*.

Neither of them spoke until they were out of earshot, and then Marcus said, 'I must apologise for hav-

ing compromised you. And having done so, I must reiterate my proposal.'

'It is very kind of you to keep on proposing.' Eloise was impressed with herself; she had regained her composure really quite admirably. 'But you did not compromise me as I am sure that they did not see us. And as we have already discussed at far too great length, I do not wish to marry. And I will not do so. A moment of madness, with no witnesses, is not sufficient reason to take a course of action with the potential to make quite so many people miserable.'

Marcus did not reply for a moment, and then said, 'I must accept your decision, but please be assured that my offer remains.'

Eloise looked up at him and failed to prevent a giggle from escaping.

'And the joke is?' Marcus enquired.

'It isn't really funny. Except, also, it is *quite* funny. You look so *torn*. You want to do the right thing, your duty.' She was certain of that; she just *knew* that he was a deeply honourable man. 'But, also, you do look *relieved*. You really don't wish to marry at all, do you?'

'Well, I...'

Eloise waited and then said, 'I have been quite plain with you and I will not be at all offended if you in your turn are plain with me. I will, indeed, be flattered, for it might demonstrate that we have become in some way friends, which I think will benefit us over the years to come.'

'Well. Yes. Or rather no. You are partially right; before meeting you again I had no wish to marry.' He paused and Eloise waited, and then he continued. 'I suppose one might say that I crave a calm existence after the trials of war.'

'A calm existence?'

'Yes. I think a number of my fellow ex-soldiers feel the same way. We need some time to recover. I don't feel that I need to spend time alone on my land, as some do. Indeed, solitude is not for me; thoughts intrude too much and I enjoy spending time with friends. But I had not wished for anything deeper than light-hearted friendship.'

Eloise nodded. 'I understand that. My marriage was of course not at all similar to being on the battlefield, but I did find aspects of it stressful and also enjoy my current calm existence. And I understand very well that you must wish to have time to recover from the night-mares to which you referred.' She looked sideways at him. 'So you feel that a wife would disturb the calm of your existence?'

'Put bluntly, yes.'

'Then you should thank me for my refusal.' She gave him her best sunny smile, and he laughed and shook his head.

'In your case and yours alone, the calmness of my existence is already disturbed. And I do wish to marry you.'

The strange thing was that Eloise felt almost regret-ful for a moment about turning him down.

Chapter Twelve

Marcus

Eloise was still smiling at him but something in her expression had shifted from humour to seriousness.

Something had shifted inside Marcus too; he couldn't believe that he'd told her about his nightmares and not previously wishing to marry. Why had he done that?

That was something he might think about later.

For now, though, he should perhaps address what had just happened.

'I must apologise,' he said. 'That is to say…'

Eloise had her head tilted a little, waiting for him to continue, which allowed him to take note of the fact that her ears were really most attractive.

What? *What?* He was finding her *ears* attractive now?

Well, yes. Everything about her was attractive.

'I apologise for having kissed you,' he said.

'Oh, no.' She smiled at him, and *damn* he loved that smile. 'It was just a moment of madness, on both our parts, which we will certainly not repeat.' And *damn* again.

'Of course,' he said, not sure that he meant it.

Maybe they should go. He really didn't know what he wanted to do or say right now.

He looked up at the position of the sun in the sky. 'We've been in here a long time. Perhaps we should leave now.'

'Without getting to the centre? Really? You're happy to fail?'

Marcus narrowed his eyes at her as she laughed. 'It takes a strong and wise person to admit to a change in intention,' he said loftily.

'I think you should at least look at the final clue in that bench.'

Marcus turned and looked and… '*Eloise*. No.' He stood up and walked around a little island of hedge in the corner of the little clearing they were in and… 'That's the *centre*. Right there.'

'I know.' She looked so pleased with herself that he couldn't help laughing again.

'You are a very hard-hearted woman.' They'd been *so* close to here a *long* time ago.

'I'm sorry,' she said, not looking at all penitent.

Marcus looked down at her and wished he could punish her by… No, the only thing he wanted to do to her was kiss her again, taste her, feel her against him, do more, much, much more. Which he must not do.

'Let's go,' he said.

Well under two minutes later, they were on top of the platform, waving at the few of the party who were still near the maze entrance.

Having memorised from the platform the route back, which was very straightforward once you could see it, they went directly to the exit and were out within perhaps ten minutes. The walk was companionable—and Marcus made huge efforts not to think about anything more intimate than their conversation as they strolled—and they were chuckling together again about having overheard Sir Walter and Mrs Heatherington when they reached the exit.

Lady Kingsbridge and Lady Morton were no longer there. No one was.

'I'm not surprised,' Eloise said. 'We were in there a *long* time. Too long for elderly ladies to wait for us.'

'I'm not sure whether I'm relieved to have escaped commentary on our time in the maze or disappointed not to have experienced the comedy of the commentary,' he said as they began to stroll towards the house.

'If you knew my grandmother better, you would know that both emotions are misplaced,' Eloise told him. 'There is no need to be either relieved or disappointed at the lack of comment; I'm sure we will just face it later this evening.'

As they smiled and laughed their way up the path, Marcus reflected that he was talking to her as though she was a *friend*. Granted, a friend with whom he felt a temptation to be intimate. But still, a friend. A good friend.

'I will leave you here,' she told him a few minutes later, at a fork in the path. 'I need to return to the dower house to see Amelia and to change for dinner.'

'Allow me to accompany you.' Marcus turned with her.

'That is very kind but there is no need. I am a dowager duchess, not a young miss.'

He looked at her. She was the only dowager duchess he'd ever met who was quite so beautiful and who could pass for a lady in her early twenties. She was also the mother of his daughter and therefore her health and safety were of utmost importance.

'I will enjoy the walk after being confined in the maze for so much of the afternoon,' he said.

'I would, however, not wish to occasion comment.'

Marcus paused. She was right. It didn't feel good, though.

Perhaps he could watch her most of the way from here, and then assume that if anything befell her just before she got inside, someone in the dower house would find out quickly.

'I walk around the estate by myself very frequently. It is one of the—many—advantages of being a widow rather than a young, unmarried woman. I will see you later, at dinner. Good afternoon.' And she walked off very briskly.

Marcus watched her until she was only a dot in the distance, before taking himself off up to the castle.

Perhaps he *did* have sun stroke; certainly something had affected his wits: when the party assembled for dinner a couple of hours later, he caught himself glancing more than once at the wide entrance to the great hall, and knew that each time he was hoping to see Eloise.

After a few minutes, he found himself embroiled in a light-hearted argument with Sir Richard and Viscount Stockall, which had him laughing out loud at various points. And still he could not prevent himself from looking two or three more times at the door.

The reason he was so particularly hoping that Eloise would arrive soon was probably that she was the only person who would be able to appreciate fully and share in the extreme enjoyment he was deriving from witnessing the interaction between Mrs Heatherington and Sir Walter. No other reason.

When—eventually—Eloise and Lady Kingsbridge entered the room, suddenly everything seemed a little…brighter. Even if they weren't able to speak very much this evening he would know that she had seen what he had seen, and they could discuss it when they went for a walk together with Amelia again, hopefully tomorrow.

Eloise had changed into a pale pink dress, with little sprigs of flowers on it, which became her particularly well.

'My lord.' Lady Kingsbridge was making her imperious way across the room, her many-bracelet-clad arm held out in his direction. 'I understand that you were quite woefully incompetent in the maze this afternoon.'

Marcus laughed and took her proffered hand. 'I was indeed.'

'I'm sure it was very good for you,' she told him. 'I doubt that you are incompetent in many other ways.' She raised her eyebrows in…was that a *suggestive* manner? Surely not.

'Erm.' He swivelled his eyes and caught Eloise sniggering behind her hand, which made him smile. 'I hope not,' he said, waggling his own eyebrows at Lady Kingsbridge.

She snorted approvingly. 'Naughty!' She rapped his knuckles with her fan.

Eloise was still sniggering.

'Lady Kingsbridge.' Sir Walter shuffled his way

into their group. 'I should be grateful if I might make an announcement.'

'Certainly.' Lady Kingsbridge leaned towards her granddaughter and said in a not-at-all-quiet whisper, 'I am quite agog,' which did nothing to dispel Eloise's giggles.

Lady Kingsbridge clapped her hands together impressively loudly and said, 'Sir Walter has an announcement to make.'

Marcus's eyes had gone to Mrs Heatherington as Lady Kingsbridge clapped, and he now saw her mouth drop open a little before she said, 'No, no, I don't think...'

Sir Walter moved towards her and took her hand, saying, 'Mrs Heatherington, you must not be coy.' Holding her hand aloft, like a trophy, and looking around the company, he said, 'Mrs Heatherington has done me the utmost honour of accepting my hand in marriage.'

'Mama!' Miss Heatherington screeched, before taking three steps to her right and crashing straight into the arms of a startled-looking Viscount Stockall. She opened her eyes briefly and said, 'I have fainted,' before closing them again and settling into her swoon.

'Congratulations, Mrs Heatherington, Sir Walter,' Eloise said over the ensuing hubbub. 'Lord Stockall, there is a chaise longue here upon which you might lie Miss Heatherington. Fenton, would you be so kind as to procure smelling salts?'

'Did I congratulate them in the correct order?' she asked Marcus in a low voice, just for him, when Miss Heatherington had been carefully laid out on the chaise longue by the still-startled—in fact frankly terrified-looking—viscount. 'I thought ladies first but then it sounded to my ears as though I was saying that she deserved greater congratulations than he on their match.'

'That is a very good question,' Marcus agreed, considering. 'I shall ask my man later on. He always knows things like that. I have to say that if you have the order wrong, you could be forgiven for being more than a little stunned.' The entire tableau, including the obviously staged faint, was quite remarkable, and, Marcus realised, there was no one he'd rather have shared it with than Eloise, even his lifelong friend Sir Richard, for example, who was on the other side of the room and with whom it had not once occurred to Marcus to share a smile, because he'd been busy laughing with Eloise. Truly, something had happened to befog his mind today.

Movement in the corner of the room caught his eye and he glanced over to see Miss Heatherington pulling at the viscount quite vigorously.

'Marcus,' Eloise hissed, pulling at *his* arm quite hard. 'We can't allow...'

Marcus nodded. It looked as though the viscount was in danger of toppling over onto Miss Heatherington, and therefore in danger of having to propose to her.

He moved fast across the room and took the viscount's other arm. The man turned a look of panicked relief on Marcus, and Marcus clapped him on the shoulder and said, 'You must tell me more about those new horses you bought last week. First, though, allow me to call your mother to you, Miss Heatherington, to assist you in your hour of need.'

Once Mrs Heatherington was installed next to her daughter, Marcus drew the viscount to safety away from the two ladies.

He couldn't help checking to see what Eloise was doing and was gratified to see her smiling at him approvingly.

A few minutes later, having decreed that this evening would consist of dancing punctuated by an informal supper, Lady Kingsbridge announced that couples should begin to take their places for the first set.

Marcus found his eyes going immediately to Eloise, who was standing a few feet away from him. He enjoyed dancing, in the right situation with the right partner, and he knew that he enjoyed dancing with Eloise.

He took a step towards her, just as Sir Walter hurried over to her and came to a halt very close to her.

'Your Grace.' Sir Walter's words rang out loudly; the man must have raised his voice purposely.

'Sir Walter.' Eloise's smile was a little tight.

'While recent events—my engagement—have changed matters, I am an honourable man, and I still intend to dance the first dance with you this evening.'

Eloise looked at him for a moment, and then said, 'Thank you, Sir Walter. I am extremely honoured. I have the beginnings of a headache, however, and wonder whether I should be well advised to rest for a few moments and allow you to dance with Mrs Heatherington and celebrate your engagement.'

'I feel quite sure that you do not have the headache and I cannot allow you to sacrifice yourself and miss this dance just for my happiness.' Sir Walter gave a theatrical bow and held his arm out to Eloise before almost dragging her onto the dance floor. 'My fiancée understands that I cannot disappoint you and has agreed to dance the second set with me instead.'

Marcus realised that he was glaring at Sir Walter's back and looked away to see Lady Kingsbridge watching him. He looked around and saw that a young lady, a Miss Denby, was standing by herself looking at the ceiling, the floor, the walls, while her aunt talked to Lady Morton. It would be outrageous behaviour in him to ignore her.

'May I have this dance?' he asked her.

'Oh, I'd be delighted,' she said, beaming.

Marcus did not enjoy the experience of dancing with one lady—who, it turned out, was particularly desirous of engaging him in regular, formal, conversation—while wishing to watch another. Eloise danced with grace and pretended—he was sure—to enjoy conversing with Sir Walter. He should really do the same himself. He looked away from Eloise and applied himself to conversation with Miss Denby, and was soon enjoying himself quite adequately.

A few minutes into the dance he did, however, find himself metaphorically gnashing his teeth when he glimpsed Sir Walter place his hand a little too high above Eloise's waist. He was on the brink of moving over to nudge them somehow, when something happened and Sir Walter lurched and yelped and dropped his hand. Marcus caught a look of pure glee on Eloise's face and nearly laughed out loud, before realising that Miss Denby had just asked him a question and he was in real danger of being quite rude to her, because, try as he might, he could not quite recall what she'd asked him.

After he'd turned his most charming smile upon her, feigned deafness in one ear and asked her to repeat her question, he began an earnest description of all he knew of the geography of Kent. While he was talking about the Garden of England, he couldn't help still watching Eloise and almost not hearing Miss Denby's next question, which seemed to relate to the geography of Essex.

He suddenly realised that he was smiling at Eloise rather than at Miss Denby, and rolled his eyes at himself. He was behaving like a lovelorn young sprig.

Eloise did not wish to marry him and he should probably accept that. He didn't, after all, wish to have any more people to care about, worry about. He did want to be able to see Amelia, though.

'Ouch,' squeaked Miss Denby. It seemed that he'd just trodden on her toe.

After another dance, the duration of which he spent again trying hard not to look over his shoulder at Eloise, who was dancing with the duke this time, Lady Kingsbridge announced that they would go through to supper in an adjoining room.

He made his way quickly over to Eloise and said, 'Allow me to escort you through to supper?'

'Thank you.' She smiled up at him and his breath caught in his throat. That smile somehow demonstrated the two sides to Eloise's character, the cheekiness and the maturity, and the combination was strikingly seductive.

'Malbrook,' someone said quite loudly, and he realised that they were blocking the doorway as they stood and smiled at each other, probably quite foolishly in his case.

'My apologies.' He nodded to Mr Forrest and held out

his arm for Eloise to take, and the two of them walked into the supper room together.

Marcus directed Eloise towards a table at the back of the room, at which they might converse without being overheard by others. He asked her if she had any preferences as to which dishes he selected for her, and then went over to the buffet table that had been set up along one corner.

When he turned to make his way back to their table, confident that he'd chosen very well for her, and looking forward to telling her about what Mrs Heatherington had just said to him about Sir Walter, he saw that Mr Forrest and Miss Denby had sat down with her, their plates laden. It seemed that they were going to spend supper as a foursome. He'd have to tell Eloise another time about the newly—but apparently not happily—engaged couple. And about some other things he'd just thought of, actually, to tell her about.

He would ask her to dance now, he decided, as he walked across the room. Just once, because, while he wished for her to accept his proposal, he did not wish her to feel that she was forced to do so.

'We were just talking about how you got so lost today in the maze,' Mr Forrest joshed him as he placed Eloise's plate in front of her.

'Yes, not my finest hour,' Marcus said cheerfully, sitting down.

And supper was very pleasant, actually. He enjoyed Eloise's humour just as much in a group as when they were alone.

'May I have the next dance?' he asked her towards the end of the meal, when their companions were distracted for a moment.

'I'm afraid I am already promised to Sir Richard,' she told him.

'The next one, then?'

'Even though the dance is informal, my card is entirely full,' she said, sounding far too happy about it for Marcus's liking. 'I think people like the cachet of dancing with a duchess and that it's particularly attractive when combined with no worry that the duchess is seeking to remarry.'

It was quite obvious that Eloise's personal attractions were a large part of the reason that people wished to dance with her, but now was not the time to say so.

'I shall have to hope to dance with you another time,' he said, as lightly as he could, hoping that he didn't sound as disappointed as he felt. He *shouldn't* feel this disappointed.

And then Lady Kingsbridge clapped her hands and they all stood up to re-enter the ballroom. Marcus found a few moments in which to agree with Eloise a final meeting with Amelia before he left the party, but beyond that there was no further opportunity for them to talk other than an exchange of a few anodyne words as they briefly partnered each other during the next quadrille.

At the end of the fourth dance after supper, Lady Kingsbridge clapped loudly and told the company that she was older than she looked and needed to retire for the night.

Eloise joined her, saying, 'I shall of course accompany you.'

'Billiards?' Sir Richard asked Marcus a few minutes later.

Marcus hesitated for a second, and then said, 'Although normally I would certainly join you, I think I should retire myself now. I am promised to the duke for a fishing trip tomorrow morning, and we are engaged to meet at the crack of dawn.' And he was likely to wake in the night again after one of his dreams. And, also, the evening seemed a little flat now without Eloise's presence.

Maybe he would allow himself one final attempt to woo her, tomorrow evening, the last night of the party.

Chapter Thirteen

Eloise

Eloise and Marcus had agreed to meet for one final walk with Amelia before Marcus left the next morning. He'd been busy during the morning fishing with the duke, so it was early afternoon when they met.

As they reached Marcus where he'd been waiting for them, Eloise had to suck her cheeks to prevent herself from smiling like a lovestruck young girl. This infatuation was silly; it was a good job he was leaving tomorrow.

'Good afternoon. How was your fishing trip?' Oh, dear. She *sounded* lovestruck, sort of breathless.

'It was very productive. The duke and I agreed that we should fish together again, and perhaps also shoot.'

'Excellent.'

'But you don't live here so you'll have to come to stay again,' Amelia said.

'Yes, I think I will,' Marcus agreed, smiling.

'Good, so we can go for more walks. Come on.' Amelia tugged his arm and he laughed. 'Mama, might we go down to the stream and see all the fish?'

'Certainly, if His Lordship would like to join us.' Eloise did entirely trust the discretion of Lucy and her footman, but she didn't want to put them in the awkward position of suspecting anything.

Marcus talked to Amelia for the entire walk, smiling down at her and answering her questions very seriously in really the most adorable way.

When they had to return, Eloise should certainly not have felt disappointed that Marcus had not attempted to flirt with her at all during the walk; she should have been pleased.

'The plans for this evening have developed gratifyingly well,' Eloise's grandmother told her when they arrived back. 'We must now make haste up to the castle to choose our costumes.'

'Costumes?'

'Did I not tell you that we are hosting a masquerade this evening?'

'No?'

'Well, we are. I had the invitations sent out two days ago on behalf of the duke, and everyone who is anyone in the county is coming. The power of a duke.'

'Oh,' said Eloise faintly. A masquerade. With Marcus. Not that it would be a repeat of their first one, obviously.

'Are you quite certain that you have your costume planned adequately?' her grandmother asked her when they returned to the dower house late in the afternoon.

'Yes, thank you; I am most happy with it.'

'What are you wearing?'

'Just a domino and a mask.' Eloise thought nostalgically of her shepherdess costume from nine years ago for a moment and then whipped her thoughts away from where they'd naturally gone from there when she caught her grandmother staring at her.

'Are you quite all right? You seemed to be dreaming of something.'

'Very much so, thank you.'

'I wonder whether you might think of wearing a costume rather than a domino. I'm sure we can find one today.'

'The domino that I have will be quite ideal. I have no wish at all to wear a costume,' Eloise lied. She'd *love* to wear a costume but she was not going to do so. There should not be any more kissing or flirting or anything else between her and Marcus, and she should behave in as staid a manner as possible this evening.

'I think you would enjoy wearing a costume.'

'I really don't think so.'

Four hours later, Eloise was, on her grandmother's insistence, attired in a Cleopatra costume—found at the last minute by Fenton in the attics of the castle— and regarding herself in the looking glass in her bed-chamber.

This gown was not scandalously low-cut in the way that her shepherdess one had been, but it was, somehow, actually *more* risqué. The cut and the fabric ensured that it clung to her form in a quite outrageous way. Well, she would go below stairs and show her grandmother, who would obviously agree that she—a respectable, widowed duchess—could not possibly wear this, and then she would return to her chamber and change into a more demure gown and put her domino on and they would go up to the castle.

'Wonderful,' her domino-clad grandmother declared as Eloise entered her drawing room two minutes later. 'Turn around for me.'

A little stunned, Eloise dutifully turned a slow pirouette.

'Perfect,' her grandmother declared.

'No. Not perfect. I look...'

'You look beautiful. The way every woman would like to look if it weren't normally unacceptable to dress in such a way.'

'Surely it is *always* unacceptable to dress like this.'

'Certainly not. Which is just one of the attractions of a masquerade. It is a huge disappointment if guests arrive attired just the way they would usually be with the mere addition of a mask and perhaps a cloak. I have held several and I assure you that no one will bat an eyelid at your costume.'

'I really feel...'

'And you don't have time to change. Come on.'

Well, if she was honest, Eloise *liked* the dress, and it was quite refreshing to be able to ignore convention. Maybe if she didn't have to inhabit her duchess persona for the evening, she might have a night as enjoyable as her Vauxhall Gardens masquerade. Well, not *that* enjoyable, obviously...

Much as she liked her dress, she couldn't help pulling her domino tightly around her for the walk up to the castle, telling her grandmother that she did not wish to catch her death of cold.

'I also do not wish to get cold.' Her grandmother wiggled her shoulders inside her purple domino and Eloise laughed.

The castle staff had clearly worked hard in decorating the ballroom. Swathes of dark red fabric hung on the walls and strategically placed candles had quite changed the feel of it. A small group of four people, two men and two women, walked past her, and Eloise realised that she really didn't recognise them at all beneath their costumes and masks. Which meant…

Which *surely* did mean, she hoped, that no one would recognise her.

And if no one would recognise her…

A delicious, long-forgotten feeling of abandon was beginning to work its way through her. She might perhaps have a *particularly* nice evening. She could almost be Ella all over again.

When a footman asked if he could take her domino, she relinquished it a lot more happily than she'd expected she would. She turned round just in time to see her grandmother sliding out of her own domino and…

'Oh, my goodness,' Eloise said. 'Grandmama.'

'Shh.' Her grandmother adjusted her full-face mask and smoothed the skirts of her truly *shocking* shepherdess costume—so much more risqué than Eloise's had been—and looked around. 'I shan't be able to behave as badly as I'd like if people know it's me.'

'Erm…' Eloise was quite sure that people *would* know who she was. No one else ever wore quite such a profusion of bracelets and bangles, for a start. But actually, if everyone was going to lower their inhibitions, her grandmother should *certainly* join in; why not? 'You're right,' she told her. 'You are completely unrecognisable.'

'As are you, my darling. So *enjoy* yourself.' And her grandmother danced off—making light use of a shepherd's crook in place of her usual stick—into the crowd of people in the centre of the room.

'My goodness,' Eloise said again, out loud.

She looked around. If she was being entirely honest with herself, she had to admit that there was only one person she wanted to see at this moment. But, assuming he was costumed—she hadn't spoken to him about it because she hadn't wanted to sound too interested—would she actually recognise him?

'I s-say, Cleopatra, would you care to d-dance?'

'Of course I would.' She smiled at the chimney-sweep outfitted man in front of her, knowing from his voice that he was the very shy son of a squire who lived on a neighbouring estate and whom she had suspected for several months of wishing to ask her to dance. The question was, did he recognise her in her costume.

As soon as they reached the dance floor, he pulled her hard against him and reached his hands very low on her back so that they were almost on her bottom. Eloise had time to think that if he *did* know who she was he was very silly given his distinctive voice, because she was *not* pleased at this moment and she *would* remember this, before she stamped on his foot as hard as she could and then waltzed herself away from him while he was gasping in pain.

She moved over to a large plant in a pot and stood behind it for a moment to gather herself, before emerging to look at the room again. She would not assume in future that shyness was a barrier to a man behaving badly at a masquerade and she might be more circumspect if anyone else asked her to dance. Except for one person, if she was honest. If she recognised him.

'Good evening, Cleopatra,' a very tall and broad Henry the Eighth interrupted her thoughts. 'I see you've left your sheep behind this evening.'

And of *course* she recognised him. He was fully masked, but he was taller and broader than every other man in the room, and anyway she would know his voice anywhere, the deepness of it that touched her every single time she hadn't spoken to him for more than a few minutes, and, so often, the hint of a laugh that it held.

'Good evening, Henry.'

'Should you not take care to call me *Your Majesty*, to avoid my having you beheaded?'

'I believe that I have progressed from sheep tending to become Queen of Egypt, and am at least equal to you in the majesty stakes.'

Marcus nodded. 'Ah, yes. My historical knowledge had deserted me for a moment there. I apologise, Your Majesty.'

'I accept your apology with all the queenly graciousness at my disposal, Your Majesty.' She twinkled up at him and then pushed her headdress back into place. It was a little too large and had a tendency to slip so that she couldn't see properly.

'Thank you. Would you care to dance?'

'I think I would.' She *really* would. She loved dancing, and it was rare that one had the opportunity to do so with abandon and with whomever one wanted.

She jumped as Marcus reached down and took her hand quite openly.

'People will see,' she hissed.

'You are *not* recognisable,' he said. That was probably true: the squire's son would not otherwise have tried to feel her bottom. 'And also...' He gestured around them. Hand holding was a very minor thing compared to what some of the other guests were already doing.

'This is a private party! And we all more or less know each other!' Eloise wasn't sure whether she was shocked or quite delighted.

'And what is so marvellous about a masquerade, as your grandmother mentioned to me earlier today when she told me that I *would* be Henry the Eighth, is that people behave with real abandon because they believe themselves to be disguised.'

Well, that was certainly true, as Eloise knew from experience. And holding Marcus's hand was...nice. It felt...right. As though their hands belonged together. She held Amelia's hand a lot when they went for walks. She vaguely remembered a governess whom she had liked a lot and whose hand she had held. And she hadn't really ever held anyone else's hand. It felt...intimate. Almost as intimate as doing the things she had done with Marcus that night, because it would just be peculiar to hold hands like this with someone you didn't *know*.

They'd reached the dance floor. Marcus tugged her gently into a waltz hold and as he did so his hand travelled up her arm and, just for a second, he rubbed his thumbs against the insides of her wrists, and, light as his touch was, and, fully clothed as they both were, it nonetheless sent shock waves of sensation through her entire body.

And then he was holding her in a perfectly innocent—

as waltzes went—hold, and directing her gently around the floor, weaving in and out of couples dancing with raucous abandon, narrowly avoiding a couple of men chasing two happily shrieking ladies in maids' outfits, *and* a certain bangle-wearing somewhat elderly shepherdess, who was very thoroughly embracing a gentleman rather boringly attired in black domino and mask.

'No!' yelped Eloise.

'Was that…?'

'Yes.'

'Good God.' Marcus steered her away from her grandmother right over to the other side of the dance floor.

'I'm never, ever going to be able to forget I saw that.' Eloise could see Marcus's shoulders shaking and she began to giggle.

Marcus nodded. 'I *want* to tell you that you will *certainly* forget it, but sadly I think you might not.'

'It's wonderful, of course.' Eloise was still giggling. 'Truly wonderful. That she's enjoying herself so much.' She gasped. 'I thought she'd planned this masquerade to…'

'To throw us together, but now you wonder whether perhaps her intention was to amuse herself?'

'Yes.'

'Or perhaps she was trying to kill two birds with one stone.'

'I don't think I'm ever going to ask her.'

'No.' Marcus pulled her back into his hold, but this time a little less decorously than before. There was something about the light pressure he was applying with his left hand to her lower back that made her stomach dip and her breath catch.

'I am very grateful to your grandmother.' He spoke

in a low voice, close to her ear, so that only she could hear. 'The evening is young and already I am enjoying myself greatly.'

'Me too,' squeaked Eloise, entirely against her better judgement. Except…no one recognised her, so…

They swayed together to the music, hardly moving their feet, and somehow, Eloise had her cheek against his chest, and their bodies were almost moulded together as they moved.

Eloise didn't know how long they stayed like that, just moving gently in time to the music, their bodies almost as one, before Marcus began to edge her further towards the edge of the dance floor, and some open doors.

'Would you care to take some air?' he asked her.

'I think I might,' she said, sure that he had an ulterior motive in asking her that question. She knew that she—they—shouldn't do whatever she suspected Marcus thought it would be nice to do outside. Even if all he wanted to do was talk, because being alone with a man outside at night, exchanging confidences, or even just banalities, was not at all respectable. But also, she really wanted to…not necessarily *do* anything with him, but just…be alone with him again, talk to him, for as long as they liked, with no fear of being seen and no urgency to finish their conversation. It would be nice to be able to talk all night if they wanted to. And again, no one would recognise her and no one would know…

And if they perhaps exchanged one or two kisses, it couldn't really hurt. They'd already kissed in the maze and been able to continue to talk quite normally when they were with other people afterwards. Apart from a little heart juddering when she was near him, but that was quite normal. She'd get over it. And a masquerade was special; people were *expected* to behave differently from usual. It didn't *mean* anything…

Chapter Fourteen

Marcus

As they dodged the hordes of unruly partygoers close to the ballroom doors—felicitations were due to Lady Kingsbridge for having gathered such a large number of enthusiastic people at such short notice—Marcus had a strong sense that this evening was going to be very important.

They'd reached the long doors open to the terrace that ran along this side of the castle. Marcus held his hand out to Ella to help her down the short flight of steps to the lower part of the terrace. She glanced up at him as she took his hand and that look from her caused his heart to beat a little faster.

'Sometimes I like to walk in the dower house garden by myself after dark and just look at the stars,' Ella told him as by unspoken agreement they walked away from the candles near to the doors towards the night's darkness, which was punctuated only by a sliver of moonlight, Ella's hand still on his arm.

They weren't just walking towards darkness, they

were walking towards danger, towards opportunity, the opportunity to do something that one or both of them might regret. Marcus hoped he would have the strength of mind to avoid doing anything they really shouldn't. He did not want to compromise Ella into marriage; that was not the right way to go about things. He wanted her to agree with him that it was the sensible way for them to proceed.

'I didn't know that.' Which was a remarkably foolish-sounding comment. 'What I meant was…'

What he meant was that he'd just realised that while he *would* like to make love to Eloise, of course he would, he would also very much like just to talk to her in private, find out everything there was to know about her, hear her jokes, her thoughts, what made her scared, what made her laugh, what she was interested in.

'I meant that I like looking at stars too,' he said.

Oh, for God's sake. Foolisher and foolisher.

Eloise laughed. 'It's an unusual person who does not.' She pulled his arm a little and said, 'This way.'

'This way to…? Do we have a destination?' He allowed her to lead him; it was beginning to feel as though *she* was his destination, and wherever she went he would follow.

'There's a rose garden over here that's beautiful in the moonlight. It also has a folly with an upper storey that affords quite dramatic views over the land, and there's something quite magical about it at night.'

Marcus nodded in the darkness. 'That sounds nice.' Nice was an understatement.

As they continued to walk, they discussed constellations and the phases of the moon. Eloise's knowledge was impressive…and Marcus liked her even more for it. Was there *any*thing she could do or say that he wouldn't like?

'Did you learn this as a child?' he asked.

'No. I received very little formal education. My father's expressed opinion was that the only good thing about a daughter was that you didn't have to pay for any tuition beyond that necessary to enable her to find a wealthy husband. I learnt to read young, though, and have always enjoyed reading, and the castle's library is very well stocked. The late duke continued to augment it and the new duke is also doing so, so I have been very lucky in that regard.'

'I'm sorry,' Marcus said. 'About your father.'

'Oh, no, I didn't mean to sound bitter. I shouldn't have said that.'

'Yes, you should. We are friends, are we not, and friends should be able to say such things to each other. You listened when I told you about my bad dreams.'

'Well, I… Thank you. I suppose I am…not accustomed to talking about these things. And, indeed, there is no reason to do so. One should look forward to the future rather than dwelling on things that are past.'

'Sometimes it is difficult to forget the past.'

'That is true. And…'

And he knew that was why she did not wish to marry him, as she'd already told him. And it was also why he had not wished to marry; his past was still causing him too many nightmares for him to wish for any new complications. Although, it seemed that talking to Eloise had helped. Last night, he'd slept the most soundly he had for a long time. It felt now as though the present might begin to mingle with the past, mitigate it. He hoped so, anyway.

'The roses are indeed beautiful,' he said as Eloise led him down a path lined on both sides by well-tended bushes.

'In the spring and earlier in the summer they are quite spectacular. If the duke invites you to a sporting party at that time of year we must certainly come here to look at them.'

The moonlight danced across her face as she smiled up at him and damn he wanted to kiss her, he really did. He wasn't convinced that that was the right thing to do, though. For Eloise's sake.

What he needed was more mundane conversation.

'The duke must keep many gardeners,' he said. That was the ticket; no one wanted to kiss people when they were talking about gardening.

'He does. And he is kind enough to send them to work on my gardens too. I had imagined that I would enjoy tending to my vegetable garden in particular but I have to confess I find it sadly dull.'

Marcus laughed. 'Each to their own.' This was good. He had almost managed entirely to stop thinking about how much he wanted to pull her into his arms and... No, if he was honest, he hadn't stopped thinking about that at all.

'Do you...garden?' Apparently Eloise was also eager to keep the conversation on unemotional topics.

'I have never gardened and am as unenthusiastic about the idea as you.' He looked more closely at her. 'You're shivering.' The temperature had dropped quite considerably from the warmth of the afternoon. He looked at the folly ahead of them. 'Let's go inside and shelter for a moment until you warm up. And in the meantime, take my cloak.' He already had his arms out of it; the Tudor way of dressing had apparently been a lot less time-consuming than the modern way with all the tight-fitting jackets that men wore today.

'But you will get cold.'

'No, I won't.' He placed it around her shoulders, taking care to avoid touching bare skin with his fingers. There was no point in tempting oneself unnecessarily. 'The Tudors wore a lot of fur it seems. I am more than happy to divest myself of some of it.'

'In that case, thank you; I am most grateful.'

He could feel her snuggling herself into the cloak next to him and for some reason he temporarily lost the ability to speak.

They walked along in silence until they reached the folly.

Marcus reached above Eloise's head to push the door open and they both entered, Marcus ducking his head to avoid the low beam above the entrance.

As they stood side by side in the middle of the small room, he could make out through the haze from the moon a short staircase in the middle of the folly, leading to an upper level, which had windows all the way round, allowing in light.

'If we…' Eloise began to say, and then she screamed.

'What is it?' He automatically put out his arms to hug her against him.

'Um…' Her voice was muffled against his chest. 'I think it was a cobweb.'

Marcus would normally have laughed, but he wasn't feeling humour right now, because he was feeling… well, lust, frankly. And…something else. Something less basic and more…honourable. The honourable, decent feeling was still strongly combined with lust, though.

Eloise was still in his arms and, suddenly, he just wanted to see as much of her face as he could in this half-light.

He turned her gently within the circle of his arms so that they were facing each other, with his arms still around her, while she now had her hands placed against his chest.

God, just the feel of her hands on his upper body, even through the tunic he was wearing, was doing alarming things to his heart rate.

He wanted to know what she was thinking, feeling, but he couldn't formulate the question out loud, and she was so much shorter than he that he couldn't see her face at all.

'Eloise?' he said after a few moments during which they just stood there, him drinking in the sensation of her being against him like this in his arms.

'Mmhmm?' She looked up at him and the expression on her face made him almost gasp out loud. Her eyelids somehow looked heavy and she wore a small smile that was half provocative, half innocent. This evening, they had done nothing more than hold hands, and dance closely and now stand in an embrace, and yet she looked as though someone had just made long, satisfying love to her.

He wanted to see the rest of her face, not just her eyes and her mouth.

He moved his hands to her hair and slowly undid the ribbons of her mask, before drawing it away from her head.

'You're beautiful,' he told her.

'Some might say you're quite handsome yourself.' Her words indicated self-possession but the slight shake in her voice betrayed her. 'Even with that mask on.'

Damn, he wanted to kiss her. And more. So much more.

As the moonlight played across her face, he knew that if she wanted this as much as he did, they were lost, because he felt as though he was running out of willpower fast.

And then she slid her hands up his chest and into his hair and pulled undone the ties of his mask.

'Really. Quite handsome,' she said. And pouted.

And *damn* that pout. Marcus couldn't do anything other than lean down to her—very slowly, so that she had ample time to stop him if she so wished, although he didn't think she would—and kiss her on the lips, very gently, more of a brush than a proper kiss.

'Marcus,' she said. It was really a sigh rather than a word.

'Mmhmm,' he said in his turn.

And then he bent to kiss her again, properly this time, and she wrapped her arms around his neck and then they were kissing urgently, desperately, passionately, as though this might be the only time they ever kissed again. And perhaps it would be.

And, God, thinking that just increased the intensity of his desire for her. But also, if they were only going to be together like this just this once, they should savour it.

Marcus sighed, judderingly, into her mouth, before drawing back and then tracing with his finger the surprised O of Ella's lips. Then he began to kiss her forehead, her eyelids, her cheeks, her nose, and back to her mouth, taking his time with each kiss. He wanted to kiss *all* of her, and he wanted to do it slowly.

Ella, though, did not seem to want to be kissed slowly; she had her hands in his hair now and was pulling his head down to hers, hard. And, *yes*, that was good.

'Over here.' She wriggled out of his hold and gave him a little push, shrugging herself out of his cloak at the same time.

'Did you...*push* me?' He caught hold of her hands and pulled her into him again.

'Yes, I did.'

'Why; what would you like me to do?'

'I'd like you to come and sit on this bench with me.' She tugged his hands and he allowed her to lead him to the bench. They sat down very close together, still holding hands.

'What would you like me to do now?' he asked.

'I'd like you to stop talking and kiss me again. Immediately.'

Marcus smiled at her. He *liked* this demanding version of her.

'And what if I don't stop talking and kiss you?' he said.

'Then maybe *I* will have to kiss *you*.' She took her hands from his and ran them up his chest, and, God, she had him shuddering beneath her touch. Reaching his shoulders, she dug her fingers in before caressing his neck and then pulling his head to hers again.

Marcus heard himself groaning into Ella's mouth.

He wanted to hold her even closer. He lifted her so that she was sideways on his lap and she sighed and kissed him again, before, *God*, she turned and straddled him and began to move against him, slowly at first and then faster and harder.

'Ella.' The word sounded guttural to his own ears. How could this be so good when they were still fully clothed?

'Yes?' She wriggled more against him and he bent to kiss her again, before sliding his hands right around her waist and then moving to weigh her breasts in his hands. 'Marcus!'

'Mmm…' He pulled a little at the fabric of her costume and achieved absolutely nothing. 'How does this gown *work*?'

'There are ribbons at the neck.' She reached up behind her and pulled something, and suddenly the dress was loose. He helped her in pulling it down, and now she was on his lap naked from the waist up and, oh, Good Lord, this was almost more than a man could bear.

Holding, weighing, teasing her breasts with his mouth and one hand, he reached beneath her skirts with his other hand and ran it up her beautifully smooth leg until he reached the softness of her thighs. As he found her most intimate parts and began to touch her, all the while caressing her breasts, she moaned and moved against him and reached for him in her turn.

'Your breeches,' she panted.

He lifted her and undressed himself and then they were almost completely naked together.

'Are you…?' he asked. Even in the heat of the passion between them, he knew that this had to be her decision.

'I am…' She arched against him and he closed his eyes for a moment before reopening them.

'You're certain?' He made himself stop what he was doing for a moment so that she could answer.

She stilled and then said, 'I don't know.'

'Then we won't,' he said, applying pressure with his fingers instead and continuing to kiss and love the rest of her body.

She began to pull away and he said, 'There are other things we can do.'

As he continued, she gasped against him and then felt for him again.

And *God* that was good. *So* good.

And then he lost all ability to think.

After some time, as their pleasure grew and grew, she moved onto him and said, 'Now, please.'

'Are you sure?' he managed to ask.

'Yes,' she panted. '*Yes*. Please.'

And then he was inside her and they were moving together and it was utter, excruciating bliss.

Several minutes later, they lay gasping against each other, their limbs entwined, their costumes spread around them, both of them hot and breathless.

'Well,' Marcus said, when he could finally speak. 'That was…' He didn't know what to say. He wanted to thank her, he wanted a moment to consider the possible implications of what they'd done, he wanted to… He wanted to carry on holding her.

'I don't… I can't…' Ella began, and then her voice tailed off.

'Shh…' He pulled her even closer to him, wrapping his arms fully round her as though to ward off the rest of the world. He still didn't know what to say. Initially she hadn't wanted to do that, and he'd thought they weren't going to, and then she'd very much wanted to, and they had, and if it resulted in another pregnancy that could make life very complicated. He should obviously have exercised greater strength of mind.

They lay there for a while longer, not speaking, just holding each other.

Eventually, Marcus began to realise that the bench was hard and that the night air was cold on their naked bodies and that this wasn't the most physically comfortable position. And yet he knew that he could happily lie like this for the rest of his life with Eloise. Because…

Because he loved her.

Well, of course he did.

Yes, he did. He loved her. He adored her.

And that wasn't actually a problem. Why had he ever thought it *would* be a problem?

Now that he thought about it more rationally, he could see that spending his life with Eloise would not make it more complicated. Well, it might, but it would be a good kind of complicated. A *better* kind of complicated.

And already, talking to her had improved matters for him; after he'd told her about his nightmares yesterday he'd slept a lot better last night. He was quite certain that if Eloise were at his side at night the dreams would reduce even more. If he continued to share his thoughts, his problems, his hopes, his happiness with her, that could only enrich his life.

'Marcus?' Her voice was small. She was probably cold too. 'We should go back. What if someone finds us?'

He nodded and exerted his muscles to push them both up to a seated position. And damn she was beau-

tiful, sitting there almost entirely naked, her hair loose
and tumbling down her back and across her breasts.

He reached to kiss her again, because he couldn't
help it.

She didn't respond immediately, and then after a second or two, wound her arms round him and returned
his kiss very enthusiastically for a long moment, before
quite suddenly pulling away.

'I think we should go back now.' She sounded odd
but maybe she was just feeling understandably self-
conscious now.

'Of course,' he said immediately.

He lifted her off him and bent to gather up all their
clothes. When he looked back at her, she was busy
pulling her undergarments back into place from where
they'd been gathered around her waist.

'Let me help,' he said as she struggled with her gown.

'Thank you. It's very lucky that we have masks. I
think perhaps I shall take my domino from the castle
and go back to the dower house immediately.'

'You will allow me to escort you.' Marcus stated it
because it wasn't a question. Who knew how the other
male guests might behave this evening while in disguise, many of them inebriated.

Eloise looked at him for a long moment, apparently
decided that she wouldn't be able to change his mind,
or perhaps agreed with him that an escort would be
wise, and said, 'In that case, I might just go directly
back, please.'

'Of course.'

Marcus led the way down the steps and across the
folly to the door, to make sure that Eloise didn't trip.
As they left the building, the moonlight dwindled for

a moment—perhaps a cloud passing briefly—and Eloise stumbled in the darkness.

'Take my arm,' he suggested.

She paused and then said, 'Thank you,' and placed her arm on his.

'It's a lovely evening,' he observed as they walked back through the rose garden.

'Beautiful.'

Silence arose between them, and—Marcus wasn't sure why—it did not feel comfortable, despite how they had spent the evening and the fact that they were walking closely together.

Searching for something to break the awkwardness, he said, 'I trust that Lady Kingsbridge will have enjoyed the evening.'

'Oh, yes, I think she will.'

'She did look as though she was enjoying herself when we saw her.'

'Yes, indeed.'

'It has probably been a successful evening all round,' Marcus persevered.

'I imagine so.'

Their stilted conversation was at least as awkward as the silence had been, but required more effort, so Marcus decided that there was really no point in it. Also, he felt as though he had a lot to think about. Probably Eloise did too; perhaps that was why she seemed suddenly to have so few words.

They walked the remainder of the way in near-complete silence other than a small shriek from Eloise when a bat flew close to them followed by a murmured reassurance from Marcus. Eloise didn't even laugh about her reaction, and he was sure that she would usually see the funny side of it.

They did both have a lot to think about, though.

Eventually, they reached the dower house.

'Thank you very much.' Eloise was walking inside as she said it. 'Good evening.'

He would have liked to have had the opportunity to hug or kiss her goodnight, but she was right not to wish to do so; it was one thing dancing in an unusually intimate manner at a masquerade, when it was accepted that guests would do that, but another embracing here where it was possible that any such embrace might be witnessed by one of the servants.

'Goodnight,' he said to her departing back.

As he walked back up to the castle, Marcus was almost relieved to be alone so that he could think.

He loved Eloise. He wanted to spend the rest of his life with her. He couldn't believe that he had until this evening thought that the reason they should marry was that it would be *sensible* to do so.

By the time he reached the steps at the terrace, he felt as though he didn't have too much more thinking to do.

'Henry the Eighth,' said a swaying, slurring man who was leaning on the walls running up the side of the steps. 'Where have you been?'

'Walking,' Marcus said, not halting at all.

'Game of billiards?' asked a drunken sailor, immediately recognisable as Sir Richard.

'Thank you but I am otherwise engaged,' Marcus told him, continuing on past him.

He sidestepped several more drunk and raucous partygoers, including two couples who really ought to find somewhere a little more private to engage in what they were doing, and made his way straight up to his bedchamber.

'Good evening, my lord.' Norris was busy with candles and water for a bath. Marcus had an unfashionable liking for extremely regular bathing.

'Good evening, Norris. Thank you very much; I shall have no further need of you tonight.'

'Was it a good party?' Norris did not look as though he was about to leave, or at least not until he had any gossip that Marcus might be able to give him.

'Yes, very pleasant.' Marcus made a big show of sitting down at the dressing table and stretching his legs out in front of him and then yawning. He was certainly not going to undress in front of Norris; he did not wish there to be any possibility of his guessing that Marcus had been engaged in lovemaking this evening, for Eloise's sake. 'I am very tired now, though, so I think I'm going to go straight to sleep.'

'Allow me…' Norris moved forward.

'Thank you; I believe I have everything I need now. Goodnight.'

'As you wish.' Norris sounded a little grumpy, which wasn't entirely surprising. Marcus had found it odd returning to civilian life after the army, and one way in which he had coped had been to dissect each evening with Norris when he returned home from social events. Well, when his relationship with Eloise became common knowledge, he would be able to explain all to Norris.

Good God. It seemed that he'd made a decision, without even realising. He wanted to have a relationship with Eloise. He wanted to…

'My lord?' Norris was staring at him.

'Sorry. I'm tired. Goodnight.'

As he began to undress himself, he thought of Eloise helping him—extremely eagerly—to divest himself of his tunic and breeches earlier.

He wanted her to help him undress every single night.

He wanted to spend every single night with her. For the rest of his life.

He snuffed his candle and got into bed, and as he did so, his thoughts clarified entirely.

Tomorrow morning, before he left, he was going to ask Eloise to marry him again. Properly. Not out of duty but out of love.

Chapter Fifteen

Eloise

Eloise's looking glass showed a woman who looked as though she'd just been dragged backwards through a hedge. Or been made love to on a bench in a dusty folly and then dressed herself in a strange costume in the dark.

She should try to go to sleep. It was probably very late. She'd dismissed her maid while standing as far out of the candlelight as she could to disguise quite how dishevelled she was, and had then just sat in the armchair next to the window of her bedchamber for a long time. And now she'd been sitting here staring at her reflection, somewhat unseeingly, for goodness knew how long.

She stood up and dragged her stupid costume off before kicking it to the side of the room. Then she sat back down again and picked up her hairbrush and began to pull it hard through her hair.

How could she have been so stupid? She'd allowed an immature infatuation to lead her into *such* idiocy.

She gave another vicious brush to her hair.

What if someone had seen them?

Yes, it was an accepted thing that people behaved with more licence at masquerades under the safety of their costumes.

But they *surely* did not make love. And those who did were surely not respectable dowager duchesses and *mothers*.

She'd run quite mad this evening.

She closed her eyes for a moment, thinking again about the horror of someone having seen them.

And then she opened them and stared straight at herself. There was another thing. It had been hovering on the edge of her thoughts the entire time since she'd come to her senses after her lovemaking with Marcus.

She was going to have to address it properly in her mind.

She put her brush down and leaned her elbows on the dressing table in front of her and put her face in her cupped hands and closed her eyes. She couldn't even look at herself while she allowed the thought prominence.

What if she became with child as a result of tonight's lovemaking?

She might already be in an interesting condition.

She didn't know exactly how or when pregnancy occurred but, unlike nine years ago when she'd conceived Amelia, she did now know that it arose as a consequence of making love. She also knew that it did not occur every time people made love. So she might or might not have a baby in approximately nine months' time.

It was a question she was going to have to consider, because if she had become with child she would not be able just to ignore the fact.

She could feel hot tears falling onto her hands.

If she were with child and she told Marcus, he would, she was sure, propose marriage to her again. If he had felt that it was his duty to do so because he was Amelia's father, how much more obliged would he feel now that she would be facing rejection by the *ton* as an unmarried mother? Of course he would again propose.

From what he had said, though, she knew that he had only proposed to her out of duty and a desire to spend as much time as possible with Amelia. He didn't really want to marry *her*, she was sure.

And she did not wish to marry him. He was certainly kinder and more honourable than many—most—men of her acquaintance, she was sure, but he was still a man. Would he expect her to submit to his will after marriage? She couldn't bear to find out. And if they did marry and were miserable together, that could only serve to make Amelia miserable too.

Perhaps they could marry in name and live separately as so many of the *ton* did.

It was quite ridiculous that a woman could live quite apart from her husband and bear a child by a lover and still be received everywhere as long as everyone pretended her baby was her husband's, but an unmarried woman could be entirely faithful to one lover and be ostracised by Society if she had a baby.

It was irrelevant, though, that it was ridiculous, because it was the way of the world, and it was the world they lived in, and she, as a woman, could do nothing about that.

She gave a honking sniff and wiped her eyes and looked at herself again in the glass before her.

What did women *look* like before their bodies demonstrated more overtly that they were with child? Was she already that way now? It was hard to tell whether she looked any different facially due to her tear-swollen eyes.

She sniffed again and stood up. She should get into her bed gown and get some sleep. Being tired never helped anyone.

She was woken a few hours later by her maid from the deep sleep she'd finally fallen into after much tossing and turning, feeling extremely un-refreshed, and dragged herself reluctantly out of bed and into a gown.

'I am quite sad to see our house party end,' her grandmother told her when they sat down to breakfast together. 'We shall miss some of our guests.'

'Indeed.' Eloise's temples were almost pulsating with the tremendous headache that she'd just begun.

'Some more coffee, please.' Her grandmother nodded at Eloise's butler, Jarvis, who immediately moved to fill her cup. 'I hope you enjoyed yourself as much as I did yesterday evening. I didn't see you at all after we arrived. Although I must say that I was quite *busy* enjoying myself.' She actually smirked and Eloise winced at the thought of her *enjoying* herself. 'With whom did you spend the evening?'

Eloise choked on the piece of toast she was eating and coughed for quite a long time, which, while physically very unpleasant, was really quite useful for gathering her thoughts.

'Several different people,' she said eventually. 'The costumes were so good that people were quite disguised. I wouldn't even be able to say exactly whom I danced with.'

Her grandmother nodded. 'Yes, people were very well disguised. Of course, not everyone can be disguised merely by a costume and a mask. The earl, for example. His height and breadth of shoulder must always give him away even masked and dressed as Henry the Eighth.'

Eloise's headache was getting worse. 'Yes, I did see the earl and speak to him for a few minutes.'

'He is a very attractive man.'

Eloise wondered if she was actually going to be sick. Her stomach was certainly churning. 'Yes, I'm sure everyone must agree that he is quite handsome.'

'And also very good company,' her grandmother pursued.

'Indeed.'

'Your Grace.' The miniscule twitch on Jarvis's face told Eloise that he was surprised about something. 'The Earl of Malbrook has called and wishes to speak to you.'

'Oh, how *exciting*,' exclaimed her grandmother before Eloise had time to wonder whether she might say she was indisposed. 'Go.'

'I…'

'*Go.*'

Eloise went.

He was waiting for her outside the house, a small smile on his face. She felt her mouth dry, her hands grow clammy and her heart beat faster at the sight. She did *not* want to have this conversation, whatever Marcus might be about to say from his side.

'Good morning.' His smile grew and it felt as though her heart cracked a little because he seemed genuinely pleased to see her.

'Good morning.' Eloise wasn't smiling.

'Shall we walk?' He held his arm out, and she took it, miserably.

'I'm afraid I cannot stay outside for long,' she said, to try to indicate that this was not necessarily going to be an enjoyable conversation.

'Then, if you don't mind, I will get straight to the point.' He was still smiling in that heart-rending way.

And suddenly she was sure that he was going to say that he wished to continue in some way doing what they'd been doing. And they obviously couldn't continue.

'May I say something first?' she asked.

'Of course.'

'I feel that what we did was a mistake and should not be repeated. We were very silly. Had anyone seen us...' She couldn't bear to look at him as she spoke.

'I think that problem could be solved.' He drew her towards a secluded corner of the garden and stopped under a beech tree.

And then... And then he stood in front of her and looked into her eyes, before—holding her gaze the entire time—kneeling on one knee.

'Eloise. Ella.'

She shook her head but couldn't find the words to say *No, please get up.* 'I...'

He took her hands in his. 'Ella.'

She shook her head again. 'Marcus...'

'Ella.' He clasped her hands more tightly, and Eloise had to fight the urge to return the pressure. 'Would you do me the great honour of becoming my wife?' His smile was simultaneously deeply sincere-looking and a little tentative, and the overall effect was such that Eloise's legs almost gave way beneath her.

She pressed her lips together. How could she say *No, unless I'm with child, in which case, sadly, I will have to accept your very kind offer, but with regret*?

Marcus was still gazing into her eyes, but his smile was now beginning to falter.

'I love you, Eloise,' he said. 'When I proposed before, it was out of duty and because I wanted to be able to spend time with Amelia. Now, it is out of love. I realised that last night.'

She couldn't reply. She just stood and looked at him. He looked and sounded entirely sincere, and she did think that at this moment he believed what he said. But—whether the love lasted for the next ten minutes, the next ten days, the next ten years or forever—it might not be enough. She *could* not relinquish her independence.

She shook her head but found no words.

Marcus was still kneeling. After a pause, during which his smile faded, he said, 'Well.'

'The thing is…' Really, it was remarkably awkward to set out her thoughts. 'That is to say…'

'Oh.' Marcus stood up. 'I see. I presume, anyway, that I see. You still do not wish to marry me, but you wonder whether you might be with child.'

Eloise wrinkled her face. 'Yes.'

'And after much consideration you have decided that if you are with child marrying me would be the lesser of the evils open to you.'

She winced. 'Yes.'

'I agree with you.'

'You do?'

'If you do not wish to marry me and you are not with child then, as we discussed before, you are right not to marry me. But if you are with child then you would be faced with terrible scandal unless you married me, and marriage would be the better option. I cannot argue with your logic.'

Eloise nodded. She couldn't speak because she felt as though she might cry if she did.

'I would like to reiterate that the reason for this proposal is that I have realised how much I love you,' Marcus repeated. 'I did propose out of a sense of duty last time. This time it was nothing to do with duty. This time it was because I can't imagine a better person with whom to spend my life.' His voice cracked a little on the last word.

Eloise's heart seemed to have moved to her throat and she felt as though she was on the brink of a truly enormous bout of sobbing. What if there was *no* person with whom one could happily spend one's life as well as being alone? There might be no one better for him to spend his life with than her, and there might be no one better for her to spend her life with than him, but they might—probably would—both still be better off alone. Certainly it was likely that she would. In which case Amelia would be better off with them both being alone.

'I love your smile,' he continued. 'I love your sarcasm. I love your devotion to Amelia. I could say a lot more but I don't want to embarrass you. I just wanted to explain, a little more fully, that this proposal was very different from my first one.'

'Thank you,' said Eloise, and immediately regretted it; it wasn't enough for the magnitude of the compliment he'd just paid her, and she would never want to hurt him, because she cared about him so much. Oh.

Yes, she did. She did care about him. And she felt as though she owed him some honesty. 'I do… I do care about you. I would never wish to injure your feelings. But I cannot marry again. Unless I have to.' She looked straight ahead as she spoke because she couldn't bear to see any misery on his face.

Marcus did not speak for a long moment and then said, 'So we find ourselves in an odd position. As you know, I had not previously thought of marriage, and indeed actively did not wish to marry until I realised that I had fallen in love with you and realised that being with you would improve my life rather than just make it too complicated. And so I would only wish to marry out of choice, on both sides. I cannot therefore hope that you are now expecting a child, as I don't wish you to have to marry for a reason that is not love. But equally, if you do have a baby, I know that that baby would be as dear to both of us as Amelia is.'

The enormous lump was back in Eloise's throat. 'For someone who jokes a lot, you're very wise.'

'I must admit that compliments on my wisdom were not what I was hoping for today.'

She glanced up at him and saw that he was smiling but in a twisted way.

I love you, she thought.

'I do care about you very much and am extremely appreciative of the compliments you've paid me,' she said.

'Appreciation wasn't what I was aiming for, either,' Marcus told her. 'No, I'm sorry. That sounded bitter. I have no right to feel bitter and indeed I do not feel bitter.' He paused for a second while Eloise searched for something to say, and then said, 'I suppose we both have to wait until you know your condition. Which of course I now realise will—if you are to tell me immediately—force you to speak to me about matters that one would never usually wish to discuss.'

'Oh, yes. I hadn't thought of that. Well, it's just one more…' Little evil arising from their impetuosity last night.

'Just one more not particularly enjoyable conversation,' he finished for her. 'I do not wish you to feel uncomfortable, however. I have a suggestion. You may write to me in a few weeks' time, or whenever you would like to do so, to let me know in which condition you find yourself.'

Eloise felt her eyes fill again. Marcus truly was extremely considerate.

'That is very kind.'

When she thought about his many good qualities, she could see that he would make someone the most wonderful husband.

And now she felt tearful again.

'Thank you.' She could hardly speak around the lump in her throat. 'Goodbye.'

He took her hand and kissed it very tenderly, before very suddenly turning and striding away.

Chapter Sixteen

Marcus

'Marcus,' Eloise called just as he reached the gate in the dower house wall.

As he turned, his heart suddenly lighter in the hope that she might have changed her mind, he thought inconsequentially that that was probably the first time she'd called him by his Christian name other than during lovemaking.

'Yes?' He walked a little way back towards her and then stopped in front of her. From the expression on her face, it was clear that she had not changed her mind.

He thought he could see tears glistening on her eyelashes, and knew that, if he were someone who ever cried, his own eyes would be moist now. In fact, maybe they were.

A strand had escaped from her thick knot of hair and had been blown across her eyes, and he lifted his hand and very carefully brushed it away from her face. As his fingers skimmed her skin for a second, she let out an audible sigh.

Then she said, 'I wanted to thank you. For your kindness and forbearance.'

He shook his head. 'It's nothing. I love you.'

'I love you too.' She spoke so quietly that her words were almost carried away on the morning breeze, but she'd definitely said them, and he felt his heart begin to soar.

He raised a hand and took a step towards her, but she said, 'No. I still cannot marry you by choice.' And then she whisked herself round the corner and out of sight, and if his heart had lifted before, now it sank to his boots.

As he walked fast up the hill, Marcus felt more bereft than he could have imagined.

Eloise was beautiful. She made him smile. She made him laugh. She made him a better version of himself. And if she was not with child he would only be able to see her again occasionally and that felt utterly heartbreaking.

Of course, they might *have* to marry. How would they navigate that?

He didn't know.

He also didn't know whether he *wanted* her to be with child.

He would—he realised—very much like Amelia to have a sibling and to have another child himself. He would also very much like Eloise to be the child's mother; he certainly didn't wish to have a child with anyone else.

But the ramifications would be immense, because she would effectively be forced to marry him when she didn't want to, and there really would be no way round that.

God.

An hour later, the company were assembled outside the castle for goodbyes. Marcus wondered whether Eloise would come.

And, yes, eventually he saw her, treading over the grass with Lady Kingsbridge, and, as every time he saw her, his heart lifted a little just at the sight of her, even though he *knew* there was no hope of her changing her mind. She did love him, though; that was good. It would be something that would help if she were with child and they had to marry. Surely it might one day transcend her reluctance to give up her independence. It would be better, though, if she made that decision without being forced to do so.

As the two ladies joined those assembled—who included those leaving and others wishing to bid them farewell—Marcus made his way immediately to Eloise's side.

'Good morning, Your Grace.'

'Good morning, my lord. I wish you a safe journey.'

'Thank you.' He took her hand and, *damn*, it was hard knowing that he might not touch her, see her again for a long time. Or that he might, but under duress on her part. What a damnable position they would be in if that were the case. He would just have to work hard to show her that he could and would, he hoped, make her happy, and hope that over time she began to believe it.

He squeezed her fingers and felt her squeeze his in return, and just could not let go of her hand.

'I…' There was so much he wanted to say.

She nodded and said, 'Yes,' in a low voice.

'I wish you very well.' Marcus just wanted to kiss her, hold her, smooth away the tightness he saw on her forehead, in her cheeks, in her smile. He just wanted her always to be happy.

'Thank you,' she whispered. 'I wish you very well too.'

And then they stood together, not speaking, for a long time, until Lady Kingsbridge poked Marcus in the ribs with her stick.

'Do you have anything important to say to my granddaughter?' she asked.

Marcus tore his gaze from Eloise and looked at Lady Kingsbridge. Her expression was so full of mischief that if he hadn't had the heaviest heart imaginable, he would have laughed. If only she knew.

'Nothing particularly important, no,' he said. 'Thank you both very much indeed for your wonderful hospitality; I have very much enjoyed myself. I must also thank the duke, of course.'

And suddenly the duke was in front of him and they were pumping each other's hands up and down and then a mass of farewells and adieux were exchanged and it was time for Marcus and Sir Richard, who had decided to travel on to Brighton together, to leave.

As they trotted on horseback down the drive together, Marcus wondered the whole time whether Eloise might be standing looking after him, or whether she had immediately turned her back on him and gone inside or back down to the dower house.

He managed not to turn round to find out, so he would probably never know.

They rode hard, which Marcus always enjoyed, and Sir Richard was one of his oldest and best friends and always good company, and the North and South Downs through which they rode were particularly beautiful at this time of year, but Marcus found himself struggling to raise a smile or any interesting conversation.

He would feel better after their arrival in Brighton, he told himself. The Prince Regent was reportedly in residence at the Royal Pavilion, and his presence always energised Brighton Society; Marcus would be able to distract himself with the many social engagements that would be available to him.

During the days that followed, he made himself as busy as possible, and tried to ignore both the continued emptiness he felt and the hope he also experienced; if Eloise was with child, they would marry immediately, and she would in time, he trusted, come to understand that marriage *could* offer benefits—love and happiness—to her.

And then one morning, as he broke his fast, a footman handed him a letter. He immediately recognised the script on the envelope as Eloise's. His heart suddenly beating a lot faster, he drew the paper out and began to read.

Dear Lord Malbrook,
I trust that you are well.
  I am writing on behalf of the Duke of Rothshire to reiterate that he would very much enjoy your presence at a sporting party in the autumn.
  In the meantime, as you kindly enquired most assiduously after my health when I was ill during your stay, I thought I should let you know that I find myself fully recovered and in excellent

health with no symptoms whatsoever. That is to say, my condition is entirely as normal.

I shall perhaps see you when you visit the duke in the autumn if I am at home at the time.

In the meantime, I wish you very well and thank you for your kindness.
Yours,
Eloise, Duchess of Rothshire

Suddenly, Marcus's appetite was completely gone.

Chapter Seventeen

Eloise

As Eloise watched Amelia being led around a paddock by a groom on the back of one of the most placid horses in the duke's stable, she surreptitiously wiped tears from under her eyes.

If anyone saw that she was crying, they would hopefully think that it was due to the slight breeze or the dust kicked up by the horse's hooves.

She was being ridiculous.

She had *wanted* her monthly courses to come. She had *wanted* not to be with child. She had. It was for the best. She did not want to have to marry Marcus. And yet...

She felt as though a future had been taken away from her somehow. She didn't know how that future would have been, and common sense told her that it would—or could—have been difficult, given that it would have involved marriage. But without that future, life felt quite empty.

She sniffed and began to walk around the edge of the paddock. She should really now be used to the fact that her fears had *not* been realised. It was nearly two days since she had found that she would not be having a baby.

She had written to Marcus almost immediately, and that…well, that was that. A man and a woman could not enter into regular correspondence. She would see him as an acquaintance when he came to the duke's sporting parties—she would make sure that she sowed seeds in the duke's mind if it appeared that he might forget to organise the parties—and they would walk together with Amelia occasionally. And other than that, well, nothing.

She felt another tear roll down her cheek and didn't even bother to wipe it away; there was no one near enough to see it, and she just…couldn't be bothered.

Amelia called, 'Mama, *look*,' as her horse began to trot, and Eloise smiled through her tears, and this time did wipe them away. She had *much* to be happy about—Amelia was everything—and should certainly not allow herself to feel miserable.

She wondered whether Marcus would yet have received her letter. And how he would have felt when he read it.

'Mama!' Amelia called again.

Eloise smiled and waved and forced Marcus out of her mind. 'You are doing marvellously well,' she told her daughter, clapping. And if the claps sounded hollow to her mind, that was utterly ludicrous. Claps *couldn't* sound hollow.

When they got back to the house, Amelia still chattering excitedly about horse riding, Eloise found that she had a letter. She recognised Marcus's firm-stroked handwriting immediately.

'Thank you,' she said to Jarvis, surprised to hear that her voice sounded really entirely normal. If it had been a reflection of how she felt on the inside at this moment, it would have been quite tremulous.

Which was of course extremely silly. There was no reason at all to feel any rush of emotion on receipt of his letter. He was probably just thanking her for her own missive and wishing her well.

She would, though, open it when she was alone, just in case.

'Eloise, my darling.' Her grandmother came almost flying out of the drawing room into the hall. 'I should like to go shopping. I need new ribbons. If we leave now, we will reach the haberdasher's before it closes, I am assured by the groom.'

'Of course.' Eloise felt almost like grinding her teeth in frustration. She was sure that the letter *wouldn't* say anything of particular note, but—just in case it did— she would very much like the opportunity to read it sooner rather than later.

Their trip to the shops was long. There was a problem with the horses so their carriage had to be changed. When they did arrive it took some time even to get inside the haberdasher's because Eloise's grandmother caught sight of all sorts of alluring objects in the windows of the shops they passed on the way, and had to go inside several other shops to enquire about the things she'd seen, and then make a number of purchases. Once they were in the haberdasher's, her grandmother was struck by indecision and spent quite twenty minutes choosing between the various ribbons that were available, before determining that the obvious thing to do was to acquire them all. And halfway through the journey home, they found that they had to turn back and take a long detour because while they had been at Farbridge a tree had fallen and blocked the road.

'Despite the small issues with the journeys, this has been a most pleasant trip, has it not?' Eloise's grandmother said, as the dower house *finally* came into view.

'Certainly,' Eloise said, thinking of the letter from Marcus waiting in her reticule to be perused. She'd been thinking of it every few minutes the entire time they'd been out; it was almost as though it was burning a hole in the reticule and clamouring to be read.

It would of course almost certainly be quite anticlimactic when she *did* read it in a few minutes' time.

'I think we should now have tea,' her grandmother said as she descended from the chaise. 'I believe we should ask Jarvis to bring it directly.'

'Wonderful.' Eloise thought again of the letter as she smiled at her grandmother through slightly gritted teeth.

When they finally finished their tea, it was more than time for Eloise to go and see Amelia in the nursery. Perhaps she would just take a moment to go to her chamber and read the letter first.

No. Just thinking about reading it made her feel a little odd—obviously there was no reason for her to feel that way but she did; maybe she was worried that Marcus had written to tell her that he was upset—and she didn't want to feel like that when she was with Amelia. She would read it afterwards.

After she'd spent an hour with Amelia, it was time to change for dinner, which they were taking up at the castle with some neighbours, and Miss Denby and the Heatheringtons, who, together with Sir Walter, seemed to be staying for weeks and weeks, with no one—not even Eloise's grandmother—quite brave enough to tell them just to *leave*.

'I wonder how dear Lord Malbrook and Sir Richard are enjoying Brighton,' Miss Denby said a little wistfully to Miss Heatherington after the ladies had retired to leave the gentlemen to their port. They talked about the erstwhile male guests a *lot*.

'I declare I am surprised that neither of them came up to scratch with any lady while they were here,' said Miss Heatherington.

Eloise immediately stared at her knees, not wishing to give away by the expression on her face that Marcus *had* come up to scratch. Twice. And the second time she was sure that he'd meant it.

Mrs Heatherington had remained in her chamber this evening with the headache, or as Eloise privately surmised, a reluctance to spend any more time with Sir Walter. Eloise was quite sure that Mrs Heatherington was regretting her betrothal, despite Sir Walter's ten thousand pounds a year.

In her mother's absence, Miss Heatherington had quite a lot to say about the various departed members of the party and about other members of the *ton*. Eloise wished quite desperately that Marcus could hear what she said because she was sure she would have caught his eye and he would have found exactly the same things funny at exactly the same time.

As it was, she had to be content with knowing that her grandmother would certainly pass comment later.

That should be enough for Eloise. It *was* enough for Eloise; she adored her grandmother's acerbic company and always had.

She really did miss Marcus, though. And she really wanted to know what he'd written to her, even though it was probably nothing at all, just a 'thank you for your note.'

She tried to catch her grandmother's eye to suggest that they leave now, so that she could read the letter. Usually, her grandmother was quite partial to an early bedtime. Not this evening, however; she was clearly enjoying Miss Heatherington and now Miss Denby's indiscreet conversation far too much.

When the gentlemen joined them and someone suggested that they play cards, her grandmother, of course, acquiesced for once.

Partnered with the squire, Eloise couldn't help wishing that they'd played cards when Marcus had been there; she was sure that she would very much have enjoyed partnering him or pitting her wits against his.

Eventually, her grandmother declared herself tired and very ready for her bed, and they began the walk down the slope together towards the dower house.

'We feel the loss of some of the members of our party, do we not?' her grandmother observed.

'Yes, I believe that it must always feel strange when a group is reduced in size.'

'I shall say just one thing to you.' Her grandmother squeezed her arm.

Eloise winced in the dark, sure that she wasn't going to want to hear whatever was going to come next. Her grandmother had had a lot of 'just one' things to say to her since Marcus had left, and they had all related to him.

'Malbrook is a good man. I believe he could make you happy. As your grandfather made me happy.' Her grandmother sounded wistful.

Eloise sighed silently in the near-dark.

By the time she had the leisure to read the letter in her chamber, alone, she was in her nightgown sitting in bed.

As she pulled it out of the envelope, her hands were almost shaking, which was *so* silly. As was the lump that arose in her throat as she saw the salutation.

> *My dear Eloise,*
> *Thank you for your note and thank you for writing so soon to settle the uncertainty.*
> *I trust that you are well and hope very much that you are now feeling content; your happiness is very important to me.*
> *Should your sentiments ever change in regard to the matter of which we spoke, be assured that my own will remain constant, but that I will not mention it again.*
> *I should be grateful if you would pass on my regards to your daughter.*
> *Your humble servant,*
> *Malbrook*

By the time she got to the end of the short letter, tears were rolling down Eloise's cheeks yet again.

By the time she'd read it at least five times, she was still crying.

From what he'd written, he still loved her and would like to marry her if she would like to marry him.

In the same way that she had experienced the loss of hope of having another baby, so had he.

He must therefore have been upset when he received her letter.

But he hadn't told her that he was upset; his own letter had been all that was thoughtful, and kind, and chivalrous, and discreet.

It was a fact that Amelia's father was a wonderful man.

He was also delightfully witty and deliciously handsome and quite wonderfully adept at kissing and... other things.

It was so sad to think of *him* being sad.

She heaved a big juddering sigh and read the letter one more time, before sniffing and wiping her eyes and carefully folding the letter and returning it to its envelope. Then she put it safely inside her book—Fanny Burney's 'Cecilia'—and snuffed out her candle.

She soon realised that that had been a mistake; she was tired but she was unable to get to sleep for a long time, and would have been much better off reading. Her mind was full of thoughts of Marcus's kindness, her own loss—she realised that she had wanted to be with child more than she had thought—and memories of what Marcus had told her about his nightmares; she hoped that they had improved.

'I have just sent word up to Fenton that to mark the final day of the remainder of our guests' stay I plan to organise an excursion to Box Hill today. I think we should leave by eleven o'clock. It would be nice to picnic there,' her grandmother told her the next morning over breakfast.

'Perhaps I could help Fenton arrange it,' Eloise said, alarmed. She now knew that when her grandmother said she would arrange something, the entire arranging was carried out by her—or in this case the duke's—servants. The castle staff were already showing signs of open rebellion in the face of her grandmother's demands. Although maybe they would be happier now that the Heatheringtons and Sir Walter and Miss Denby were *finally* leaving. 'I think I will walk up to the castle now myself. I will take Amelia.'

'I'm sure they don't need your help.'

Eloise decided to remain firm. 'I am very happy to go.'

It was a pleasant morning to walk up to the castle hand in hand with Amelia, and when they got there, Eloise became very fully occupied both in mollifying wounded housekeeper and butler sensibilities and in making her own suggestions for ways in which her grandmother's plans could be carried out with the least possible extra work for the castle servants.

She realised when she began her return to the dower house with Amelia that an hour and a half had passed without her noticing, and that she felt quite rested as a result, because it was the first time since she and Marcus had made love that she hadn't thought about him for any appreciable length of time.

She just needed to continue to make herself busy, therefore, ideally in talking to others, and she would soon forget all about her ridiculous infatuation with him.

When the remaining party assembled half an hour later to set out for Box Hill, and Eloise joined three other members of the party in a chaise, she found herself reflecting that she'd never been inside a chaise with Marcus.

And when she saw some of the men riding alongside the ladies, she couldn't help thinking that Marcus made a finer figure of a horseman than most people.

And when someone pointed out a hawk hovering in the sky above them, she couldn't help thinking about all the bird conversations she'd had with Marcus even though neither of them was a particular bird fanatic, and then she couldn't help smiling.

'Are you quite all right, Your Grace?' Mrs Heatherington's voice cut across her thoughts. Oh, dear; she'd been ignoring her companions.

'Quite all right, thank you.' Eloise needed to try harder to put Marcus out of her thoughts, clearly.

Mrs Heatherington leaned in towards the middle of the carriage, and the other three ladies—including Eloise in a reflexive action—leaned in with her.

'I heard the most interesting *on-dit* today by letter from a friend,' Mrs Heatherington told them.

Eloise never liked group gossip of this nature. It was one thing sharing confidences with a close friend whom one trusted, and another telling anyone and everyone about things.

She sat back a little and looked towards the window.

'Lord Beechley, who is recently affianced to Lady Edwina Marson, has just discovered that he has a—' Mrs Heatherington leaned further in and lowered her voice '—if I might be crude, an illegitimate daughter, by the daughter of the squire whose land runs next to his in Hampshire. The girl, of course, is quite ruined. Beechley has behaved most magnanimously; I believe that he has deigned to send her a sum of five hundred pounds to allow them to live most comfortably.'

'What is the size of Lord Beechley's fortune?' Eloise immediately despised herself for joining in the conversation, but she hadn't been able to resist. The contrast between a single payment of five hundred pounds and whatever means Lord Beechley had must be great.

'Quite twenty thousand a year, I believe.'

A single sum of five hundred pounds out of an annual income of twenty thousand. To last the girl and her daughter for the rest of their lives.

'How very generous of Lord Beechley,' she said sarcastically.

'Indeed,' Mrs Heatherington said, not sarcastically, Eloise was sure.

Eloise knew Lord Beechley a little, and he was a perfectly average—she thought—man of perhaps her own age.

Marcus was not average.

Most men would probably do what Lord Beechley had done, at best, and would count themselves most generous.

Eloise was sure that Marcus would have proposed marriage to her had she been the gently born squire's daughter rather than a dowager duchess. She was also sure that he would not make love to another woman while affianced. He was really not an average man. He had not wished to get married and yet he had done what he perceived to be his duty. He had, she was sure, immediately become quite besotted with his daughter, but she didn't think he had expected to do so.

He was a good man.

* * *

The rest of the trip passed without incident other than the continued far too frequent intrusion of Marcus into her thoughts.

The next day, she took a slow promenade with her grandmother in the first part of the morning and then played shuttlecock and battledore with Amelia before luncheon. In the afternoon, she read with Amelia and then walked with her. It was lovely to spend so much time with Amelia, but she did find herself wishing that she could tell Marcus what Amelia had been doing. He and her grandmother were, after all, the only other two people in the world who were as interested in Amelia as she was.

'Mama, I enjoyed our walks with Marcus,' Amelia told her as they rowed on the lake. 'I want to go rowing with him when he returns to visit.'

'That sounds like a lovely idea.' Eloise very much hoped that he would indeed return and that Amelia wouldn't be disappointed.

She'd like to go out in a boat with him too. She'd enjoy doing anything with him, she was sure.

As they walked back to the house from the lake, she reflected that a couple of weeks ago she'd been very happy, but now her daily life felt...a little flat.

She stared down the hill and wondered why she had decided that she didn't wish to marry Marcus.

It was because she'd been worried that she and Marcus wouldn't be happy together after she gave up her independence and together they would then make Amelia miserable.

But Marcus was not like her father and he was not

like her late husband and he was not like Lord Beechley reputedly was, and many other men were. He could have ignored Amelia, but he hadn't done that. His actions had demonstrated that he was a good man, a decent man. A *rare* man.

He *would* treat her well. And he would treat Amelia well. He'd demonstrated that.

And Eloise was in danger of becoming a boring mother if she continued to feel as flat as this. Marcus made her happy and he made Amelia happy.

They'd arrived at the house.

'Good afternoon,' her grandmother said. 'Shall we take tea?'

'Certainly.' Eloise did not want to take tea; she wanted to continue thinking.

Eventually, lying in bed that evening, she had the leisure to examine her own thoughts again.

It seemed that they had been percolating inside her while she'd been otherwise occupied.

Before she snuffed her candle, she took Marcus's letter out and read it one more time.

And then she went to sleep very easily, feeling happy for the first time since she and Marcus had made love in the folly.

She'd come to a decision.

When she awoke in the morning, feeling blissfully refreshed after an excellent night's sleep, she immediately thought of Marcus.

And her decision...

She sprang straight out of bed; she wanted to be ready as soon as possible.

She did spend a few minutes choosing her dress with

care, however. She eventually settled on a cream and rose muslin newly arrived from her dressmaker. She asked her maid to arrange her hair in a chignon with a few ringlets falling artfully from it.

It seemed to take an infinity for her to be ready, but she did want to look her absolute best, so she must not give in to her impatience to break her fast and go immediately.

'Good morning,' her grandmother greeted her when she sat down to breakfast. 'That's a most becoming dress. Is it new? I don't think I have seen it before.'

Eloise smoothed her skirts, delighted to have her grandmother's approbation.

'Yes, it is new,' she said.

'Do you have anything special envisioned for today?'

'I'm going to Brighton.'

Chapter Eighteen

Marcus

'Malbrook. The Prince Regent requests our presence at supper this evening.' Sir Richard slapped Marcus on the back as he groaned internally.

Despite his best intentions, he was finding it very difficult to feel particularly enthusiastic about Brighton Society. He shouldn't have come here; he should have returned home immediately, found solace in his lands. He had the sense that it would take him some time before he regained the ability to enjoy making inane small talk with decadent princes. Everything felt a little pointless right now.

Returning home might remind him of some of the many positives that life held.

Or of course it might remind him of being in the country with Eloise and Amelia, and depress him. Or just bore him. It felt as though he had little to lose though.

'I am afraid that I need to return to Hampshire.' He put his napkin on the table and stood up. 'You will have to apologise on my behalf and say that you were unable to get hold of me as I had already left, having only ever intended to remain in Brighton for a night or two.'

Perhaps he would take the small detour necessary to stop at Farbridge to break his journey.

That thought was extremely appealing.

He couldn't, though; he could not harass Eloise with his company. If she did not wish to see him, he had to respect her decision. He would go straight home.

An hour and a half later, as he rode as fast as his horse, Calypso, would happily take him, he wondered whether the stinging in his eyes was from the dust and wind, or whether it was something else.

Usually, he loved riding. Today, though, it just seemed as empty a pursuit as everything else did.

He really needed to get over this. Maybe he would stop in a minute, take a moment to enjoy the scenery, calm himself. Maybe he would even walk with Calypso for a mile or two.

Ten minutes later he was walking—trudging— along a country road leading Calypso by the reins. It was a beautiful day. White-flowered cow parsley lined the verges, the occasional rabbit ran past, birds were singing. It was quite idyllic.

It was boring.

Really, everything felt boring.

God, he needed to pull himself together.

He should ride again. Walking was not working to improve his mood; it would serve merely to lengthen his journey towards home. Maybe spending the evening with a bottle of whisky would help. Well, it probably wouldn't, but it felt like a more enticing prospect than either spending more time with his thoughts or in making inane polite conversation.

As he hoisted himself back into the saddle and nudged Calypso to a walk with his heels, he wondered how Eloise was feeling today.

He didn't want her to be sad, of course he didn't. He *really* didn't. He wanted nothing but happiness for her. In truth, though, he'd be hurt if she was entirely happy now that he'd left. No, that was awful. He really didn't want her to experience any of this emptiness. He did want her to be happy; it would be much better if she weren't missing him.

As he re-joined the main trunk road, he saw a crested chaise pass on the other side of the road. He frowned, following it with his eyes. He'd only caught it at an angle, but that crest had looked remarkably similar to Eloise's, which he had seen several times, and indeed had studied briefly at the balloon ascension.

The chaise looked similar to hers too. It looked exactly the same, in fact, from what he remembered.

Was it in fact hers?

Was she going to Brighton?

She might well be going to Brighton. If the remainder of their guests had left, perhaps she—with Amelia and her grandmother—would be travelling to Brighton to enjoy the seaside. The duke would no doubt have a house there.

That was probably what it was.

What if she'd been travelling to see him, though?

What if something had happened to Amelia? And she wanted to tell him but didn't feel she could entrust the message to a footman?

What if she needed his help for some other reason?

What if…?

Well, he didn't know what else. But he was worried, he realised.

Obviously, he should turn around and overtake the coach to confirm that its occupant was indeed Eloise.

It didn't take long to reach the chaise; it had clearly been built with extreme comfort but only moderate speed in mind.

As he approached the vehicle, and determined that it was indeed Eloise's carriage, he realised that it was extremely unlikely that the reason she was travelling in this direction was that she was intending to visit him. There were any number of other things she might be doing. And if something had happened to Amelia, would Eloise really leave her side to visit him? Of course not. She could send a sealed letter to him.

It was clearly mere coincidence that they had passed each other in the road.

He should, therefore, probably not speak to her. Although maybe he could; maybe she wouldn't mind. He would very much like to see her, speak to her, confirm to himself that all was well with her.

As he hovered indecisively in the middle of the road—which was not pleasant because indecision didn't feel good—Eloise's face appeared at the window of the chaise. Her almost jaw-dropped look of astonishment told him that she hadn't been expecting to see him. Of course she hadn't; he'd been ridiculously self-absorbed in his initial assumption that she was on her way to visit him. And, actually, of course he shouldn't speak to her.

He raised one hand in a semi-salute and pulled on Calypso's reins to turn him.

As he did so, Eloise smiled at him and mouthed something. He couldn't decipher what she was saying, but from her demeanour he didn't think it was anything of any great import. She was probably just saying a hello. She looked very well, which was good to see.

And now he should go. He smiled back at her, turned again and spurred Calypso forward in the opposite direction from Eloise.

He did not enjoy the remainder of his journey; he was miserable about Eloise all over again, as though seeing her had just reinforced his loss.

It was good that she had looked well, though, he told himself as he cantered up the long drive to his house.

Dismounting, he reflected that it was good to be home. It really was. He would immediately make himself busy and very soon—now that he was at home, a place that Eloise had never been—he would feel a lot happier again. He would of course miss Amelia, but he would no longer feel this constant desire to see Eloise.

It was early evening. Ideal timing to have dinner, perhaps look over some correspondence this evening, accompanied perhaps by a whisky or some port, and then in the morning he would work hard on his estates, throw himself back into his real life, of which Eloise did not form a part.

He ate a solitary dinner at his desk in his library, while beginning to go through his correspondence. Most of it was not particularly interesting. That part of it that did hold some interest for him made him think of Eloise; he would have liked to have discussed it with her, laughed about some of it with her.

He took a further glass of port and looked at a couple of invitations before discarding them. He had no interest in attending local dinners.

He ought to attend them. He was very sure that this emptiness would pass soon.

He finished his glass of port, and drank another quickly, and then decided that he should go to bed. Drinking too much would certainly not make him feel any better.

He woke up early, after a not particularly good night's sleep again, and went out on his land for an early morning gallop before breakfast.

That was actually quite enjoyable.

Breakfast felt lonely, though. And, once it was done, he realised that, while he did—usually—enjoy being involved in the management of his own estates, he didn't *have* to be. His man of business and steward were most effective and quite capable of running things in his absence. There were no genuinely pressing demands on his time, and today he didn't feel particularly inspired to begin work again himself.

Perhaps he should in fact have stayed in Brighton.

He placed his tankard down on the table hard.

He needed to stop this immediately. Before he'd met Eloise again and found out about Amelia, he'd been perfectly happy. He would be happy again if he resumed his previous ways. So, even though his man of business and steward *could* continue without him, he would speak to them both today and involve himself again with the running of his estates. The duke had mentioned some agricultural advances that were in practice in Sussex, and he was particularly interested in investigating whether it would be possible to apply those methods here in Hampshire, despite the differences in the soil and climate.

The morning passed tolerably well, in fact. He even worked up quite an enthusiasm at one point when discussing the construction of a new school for his tenants' children.

This was going to work. He was going to go back to normal. He was sure he would.

This afternoon he would ride out to visit some of his tenants, make sure that those who were infirm or elderly had everything they needed. That would also serve to remind him of how lucky he was.

Just as he was leaving the house in order to set off in the early afternoon, though, there was a commotion as a carriage drew up outside. For a mad moment, Marcus thought—hoped—that it might be Eloise, before he realised that there was no reason whatsoever that she would come to visit him and that of course it wasn't her.

'Marcus.' His sister Lucretia was descending the steps of the carriage. 'We are come to spend a week or two with you.'

'Good God,' Marcus said. His first instinct told him that he really did not wish to spend a week or two being informed yet again by Lucretia—of whom he was very fond, but at a distance—that in her capacity as much older sister she could see clearly how he should spend his life, and what he needed to do now was marry.

As her three oldest sons—aged about twenty, eighteen and fifteen if memory served him right—appeared one by one out of the carriage, however, it occurred to him that perhaps they might prove a useful distraction.

'Marcus.' Lucretia kissed him vigorously on both cheeks. 'You seem surprised. We agreed this visit, did we not?'

Marcus frowned, trying to remember.

'We discussed it the day we went to the Royal Academy.'

'Oh, yes.' He did now vaguely recall the discussion. It had gone clean out of his mind, though.

'When we have taken some refreshment, I suggest that you ride out with the boys to show them your estates,' Lucretia commanded.

Marcus nodded. It seemed like a reasonable way to pass the time. And since he would not be marrying Eloise—and he certainly wouldn't be marrying any other woman—he would not be having any sons, so unless his younger brother and his wife produced a son—his sister-in-law had just given birth to a fourth daughter—Lucretia's oldest son, Jack, would in due course be heir to the earldom, so it would be important to show him the estates.

Jack and his two younger brothers, Max and Felix, proved to be excellent company, to the extent that as they reached the highest point of his land, Marcus could honestly say that he was actively enjoying his afternoon with them.

He'd been anticipating having to while the evening away with a liquid supper of whisky, followed by a digestif of more whisky. As he and the boys completed a visit to an elderly farmer, Marcus reflected that it would certainly be much more palatable spending the evening with his sister and nephews.

They arrived back at the house towards the end of the afternoon, and if Marcus had not entirely succeeded in putting Eloise out of his mind—images of her continued to crop up in his mind at the most ridiculous times—he had enjoyed himself sufficiently to be able to believe that he would in time be able to accept the situation with her as it was without being too depressed about it; and indeed as he walked into the house with his nephews, he was almost able to believe that it might all be for the best that Eloise had refused his proposal. Really, he could genuinely say that he'd enjoyed himself this afternoon.

'Marcus.' Lucretia swept into the hall in a rustle of silks. 'We have company.'

Marcus managed not to close his eyes or sigh in annoyance, but *really*? He could see now that it would be a good thing having his sister and nephews to stay, but they were family; he had no desire whatsoever to host a larger party.

Looking hard at his sister, he realised that despite his irritation he would actually like to know who the guests were, because Lucretia was behaving really quite oddly. She was smiling widely while indicating the saloon to her right with eye rolls so strong it was a wonder she didn't cause herself to topple over.

'The company is perhaps…in the saloon?' he asked when she continued with the bizarre smiling and eye rolling.

'Indeed. Let us go.'

'I am not dressed…' He was fairly sure that he was mud-spattered from where they'd waded the horses through a shallow ford earlier in the afternoon.

'No matter.' Lucretia stepped forward, took his arm, gave it a forceful tug and almost shoved him into the room ahead of her.

Marcus stopped short when he saw who was in the room and Lucretia bumped into him.

'Eloise,' he said inanely.

'Eloise?' Lucretia said from behind him. 'Her Grace, you mean?'

Marcus ignored her and stepped forward, his heart suddenly beating fast in fear. 'Is everything all right? Amelia?' Eloise didn't *look* as though she was there to impart bad news, but he couldn't imagine a reason for her to visit other than for her to discuss their daughter in some way.

'Amelia is very well, thank you.'

'Amelia?' asked Lucretia.

'Lucretia.' Marcus turned round and looked her in the eye. 'I wonder if you might…'

He wanted very much to find out why Eloise was there and he wanted very much to do that without his older sister joining in the conversation. Lucretia did not look, however, as though she wished to leave the room.

'Yes, Marcus?' His sister grinned at him and then moved round him into the middle of the room and said, 'Shall we all sit down? I shall call for tea and cakes.' She lifted a small bell on a side table and rang it, and Marcus's butler, Sands, appeared within seconds. He was, no doubt, just as agog as Lucretia.

'Tea, please, Sands,' Lucretia said. 'Please do sit down, Your Grace.'

'Thank you,' Eloise said, a little faintly.

When the three of them were seated—each on a separate sofa—both Marcus and Eloise fell silent. Fortunately—or unfortunately—Lucretia was never, in Marcus's experience, dumbstruck, and she certainly wasn't now.

'We met recently in the park, Your Grace, and I now remember meeting you in London several years ago, with Lady Kingsbridge, I think immediately before your marriage. I think we met at the pleasure gardens at Vauxhall. Do you remember that evening?'

'Oh, yes!' Eloise's eyes opened quite wide and she pressed her lips together. 'I do remember that evening.'

'Yes, I have to admit that I have always very much enjoyed a masquerade. Although of course at Vauxhall one must stay in one's box to avoid witnessing quite licentious behaviour.' Lucretia smiled at them both and Marcus wondered for a moment if she could possibly *know*. She couldn't. Surely.

'Indeed.' Eloise nodded several times. She took a deep breath, and said, 'I have not spent a great deal of time in London. I am mainly in the country, in Sussex.'

'What brings you to Hampshire?' Lucretia enquired.

'I am in Hampshire because—' Eloise was enunciating very slowly, as though to allow herself time to think '—I am on the way to visit an elderly aunt. And my horses were tired and my groom suggested that we stop here.'

Lucretia nodded. 'This is certainly more comfortable than a staging inn, although it must have been quite a detour for you from the main road, unless your aunt lives close by?'

'I am not entirely certain,' Eloise said, 'as my knowledge of the geography of Hampshire is not what it might be, but I have every confidence in the competence of my groom.'

Marcus nodded. 'Grooms certainly do have excellent geography.'

'Very true.' Lucretia paused and then said, 'You

were recently at Farbridge, were you not, Marcus?'
She tilted her head quite a long way to the right and
looked at them both with a bland smile, and Marcus
suddenly remembered being a little boy and watching
his sisters argue. Lucretia had always won, and straight
before she delivered her killer verbal blow, she would
always do the head tilt and the smile.

'Yes,' he said. 'Her Grace fainted at the balloon ascension to which I took two of Sybella's daughters, and
when I called to enquire after her health, Lady Kingsbridge invited me to a house party at Farbridge. Hearing that my great friend Sir Richard Elliot, amongst
others, was to attend, and hearing that the sport at Farbridge is second almost to none, I accepted the invitation, and passed a most enjoyable stay.'

'How delightful,' Lucretia said. She turned the head
tilt and smile on Eloise. 'We are so pleased to receive
you here, Your Grace.'

Marcus was certain that she'd been intending to ask
what Eloise was doing there—and that was a question
to which he very much wanted the answer himself, but
in private—but that she had found herself unable to
continue due to the haughty expression now on Eloise's face. It wasn't one Marcus had seen before, and
he was impressed.

'Thank you,' Eloise said.

A footman opened the door and Sands entered with
their tea.

'I will pour,' Lucretia said.

'You will find that my housekeeper and cook are at
all times able to provide us with excellent sustenance,'
Marcus said, determined to direct the conversation
away from the personal while Lucretia was with them.

The three of them exchanged pleasantries on the subjects of afternoon tea and the weather, and then began to eat.

Eloise took one nibble of a small madeleine and then placed it back on her plate, before addressing Lucretia.

'Thank you so much for the tea. I hope that I do not appear rude, but I should be grateful for a few moments alone with His Lordship.'

'Oh.' Lucretia choked quite severely and Marcus, alarmed, rose to pat her hard on the back. 'Thank you, thank you.' She waved him away. 'I swallowed a crumb the wrong way; that was all.' She looked between the two of them and then smiled, before putting her half-eaten sandwich on her plate. 'Certainly.' She stood up and walked towards the door of the room, paused for a moment before doing her head tilt and saying, 'I wish you both the very best,' and then took herself out of the room, closing the door very firmly behind her.

And, contrary to all expectation, here they were, just the two of them, alone together.

Chapter Nineteen

Eloise

Eloise suddenly felt a little…odd. Light-headed. She put out a hand to hold the arm of the sofa for support, just for a moment. Surely one couldn't faint while already seated. She took two or three deep breaths, to regain her composure.

She and Marcus were alone. They were in a room, together, with the door closed, just the two of them.

Perhaps she would just take another few sips of her tea.

Marcus was regarding her from the sofa opposite, with a slightly raised eyebrow and no other expression on his face.

Eloise took another sip. She had certainly had time to prepare for this meeting—after her journey halfway to Brighton, the return home, the enquiries about Marcus's whereabouts and then the journey here—and she knew broadly what she wished to say, but in this moment her ability to start a conversation appeared to have deserted her.

Eventually, Marcus broke the silence. 'I was surprised to see you here,' he observed.

'Yes,' Eloise replied. She nodded a couple of times and then drank some more.

And then they continued to stare at each other.

Marcus's thick, wavy hair was a little mussed, as though he'd been riding in a breeze, and his riding clothes were a little muddy. She hadn't seen him with such heavy stubble before; it looked as if he hadn't bothered shaving that morning.

Eloise moistened her lips, and just…looked at him. He looked, well, perfect. She loved his eyes.

What if this conversation did not turn out the way she wanted it to and this was the last time she would ever be alone in a room with him?

It was also the first time they'd ever been alone in a proper room together, she realised. How odd, considering that they had made love twice.

Marcus's voice pierced her thoughts. 'Did you have a reason for coming?'

Oh. This was the moment. This was it.

She placed her cup very deliberately on the little table just to her right and drew a deep breath.

'Yes, I did.' And now she should just ask him. What if he'd changed his mind, though? He'd assured her that he wouldn't, but people didn't always know how they would feel in the future. His sentiments might have changed now that he was back on familiar territory; his professed love for her might have been a transient emotion. Why, for example, had he ignored her wave and hello from the coach?

'Why did you ride off when we saw each other?' she asked.

Marcus frowned. 'Is that what you came here to ask me?'

She shook her head. 'No. But why did you?'

'Because we had no reason to speak to each other.' He almost shrugged as he spoke. 'And I did not wish to make you feel as though I was pursuing you in any way.' Funny, because she was now the one pursuing him.

It was also funny that she'd spent the entirety of the journey in her agonisingly slow-moving chaise just desperate to speak to him, and that desperation had continued when she'd arrived, but now... Now she almost just wanted to turn tail and run, because what if this conversation did not end the way she'd like it to?

He really didn't seem as pleased to see her as she'd hoped he would.

Perhaps she should just leave.

No. Leaving now would be ridiculous. She had nothing to lose in telling him how she felt. She'd been naked in front of him. She'd seen him naked. They'd done... well, what they'd done together. He was a very kind person. He'd been honest about his feelings for her. If he no longer reciprocated the feelings she now knew she had for him, he would be nice to her. And she would at least have tried. It would not be humiliating.

'I love you,' she said, very suddenly.

'You love me?' he echoed.

'Yes.' She felt her face scrunching up. That was *not* the response she'd hoped for. Clearly he *had* suffered a change of heart. She opened her eyes very wide in a bid to prevent tears from forming. It was obviously, it turned out, a very good thing that she had not agreed to marry him.

'And?' he asked. Demanded, really; he had said the word very forcefully.

'And?' She stared at him.

'I wondered,' he said, stating his words very clearly as though she might not understand basic English, 'whether you had anything further to say beyond that? And what your reason in travelling here was.'

'I travelled here to tell you properly that I love you.' Eloise was beginning to feel a little irritated.

'I see.'

'You see?'

'I apologise. I should have thanked you.'

'Thanked me?'

'No.' He shook his head. 'What I meant was I love you too.'

'Oh.' Eloise felt as though her whole body had suddenly relaxed a little. 'Good.'

'So...' Marcus wasn't really smiling and his stance was quite rigid. 'We both love each other?'

Eloise nodded, confused by his still quite unhappy-looking demeanour.

'Why were you travelling towards Brighton when we crossed paths?' he asked.

'I was looking for you. I wanted to see you. And that is why I am here now.'

Marcus visibly took a deep breath. 'And you wanted to see me to tell me...that you love me?'

'Not just that.' This was the moment. If Eloise were a man she would go down on one knee. But she wasn't, and she couldn't think of an alternative, so she didn't move. 'Would you like to marry me?'

'Would I like to marry you?' The man had turned into a parrot.

Eloise glared at him. 'I am going to clarify what I am asking, and then if you like I will leave. I came here to tell you that I love you and to ask you if you would still like to marry me. Because I would like to marry you.'

'Well, I…' Marcus appeared to be struggling to find words, and not in a particularly good way. This was not the outcome Eloise had been hoping for. Perhaps she should indeed just leave. She reached to her side and picked up her reticule. 'Is this because you have discovered that you are after all with child?'

'No. I am not with child.'

'Could I ask then what has caused this change of heart?'

'It isn't so much a change of heart as a change of mind,' Eloise told him.

'I see. And what has caused that change of mind?'

'I couldn't help thinking about you when you weren't there. I heard some *on-dits* that caused me to reflect on what an honourable, kind man you are. I missed you. I realised that without you I felt miserable and lonely. Whenever something funny happens, I want to tell you about it. I know that you are—will be—a wonderful father to Amelia. I want to be able to talk to you about her all the time, share experiences together as a family. I already knew that I loved you but I was too scared to marry you because I wasn't sure that you could love me and I was worried that all men might be like my father and late husband, so I didn't wish to surrender my independence. But that is of course nonsense; you aren't like them. So.' She'd been talking for a *long* time. 'In summary, I love you and I miss you and I would very much like to marry you and spend the rest of our lives together.' She'd said everything now. That was it.

'I…' Marcus pressed his lips together.

'You?' Eloise was surprised she managed to say the word without screaming.

And then his eyes began to crinkle and his lips parted into a smile.

'If you would genuinely like to marry me, I should be delighted to be your husband.' He stood up and moved towards her and Eloise felt butterflies begin in her stomach and her heart move to her mouth.

'I would like that so very much,' she managed to say.

Marcus's smile broadened even further as he sat down on the sofa next to her.

'I'm sorry for not having immediately realised what you meant.' He slid his arm around her waist and moved closer to her. 'I have missed you greatly since I left Far-bridge and have been feeling a little melancholy. I didn't wish to allow myself false hope. I love you, Eloise, and I believe that we can make each other truly happy.'

'I believe so too.'

Marcus lifted his free hand and touched her cheek, before very gently turning her face so that it was close to his.

He dropped kisses on her forehead and nose before brushing her lips with his and lifting his head to say, 'Do you remember when I proposed to you for the first time out of—I fully admit—a sense of duty, and then I found myself unable to stop talking about how very well matched we are in a physical sense?'

'Mmhmm.' Eloise smiled and then reached up to pull his head back to hers. 'This,' she said between kisses, 'is what I wanted to do then. Which was so very wrong.'

Marcus moved his hand up so that it rested on the

underside of her breast, and kissed down her chest towards the neckline of her dress.

'Is that *all* you wanted to do then?' His voice was deliciously low and the stubble on his chin was grazing her skin most delightfully and Eloise felt as though she could barely breathe in anticipation of what might happen next.

'It might not have been all.' She slid her hands up his solid chest, and then reached one of them much lower, inside his breeches.

'Eloise.'

'Yes?' She smiled and then gasped as he pulled on the skirts of her dress and then moved his hand underneath.

'You have made me the happiest man in the world,' he told her between deep and very satisfying kisses.

Eloise opened her eyes for a moment from where, somehow, she was now lying on the sofa, with Marcus above her, and saw the tea tray next to her.

'Marcus,' she said through a long shudder of pleasure, 'your servants.'

Marcus paused and said, 'They are very well trained.'

'But I would not wish to embarrass them.'

Marcus sighed and said, 'You are of course right.' He sat up and lifted her so that she was half on his lap and kissed her again. 'Like this, we are able to look quite decorous very quickly.' He kissed and nipped at her breast—somehow he had very cleverly pulled her dress down a little—and she moaned a little against him.

'Also.' She allowed herself to stroke him another time and he groaned. 'I think we should not do this until we are married. In case we do have another baby.'

'You are of course again right.' Marcus didn't stop

kissing her, though. 'There are things we might do that would not lead to a baby. Perhaps we might...'

'Mmm, *yes*,' Eloise said. She *loved* talking to him and laughing with him and just *being* with him, and his mouth and fingers were *extremely* clever.

Some time later—she was really not sure how much time had passed but she did know that they had spent that time very enjoyably—they were sitting on the sofa together and Marcus was attempting to straighten Eloise's bodice while she tried to pat her hair into place.

'We should probably tell Lucretia our news now.' He gave her bodice one last tweak and then kissed her full on the lips again. 'I seem to remember that she counts at least two bishops amongst her personal friends. We need to get a special licence because we need to get married very, very soon, because that was *good* but there's a lot more that I would like to do and I would like to be able to do it as often as I like with no fear of interruption.'

'I would like that very much.'

Epilogue

Eloise

Eleven years later—July 1828

As their coach drew up to Vauxhall Gardens, Eloise's dear friend Anne, Viscountess Bakewell, grinned at her.

'Are you ready?'

'I am indeed.' Eloise checked that her mask was securely in place and adjusted her shepherdess gown under her domino. Truth be told, the dress was somewhat tighter than it had been exactly twenty years ago, the first time that she'd attended a masquerade here.

'Are you worrying about your dress again?' Anne tutted. 'It looks even more alluring than it did before. I really do not understand why people consider women to be remotely old as they approach the age of forty. We are in our prime, Eloise.'

'Anne, you are always right.' Eloise pouted for her friend beneath her mask and they both snorted with laughter. She looked out of the window. 'Oh, my goodness. We're here and it will soon be time to descend from the carriage.'

How was it possible that after nearly eleven years of marriage she could still feel butterflies at the thought of seeing her husband?

She caught sight of some young bucks waving and winking cheekily at some young ladies in a carriage and her entire stomach flipped at the memory of Marcus winking at her for the first time twenty years ago. If he hadn't winked, she might not have chosen to dance with him, and they wouldn't now have Amelia, or their four younger children, or be here today.

As she and Anne were shown into their box, Eloise's butterflies persisted. Her stomach was veritably *churning* now. What if she and Marcus didn't *recognise* each other in their masks and costumes?

'I think it's time to go,' Anne told her a few minutes later.

Eloise took another long draught of champagne, drew a deep breath and stood up.

As they left their box and joined the—really *remarkably* lively—throng ahead of them, Anne said, 'Dominos off.' She removed her own domino and Eloise gasped for a second time that day, because if her shepherdess gown was bordering on indecent now that she was a little bit more voluptuous than she had been twenty years ago, Anne's maid costume was truly outrageous.

She hiccupped with laughter as Anne did a ridiculously risqué wiggle for her, before Anne pointed to the ties of her domino and she removed her own.

The reaction of the men around them told them that Anne's assessment that women approaching their fortieth year were at least as alluring as younger women had been quite accurate.

'Lady Kingsbridge will be *very* pleased to hear about this,' Anne said into Eloise's ear as yet another much younger man smiled at her and asked if she would like to dance. 'She asked me quite particularly to report back to her on this evening.' Eloise's grandmother was still in remarkably good health for a woman of her years—or indeed for a woman of twenty or thirty years younger—but after attending a very large number of balls recently with Eloise as they both chaperoned Amelia on her coming out, she had decided that she might take a rest this evening.

Her grandmother was still convinced that it was her matchmaking that had caused Marcus and Eloise to fall in love, and that it had been the masquerade at the castle that had caused them to begin to realise their love for each other, and that was why she had been so taken with their idea to meet at this masquerade tonight to re-celebrate their love for each other. Eloise had *not* told her that it was in fact the twentieth anniversary of the first time they had met.

'What if we don't recognise each other, though?' Eloise was becoming increasingly worried that Marcus would mistakenly dance with another woman.

And then she felt strong arms seize her from behind around the waist and gasped.

'How dare you?' she hissed as she was spun round. And then she looked into the laughing eyes of a masked Henry the Eighth and sighed with pleasure. 'How did you know it was me?' she asked Marcus as he drew her into a space so that they might dance together. 'From behind?'

'If I didn't know my own wife's delicious behind after all this time, I'd be an idiot of a husband.' Marcus placed his hand on her bottom as he spoke and Eloise squeaked.

'*Marcus*. What if someone sees us?'

'*Ella*. No one will recognise us. In that dress you look *particularly* different from the very proper Countess of Malbrook. And we are masked. And other people are doing *far* more indecorous things than we are. And we are a long-married couple.' He took her into a waltz hold and they began to move together in time to the music. And if dancing together like this had been exciting twenty years ago, now their dancing was even better, with the knowledge of how their bodies worked together, the pleasure they gave each other, and of course the *love* they shared.

Their first meeting had been all about adventure. This was all about love.

As they danced, they kissed sometimes, and at others just held each other.

'Shall we walk?' Marcus asked some time later.

'Yes, let's.' Eloise put her hand in his and he led her through the crowds, forging a path with ease due to his superior height and breadth, as he had done here at Vauxhall half a lifetime ago.

'Oh,' she said suddenly, 'I can't believe I forgot to tell you. Ludo walked all the way across the drawing room this afternoon, without any support, all the way from the door to where I was sitting at the opposite side.'

'I can't believe I missed it.'

'I know. Sorry. But I was there and it was *so* sweet. He had the most wonderful look of concentration on his face throughout and then when he reached me he laughed and laughed and laughed.'

'I know I've said it before,' Marcus said, 'but I have

to say it again. That boy is going to be an excellent sportsman.'

Eloise smiled up at him. She *loved* what a besotted father he was. Ludo was fifteen months old and while he was the most *adorable* toddler, it was in no way remarkable that he could now walk.

'Down here, I think.' Marcus drew her down a side path, towards a bench set into the hedge. 'Yes, this is definitely it.'

'You have a very good memory,' Eloise said, impressed.

'Come here.' Marcus sat down on the bench and pulled her onto his lap. Eloise wriggled and he said, his voice suddenly hoarse, 'Twenty years on and still I can barely think when you do that.'

Eloise wriggled again and he groaned.

'I am truly the luckiest man in the world,' he told her between kisses.

'And I the luckiest woman.'

* * * * *

*If you loved this story,
you'll be sure to love
Sophia Williams's debut title
for Harlequin Historical*

How the Duke Met His Match

*Watch out for more stories from
Sophia Williams, coming soon!*